DECeiVed

JERRY B. JENKINS
TIM LaHAYE

with CHRIS FABRY

TYNDALE HOUSE PUBLISHERS, INC.
WHEATON, ILLINOIS

Visit areUthirsty.com

Visit Tyndale's exciting Web site at www.tyndale.com

TYNDALE is a registered trademark of Tyndale House Publishers, Inc.

Tyndale's quill logo is a trademark of Tyndale House Publishers, Inc.

Discover the latest Left Behind news at www.leftbehind.com

TYNDALE is a registered trademark of TYndale House Publishers, Inc.

Tyndale's quill logo is a trademark of Tyndale House Publishers, Inc.

Deceived is a special edition compilation of the following Left Behind: The Kids titles:

#29: Breakout! copyright © 2003 by Jerry B. Jenkins and Tim LaHaye. All rights reserved.

#30: Murder in the Holy Place copyright © 2003 by Jerry B. Jenkins and Tim LaHaye. All rights reserved.

#31: Escape to Masada copyright © 2003 by Jerry B. Jenkins and Tim LaHaye. All rights reserved.

Cover photo copyright © PunchStock. All rights reserved.

Left Behind is a registered trademark of Tyndale House Publishers, Inc.

Published in association with the literary agency of Alive Communications, Inc., 7680 Goddard Street, Suite 200, Colorado Springs, CO 80920.

Scripture quotations are taken from the *Holy Bible*, New Living Translation, copyright © 1996. Used by permission of Tyndale House Publishers, Inc., Wheaton, Illinois 60189. All rights reserved.

Some Scripture taken from the New King James Version. Copyright © 1979, 1980, 1982 by Thomas Nelson, Inc. Used by permission. All rights reserved.

Designed by Jessie McGrath

Library of Congress Cataloging-in-Publication data

Jenkins, Jerry B.
  Deceived / Jerry B. Jenkins, Tim LaHaye ; with Chris Fabry.
    p. cm. — (Left behind—the kids)
  Special edition compiliation of the following three previously published works: Breakout!; Murder in the Holy place; Escape to Masada.
    Summary: Four teens battle the forces of evil when they are left behind after the Rapture.
    ISBN 1-4143-0270-3 (hc : alk. paper)
  [1. End of the world—Fiction. 2. Christian life—Fiction.] 1. LaHaye, Tim F. II. Fabry, Chris, date. III. Title.
PZ7.J4138De 2005
[Fic]—dc22   2004018503

Printed in the United States of America

10 09 08 07 06 05
 9   8   7   6   5   4   3   2   1

1

VICKI and the others in the Dials' underground Wisconsin hideout gathered around the television. It was two in the afternoon, and the kids expected the worst about Zeke Sr. Vicki held the phone while Mark Eisman monitored e-mail, both hoping Natalie would find a way to contact them.

An earlier news report had said the first mark application had begun at a GC facility in Wheaton, formerly known as the DuPage County Jail. Other mark applications were scheduled that afternoon in various local jails and prisons.

The kids had rejoiced when Conrad called with the news of the escape of Ginny and Bo Shairton, Maggie Carlson, and a former gang member who was now a believer, Manny Aguilara. All four were now in the home of Jim Dekker, a GC satellite operator from Illinois who had helped the kids.

Vicki prayed for Natalie. As far as Vicki knew, Global Community Peacekeepers hadn't discovered that the four former inmates were actually free.

Mark fiddled with the TV antenna to pull in the Chicago station.

Finally, a reporter in Wheaton, Illinois, broke into the newscast. "As we've reported, the mark applications began here a little after noon today. With the new technology, Peacekeepers wondered if there would be any glitches in the system. We're told that everything went fine until the last prisoner was brought into the application room and refused to take the mark.

"That set in motion a series of events that local Peacekeepers say was regrettable, but necessary."

The broadcast cut to a video feed of an interview with Deputy Commander Darryl Henderson. The man pursed his lips and shook his head. "We brought this prisoner from Des Plaines and gave him every chance to comply with the simple requirement of taking the mark of loyalty. When he refused, we had no alternative."

"Is it true you didn't expect to need the guillotine?" the reporter said.

"It's a loyalty enforcement facilitator," Henderson corrected. "No, we assumed that our prison population would all take the mark. Everyone did except for this one man."

The scene switched to the reporter looking at his notes. "That one man is identified as fifty-four-year-old Gustaf Zuckermandel, formerly of Des Plaines. He had been charged with black market trafficking of fuel oil, but sources inside this facility tell me he was a follower of the dissident Tsion Ben-Judah. Officials say they hope this execution will serve as a warning to other Judah-ite followers that this kind of defiance of the Global Community will not be tolerated."

Mark turned off the television and the kids sat in silence. Vicki thought of Zeke Jr. and wondered if he knew about his father's death. There was no denying the clear facts. They had now entered a bloody season when believers in Christ would be hunted and if caught, executed. Vicki shuddered. If she and Darrion had been caught in Des Plaines, they would have been forced to choose Carpathia's mark or the blade. Would she have chosen to die for what she believed? Would she have to make that choice in the future?

The phone rang and Vicki answered it. Conrad wanted to know if the kids had heard about Zeke, and Vicki said they had.

"We're staying at Jim Dekker's farmhouse until things settle," Conrad said. "He wants us to take supplies with us when we go."

"What do you mean?"

"GC uniforms, ID cards—you name it, he's got it."

Mark talked with Conrad after Vicki was through, and then the kids met to discuss their next move.

"We can't slow down now," Melinda said. "We have to tell as many people as we can before they take the mark."

"Pretty soon there won't be anyone left who's unde-cided," Janie said. "Then we'll just have to try and survive."

"What's important right now is getting the message to

as many unbelievers as possible," Darrion said, "and our best tool is The Cube. It's high-tech and gets people's attention. We should send the file and look for any other ways to get the message out."

The phone rang again and Vicki jumped. Mark answered and handed it to her. "It's Natalie."

Lionel Washington hid in some bushes near the Global Community apartment building where Chang Wong and his parents stayed. Judd had given him Chang's description, but Lionel was nervous. What if someone who looked like Chang came out of the building? Lionel was glad Judd would be back early in the morning.

Nights in New Babylon felt eerie to Lionel. The blistering heat of the day gave way to cool air once the sun went down. A breeze blew through the bushes, and Lionel hunkered down in his hiding place.

Lionel had witnessed incredible things in the past few weeks. He had seen the deaths of the beloved prophets, Eli and Moishe, and a few days later had watched them ascend into heaven. That had been one of the high points of their trip to Israel. But soon after came Carpathia's murder and his eventual rise from the dead. Every time Lionel thought about it, he recalled the lightning of Leon Fortunato and the bodies of innocent victims lying in the palace courtyard.

The door opened at the front of the apartment building, and a guard strolled out front, lighting a cigarette. He walked to within a few feet of Lionel's hiding place and flicked cigarette ashes into the bushes.

Thanks for using our world as your ashtray, Lionel thought, recalling the words of his father. Lionel smiled as he remembered driving in the car with his dad. A motorist would pass, flicking ashes or a spent cigarette to the pavement, and Lionel's dad would shake his head. Once Lionel's father had stepped out of the car at a stoplight, picked up a smoldering butt off the ground, and handed it to the driver through the open window.

"I think you dropped this," Lionel's father had said, then returned to the car before the light changed. He buckled up and stifled a smile. "Don't tell this to your mother."

Lionel missed his dad more than he wanted to admit. They had missed so many things. With each birthday or holiday, Lionel ached for some kind of celebration, a cake, or some presents. But the truth was, the kids didn't have time for things like that. Life was a constant struggle.

At moments like these, when Lionel was alone, he thought about his family, his mother's smile, his father's strength. Most of the kids he knew from school had parents who were divorced. His mom and dad had stayed together through some rough times and Lionel was glad.

The guard flicked the spent cigarette into the bush where Lionel was hiding and walked away. The glowing ashes faded and finally went out. It was just like the world, Lionel thought, dying and almost dead.

He drew his knees to his chest, wrapped himself in the light jacket he was wearing, and leaned back. The night chill and lack of activity inside the building made his eyelids droop.

When he fell asleep, he was thinking of his father.

5

Vicki tried to comfort Natalie, but the girl was nearly hysterical. When she finally calmed down, Vicki discovered that Natalie was at her apartment, having told her boss she wasn't feeling well.

Natalie told Vicki about her experience at the old DuPage County Jail. She had heard Zeke protest about the mark of loyalty. She had followed the man and had watched from an observation room when the Global Community ended Zeke's life.

"You actually saw the beheading?"

"I couldn't watch, but I heard the blade come down. One guy in the room raised his fist and said Zeke got what he had coming to him. How can people be that cruel?"

"I don't know. Are you all right now?"

Natalie sighed. "I just feel so alone. The GC are all saying everything went exactly as planned, but I know the truth. All those prisoners who took the mark can *never* become believers now, and they killed the only one who had the sense to not take it."

"Does Henderson suspect anything about the four who escaped?"

"Not that I can tell. He's been too busy with the mark applications to notice much, but I heard they're still looking for you."

"We're safe. Any idea how long before employees get the mark?"

"Henderson's sending a report to other facilities throughout the country. Jails and reeducation facilities will apply the mark for the next couple of days. Then employees are eligible. We have two weeks to comply after it's up and running."

"Then you have to come here."

"Believe me, I can't stop thinking about it. But I'm so mad. After what I saw Zeke go through, why does God let this happen?"

"I understand how you feel. I felt the same thing when my friend Ryan died."

"Why couldn't somebody have told us about God before all this happened?"

"They tried, at least they did with me," Vicki said. "I wouldn't listen."

"So we just have to sit back and watch all of these good people get their heads chopped off? Is that what God wants?"

Natalie broke down and sobbed. Vicki listened and tried to calm her. Suddenly, Natalie put her hand over the phone and said, "Hi, Claudia. Yeah, you should have been there." When Natalie uncovered the phone, she whispered, "My roommate's here. I'll call you later and we can talk."

Vicki gathered the other kids to pray for Natalie. She knew the girl's time was running out.

Judd Thompson Jr. crept through the darkened streets of New Babylon. A few cabs sat parked by the street, drivers slouched and snoring in their seats. A strip of yellow and white shone on the horizon as Judd looked at his watch. *6:30 A.M. I should have relieved Lionel an hour ago!*

Judd located the shrubs and found Lionel sleeping.

Lionel awoke with a start, and Judd put a hand over his mouth. "How long have you been asleep?"

Lionel rubbed his neck and yawned. "I don't know. It was so cold and I just couldn't keep my eyes open."

"I can't blame you. I'm late myself."

"No word from Chang?"

"Nothing," Judd said. "But Z-Van came in late last night jazzed up."

"About his recording?"

Judd shook his head. "He was crowing about getting to take the mark today. They're taking pictures for the album cover, and he wants to make sure he has Carpathia's mark. And get this. He's supposed to have a picture taken with Carpathia."

"If they're letting Z-Van take the mark, that means—"

Judd pointed toward the front door of the apartment building. A man with a briefcase walked inside. The guard checked the man's credentials and waved him through.

"I saw that guy at Carpathia's funeral," Judd said. "Moon, I think. He's in Carpathia's inner circle."

"Maybe he lives there."

Judd shook his head. "I wish we had some binoculars."

Lionel reached inside his jacket pocket and pulled out a tiny telescope. "Westin gave it to me before we left last night. Works pretty well."

Judd set the digital meter for the distance and zoomed in on the scene. The scope was so powerful he could see the badge of the guard at the front door. He focused on the elevators and saw one had stopped on the fourth floor.

"That's Chang's floor," Judd said.

Vicki had trouble falling asleep, a thousand thoughts swirling through her mind. It had been some time since they had heard from Judd and Lionel, and she was worried they might be in trouble. And she thought of Zeke. She couldn't shake the image of the razor-sharp blade falling.

She had just gotten to sleep when Shelly shook her. "You need to come see something."

Vicki dressed quickly and walked into the meeting area of the underground hideout. Mark had the kids' Web site up on the large screen at the front of the room.

"You'll want to sit down for this," Shelly said.

"What's wrong?"

Mark showed Vicki the number of messages from people who had received The Cube. Many of them had prayed to become believers because of the 3-D tool. Mark scrolled to the bottom and pulled up a message whose subject line simply said *Help!*

> *Vicki or anyone else working with the Young Tribulation Force,*
>
> *I'm typing this fast, so if I make mistakes forgive me. I'm Kelly Bradshaw from Iowa. You came to our meeting place at an abandoned college. I hope you remember us.*

"I remember Kelly," Vicki said. "She was the first to meet us when we got there."

> *We've had incredible growth since you came and taught us. Word spread and people came from all over to*

meet other believers and read the notes we'd taken. Then, when you sent The Cube, we almost doubled in size. People brought friends who hadn't seen it to the locker room under the gym where we meet.

Someone must have tipped off the Global Community because several Peacekeepers burst into one of our smaller meetings tonight and arrested everyone. I was on my way back to our farm when I heard them coming, but there was nothing I could do. They raided the house where some of us live, too, and took computers and supplies. We had printed copies of Buck Williams's The Truth to hand out to people who were interested.

We had a computer hidden in a secluded room. That's where I am now, but I'm so afraid for my friends. Can you help? I'm hearing they are forcing prisoners to take the mark, so we don't have much time. Please, if there's anything you can do, let me know quickly.

"Have you written her back?" Vicki said.

Mark nodded. "I told her we'd be back to her within the hour. What do we want to say?"

Vicki looked around the room. "I say these are our brothers and sisters. We have to try."

Mark smiled. "That's what I thought you'd say."

JUDD kept the scope focused on the elevators and tried to remember as much as he could about the man named Moon. Judd hoped that the elevator stopping on Chang's floor was just a coincidence.

"Is Moon head of security?" Lionel said.

Judd racked his brain but couldn't recall anything more than Moon's face on the official GC Web site. A few minutes passed and Judd felt better. "I was probably over-reacting."

Lionel took the scope and looked toward the tinted windows that lined the side of the building. He focused on the lobby and handed the scope back to Judd. "Elevator's coming down."

Judd quickly focused on the elevator doors and saw Mr. Wong and the GC official helping someone out. They headed toward the front door and Judd strained to see. The third person wore khakis, a light jacket, and had a red baseball cap pulled low over his eyes. The three turned before they reached the front door and headed down a corridor. "That has to be Chang."

Judd and Lionel darted out of their hiding place and walked to the side of the building to get a better look.

"Westin said there are tunnels that connect these buildings," Lionel said. "No telling where they're going."

Judd studied the structures behind the apartment complex. "It could be in any of those, and they're all guarded."

The two ran back to the hotel and squeezed into a phone booth. Judd dialed the Wongs' apartment, and Mrs. Wong answered on the first ring. She sounded upset.

"Mrs. Wong, where's Chang?"

The woman sniffed. "Who is this?"

"I'm Chang's friend. I know your husband didn't want me to call, but I'm concerned about—"

"They take him away just now. He so scared, they give him something to make him calm."

"They drugged him? Why?"

"He afraid of needle. They only try to make him calm."

"What needle? Where did they take him?"

"I'm not sure which building. They have meeting later, after Chang get mark."

Judd felt the air go out of the phone booth. Lionel asked what was wrong, but Judd couldn't speak. If they tried to give Chang Carpathia's mark, he wouldn't accept it. They would find out he was a believer in Christ and use the guillotine.

"You still there?" Mrs. Wong said.

"Yes," Judd choked.

"Everything will be all right. I talk with Chang. He take mark and everything be okay."

Judd placed the phone on the cradle and muttered, "No, it won't be okay." He told Lionel what Mrs. Wong had said.

Lionel slammed his fist against a wall, and several guests in the hotel glared at him. He slumped over. "I guess we're too late."

Judd and Lionel went up to Z-Van's penthouse suite and found Westin Jakes, Z-Van's pilot. The man grimaced when he heard about Chang. "We can't give up. Maybe they haven't given him the mark yet."

"There's nothing we can do," Lionel said.

"Do you know anyone else inside the GC?"

Judd shook his head. "Wait. I met this Peacekeeper a few days ago and promised to get Z-Van's autograph. Maybe he could help us."

Judd dug a card out of his pocket and read the name Roy Donaldson. "He told me he was originally from Florida."

Westin took the name and grabbed a pen and some paper from a nearby desk. "Call him and ask him to meet you in front of the apartments. I'll see if Z-Van's in good enough shape to scribble his name."

Vicki immediately called Jim Dekker's house in Illinois and explained the Iowa situation to Conrad. After she had talked with Jim, the man agreed to supply uniforms and IDs. Colin Dial would continue to pose as Commander Blakely, and they would travel in the van that already bore the GC insignia.

"How fast can you guys get here?" Conrad said.

"We're on our way," Vicki said.

Judd and Lionel found Peacekeeper Roy Donaldson pacing in front of the GC apartment building. Lionel shook hands with him and said, "So you're a big Z-Van fan?"

Roy smiled. "You bet. I liked him even before he started singing about the potentate, but I can't wait for his new album."

Judd pulled a slip of paper from his pocket and gave it to Roy. He unfolded it carefully, like it was a priceless artifact. "'To Roy,'" he read aloud. "'He is risen.'"

At the bottom of the page was Z-Van's scrawled signature. Judd wanted to tell Roy that the singer's real name was Myron and that he was a jerk, but Judd didn't have the heart or the time.

"How about a little favor?" Judd said.

"Name it."

"Where are they giving employees the mark?"

Roy pointed to a building behind the apartments. "Building D. Man, I can't wait to get mine. I'm scheduled for this afternoon, but they may not be able to get to me until tomorrow."

"Could you take us there?"

Roy studied the autograph again. "After this, I'll do anything for you guys. Come on."

As they walked, Judd asked if Roy had heard anything about a potential employee named Chang Wong.

Roy stopped. "Don't tell me you know him too."

Judd smiled. "Yeah, he's a friend of mine."

Roy shook his head. "Kid's just a teenager like us and he's already a celebrity. A friend of mine works in the department looking at him. I hear this Wong kid's a genius with computers."

"He's a pretty nice guy too," Judd said.

"He seemed kind of uppity to me."

"You've met him?"

"I just saw him earlier." Roy pointed out the entrance and a line of employees snaking through the front door. People on the sidewalk craned their necks to see how much farther until they were inside.

"Wait," Judd said, grabbing Roy's arm. "You saw Chang?"

"Yeah, I got a look at him walking with Walter Moon and some other guy heading upstairs. I know it sounds like sour grapes and all, and I understand why new hires are getting the mark first, but—"

"Chang already has the mark?"

Roy rolled his eyes. "Yeah, I saw it, even with that stupid baseball cap he was wearing. He got a little 30 next to his eyebrows, nothing like what I'm going to have."

"Are you sure it was him?" Lionel said.

Roy cocked his head. "You don't see too many Asian kids around here who have the mark before other employees, do you? Of course I'm sure."

Judd looked at Lionel and cringed.

"You want me to see if I can get you guys in D?"

"Not now," Judd said.

"Well, don't think you're going to get a mark before us employees. Have you decided which one you're getting?"

Judd shook his head and glanced at the employees waiting to seal their fates. They were like sheep being led to the slaughter, and they didn't even know it.

Judd thanked Roy, and the Peacekeeper walked away clutching Z-Van's autograph.

Lionel sat down hard on a bench. "I don't get it. Tsion said God would give believers the strength they needed to resist taking the mark."

"Maybe it's not real," Judd said. "Maybe Chang came up with a fake that convinced everybody."

"Maybe. But there's another possibility."

"What's that?"

"Maybe Chang is fake himself."

Vicki rode with Mark and Shelly toward the farmhouse in McHenry, Illinois. Though the others had put up a fight, everyone finally agreed that it was best for a smaller group to help the teens in Iowa. Vicki felt tired but knew she wouldn't sleep until they were in the van and headed west.

Vicki wept when she saw Bo and Ginny Shairton and Maggie Carlson. They hugged and shared stories. Maggie said she was worried about Natalie and wished the girl would leave the Des Plaines jail.

Vicki greeted Jim Dekker, the satellite operator who

had helped her escape the GC chase, then shook hands with Manny Aguilara, the prisoner who had become a believer after talking with Zeke. She handed Colin Dial a letter from his wife.

Mark shook hands with Jim Dekker. "It's a pleasure meeting the guy who came up with The Cube."

Dekker smiled and thanked him.

"I hate to break up this admiration society meeting," Conrad said, "but we don't have much time." He took the others to the basement and fitted them with Morale Monitor uniforms while Jim took their photos and created new ID cards.

Jim provided walkie-talkies and gave Mark a cell phone. "Make sure you keep in contact with us. Natalie will do what she can on her end, but we have to work together."

The night was still and a wind had come up in the east as the kids loaded supplies and equipment into the van. Everyone gathered and joined hands. One by one they prayed for safety for the rescue group and the believers in Iowa. Manny, who had been part of the group only a short time, prayed, "God, we trust you to help your children. Show them where to go and what to do."

Mark got behind the wheel for the first leg of the trip as Colin and Conrad explained the plan.

"How do we know they haven't already applied the mark?" Vicki said.

Colin shook his head. "Jim and Natalie diverted a shipment of injector machines. They were going to do the same thing to the guillotines, but for some reason shipments have been delayed in North Carolina, Florida, Iowa, and Tennessee. We don't have any idea why."

Vicki put her head on the seat and pulled a Morale Monitor jacket over her arms. The uniform felt stiff, and Vicki wondered about the girl who had worn it. Was she dead? Did the horsemen get her or perhaps the earthquake?

As the conversation continued in the front, Vicki felt sleep come over her. She thought of the kids in Iowa. They had to be terrified. And how long would it take the GC to realize that Commander Blakely was really Colin Dial, a Judah-ite in disguise?

Vicki prayed for the believers behind bars and asked God to help them. She also remembered Natalie and the shock she had gone through witnessing Zeke's death. When Vicki had prayed for all the names and faces she could think of, she thought of Judd. She always kept him last. Sometimes she fell asleep praying for him and thinking of what he might be doing. She wondered if he missed her as much as she missed him. There were nights when she would dream of Judd standing up to Carpathia or telling strangers about God. Once she dreamed about his speech in front of Leon Fortunato at Nicolae High, and she woke up in a cold sweat.

Now, as she drifted in and out of sleep with the droning of the van's engine, she prayed that God would protect Judd from the evil forces loose in New Babylon and the rest of the world. She knew from reading Tsion Ben-Judah's letters that they weren't just fighting against the Global Community.

Tsion had often quoted a verse from Ephesians, chapter 6 which said, "For we are not fighting against people made of flesh and blood, but against the evil rulers and authorities of the unseen world, against those mighty powers of darkness who rule this world, and against wicked spirits in the heavenly realms."

When Vicki thought of doing battle with those wicked spirits, another verse from Ephesians came to mind. "Put on all of God's armor so that you will be able to stand firm against all strategies and tricks of the Devil." Carpathia's mark was a deadly trick of the devil himself.

Mark tuned the radio to a news station and kept it low. The reporter repeated several stories about mark application sites in the United North American States being behind in their application of the mark on prisoners.

The cell phone rang and Mark picked up. After a few moments he hung up and slowed the van.

"What's going on?" Vicki said.

"That was Jim Dekker. He's changing our route."

"Is something wrong?"

Mark shrugged. "Maybe it's a roadblock."

Vicki laid back and prayed again that God would protect them until they could help their friends in Iowa.

3

VICKI wanted to ask Jim Dekker why they were turning, but Mark shook his head. "Dekker said we'd understand when we got there."

"But the kids in Iowa are going to die if we don't get there in time!"

"I understand. Jim does too. But he still told us to take a different road."

Headlights flashed on downed trees and an open field. Crude crosses rose from mounds of earth. Vicki guessed it was a graveyard filled with bodies of people killed by the earthquake, the horsemen, or some other disaster.

Mark had planned on taking back roads, concerned that a GC squad car might stop them, but Jim Dekker's call had taken them onto an interstate. They passed an 18-wheeler and a few cars but saw no GC.

They had been driving on the interstate a half hour

when they came to the mile marker Dekker had given. Mark pulled into the entrance of an abandoned weigh station and stopped.

"What now?" Vicki said.

Mark took out the cell phone. "I don't like this any more than you. I'm calling Dekker."

Mark had the phone opened and was dialing when Vicki noticed headlights behind them. Colin Dial told everyone to get down.

"He led us into a trap," Conrad said.

"Just stay calm," Colin said.

Air brakes whooshed behind them. Mark stayed behind the wheel, ready to pull away. Colin got out of the van and walked back toward the truck.

"Can you see who it is?" Shelly whispered to Vicki.

Vicki crawled to the rear of the van and peeked over the equipment and uniforms stacked on the backseat. She shielded her eyes but couldn't see anything because of the glare. "I think it's the truck we passed a few miles back."

Colin's footsteps crunched in the gravel by the road. He wore his commander's uniform, and Vicki thought he played the part well. He walked confidently toward the truck, shielding his eyes, and yelled, "Cut your lights!"

A man yelled something to him, and Colin approached the driver.

"I don't like this," Shelly said.

Colin trotted up to Mark's window and told him to move farther into the weigh station. Colin stood on the running board and stuck his head in Mark's window. "Vicki, I need you out here."

Judd and Lionel found a film crew and several security
personnel clogging the hallway in front of Z-Van's hotel
suite. When they finally made it to the door, a man held
up a hand. "Move along. This is a closed set."

Judd scowled. "We're staying here."

"Right." The man spoke into a walkie-talkie and two
burly men approached.

"Westin, are you in there?" Lionel yelled.

The man at the door clamped a hand over Lionel's
mouth. "You want to make this easy or hard?"

Lionel struggled free, but the two men were on him.
"Escort these gentlemen outside," the man at the door said.

"Hold it," Westin said, pushing his way through the
crowd. "Those guys are with me."

Judd and Lionel shook free of the men and stepped
over cords and cables as they entered the room. Bright
lights were set up near the piano, and a man with a
handheld light meter moved around the room.

"What's going on?" Lionel said.

"Ever heard of Lars Rahlmost?" Westin said.

Judd nodded. "I've seen a couple of his movies."

Westin pointed to the corner where a blond-haired
man in a leather jacket stood stroking a stubbly beard.
His hair was pulled back in a ponytail that swished
as he talked. Z-Van was next to him, smiling and laugh-
ing. "That's him. He's doing a documentary about
Nicolae called *From Death to Life*. They're interviewing
Z-Van and are going to film some of his appearances in
Israel."

Judd took Westin into the next room and explained what they had seen and heard about Chang.

Westin sat on the bed. "I'm new to this. You've been telling me you can't take this mark and still be a believer. What gives?"

"I don't know," Judd said. "Maybe we'll clear the whole thing up when we talk to Chang."

"You think that's smart?" Lionel said. "He could be a plant by the GC."

"He has the mark of the believer. There has to be an explanation."

"Set up a meeting," Westin said. "I'll still get him out of here if he wants help."

Judd phoned Chang's number but there was no answer. He sent an e-mail asking Chang to get in touch as soon as possible.

Vicki climbed out of the van, her heart beating like a locomotive, and followed Colin. She noticed the truck had official GC insignias on its side and on the front license plate.

"What's going on?" Vicki said.

"You'll see," Colin said, leading her to the front of the truck.

The driver's door opened wide and a brawny man stepped out, his back to Vicki. He shook Colin's hand and patted him on the shoulder. When he turned, Vicki's mouth dropped open and her knees felt like they were going to buckle. "Pete!"

"Surprised to see me?" Pete Davidson said, hugging Vicki tightly.

"I haven't seen you since before our trip west!" Vicki said.

"I read about that on the Web site. You did pretty well for yourself, young lady."

Vicki explained to Colin how Judd had become friends with Pete after the wrath of the Lamb earthquake.

"I've been driving for Chloe's Trib Force co-op the last few months."

"How did you—?"

"I'll tell you all about it in the truck," Pete said. "Hop in."

Shelly joined Pete and Vicki as they got back on the road. Pete said he had e-mailed the kids and was going to stop at the schoolhouse, but Darrion had called his satellite phone and told him about the situation in Iowa. They had gotten the van and truck together using Jim Dekker's satellite connection.

Vicki wanted to hear the latest from Pete, but she guessed Darrion hadn't told him about Zeke Sr. Since Pete had known the man, he nearly drove off the road when he learned Zeke was dead. He got the rig back under control and drove in silence for a few minutes. The big man's chin quivered when he finally spoke. "I called him Gus just to get on his nerves. His first name was Gustaf, you know. If there was any better man on the face of the earth, I never met him. He and his son took me in and never charged me a Nick for any fuel or supplies."

As the miles rolled on, Pete told stories about Zeke and how generous he was. "You'd never know it by looking at him, but God made him real tender towards people. First time I met him I told my story of looking for my girlfriend after the earthquake. He listened for the longest time, then put his head down. I thought he had fallen asleep, but he was crying. He'd never met her, and he was sobbing like she was his own daughter."

After a few more stories, Vicki asked what Pete was hauling in the truck. He smiled and said, "Firewood."

"Who would need firewood this time of year?"

"The GC. You see, they don't call it firewood, but I do."

"What do they call it?"

"They call it loyalty silly taters or something like that."

Shelly gasped. "You mean guillotines?"

Pete nodded. "That and some of the injector thingies. There are trailers full of these head choppers all over the country, but somehow they keep getting destroyed by the Judah-ites. It's the weirdest thing."

Vicki shook her head. "I should have known when I heard about the missing guillotines that it was something like this."

"Problem is, they're easy to make. The ones we destroy get replaced by local companies in a few days. We've slowed the GC down a little, but not much."

"Won't the GC know you're destroying them?" Shelly said.

"Sometimes we change the shipping records so me and my buddies aren't even on the list. Other times, like this one, I borrow the trailer from an official GC driver."

"You mean steal it?"

"I guess you could call it that. I know some people might think it's wrong, but I figure the only reason these contraptions exist is to kill believers. If I can do something to stop it, I will."

"What happened to you after you left the schoolhouse and went back east?" Shelly said.

"I actually headed south for several runs to believers down there. Oh, your friend Carl Meninger says to say hello. He's still hiding from the GC in South Carolina with the people on that island."

"You mean Luke and Tom?" Vicki said.

Pete nodded. "The GC got pretty close to them while they were hunting for Carl, but they've got a good hiding place. And more and more people are becoming believers down there."

"How did you get official GC stickers for your truck?" Shelly said.

"Zeke Jr. arranged that a while ago. I'm on their official roster of freelance truckers available for 'sensitive loads' as they call it. I've hauled everything from uniforms to computers to those guillotines back there."

Pete took Vicki's walkie-talkie and radioed the van to take the next exit. They drove a few miles into the countryside to a long, metal building. Pete flashed his lights twice, a door creeped open, and Pete drove in.

A wrinkled little man wearing a green hat with a deer on the front helped Pete unhook his trailer and put on a new one. They loaded the injector devices into the new trailer and were back on the road in a few minutes.

"What will that guy do with the guillotines?" Vicki said when they reached the interstate.

"He and a couple of friends will unload them, pull them apart, and burn the wood. They'll keep the metal until they can figure out what to do with it."

Pete asked the latest about the kids, and Vicki detailed the GC chase and the hideout in Wisconsin. Pete was excited to hear about The Cube and asked about Judd.

"He and Lionel were in Israel for a long time, but now—"

"No, what about *Judd and you?*"

Shelly rolled her eyes. "She doesn't think anybody knows."

Pete laughed. "Doesn't take a rocket scientist to see you two were meant for each other."

Vicki blushed. "This isn't anybody's business."

Pete playfully socked her shoulder. "When it's my sister, it's my business, you get me? You can deny it all you want, but just the way you're reacting now tells me a lot."

Vicki smiled. "Can we change the subject?"

While Judd waited for a return message from Chang, Lionel stood in the doorway to the bedroom and watched Z-Van's interview. Lars, the filmmaker, sat with his back to the camera and asked Z-Van about his music, his past, and what attracted him to Carpathia.

"My music was going well, and I suppose everything would have kept going just as it had, but finding something to sing about, to write about, that has so much meaning makes me understand what my life is all about."

"Explain," Lars said.

"Well, making money is wonderful, selling lots of recordings, and having fans think you're a god is fantastic, but it's not until you find what your life focus is about that you really understand the meaning of art. The best paintings, the best music, even the best films, don't really come from you, they come from observing something *bigger* than you. When I first heard His Excellency, his speeches blew me away. He has a grasp of every detail of life. He knows how to point people toward a goal, which is peace, and take them there."

Z-Van talked about Nicolae's resurrection and what it was like to actually see it happen. When the interview was over, Lars turned to his staff and looked at his watch. "We have about two hours to get the equipment to the next site. Let's make it happen."

Lionel turned to Westin. "What's the next site?"

"Building D. Z-Van's going to be the first civilian to take Carpathia's mark."

4

LIONEL and Westin followed Z-Van and the camera crew to Building D. Lionel offered to help move some of the heavy road cases filled with equipment, but the workers wouldn't let him.

It was a festive atmosphere inside with people stepping out of offices or lingering by watercoolers to get a glimpse of one of the most famous musicians in the world. People whispered and pointed when they saw Z-Van, and a few recognized the film director as well. When someone held out a pen and a piece of paper for an autograph, one of Z-Van's bodyguards pushed the person away and Z-Van waved. "Sorry."

As the camera crew set up, Z-Van and Lars ducked into a private office. A few minutes later, a uniformed Peacekeeper rushed into the room, followed by a full detail of Peacekeepers that stood guard by each entrance.

Lionel recognized Roy Donaldson, the Peacekeeper

Judd had met earlier, and walked up to him. "Looks like you'll get to see Z-Van in person."

Donaldson smiled. "Better than that. I get two for one."

"What do you mean?"

"The potentate is on his way. He's going to watch Z-Van take the mark."

———————————————————

Vicki and Shelly talked with Pete as the truck rolled across the Illinois border. Vicki explained how they had met the Iowa group at a college about fifty miles from Des Moines. Though the campus was in ruins, the kids had organized a group to hear Vicki explain the message.

"Did many people believe?" Pete said.

Vicki nodded. "And as we moved west, it seemed like the crowds got bigger. People were desperate to hear the truth."

"I wish I had had the same success. I went south to tell some friends what happened, thinking they'd want to hear what I had to say, but most of them were either caught up with Carpathia or they just wanted to be left alone."

"I don't understand that," Shelly said. "We have something that will give them meaning, purpose, and life that won't end."

"I guess that's how people felt about me before the vanishings," Pete said. "They tried to tell me about God, and I labeled them religious nuts."

Shelly frowned. "I hadn't thought about it that way. I did the same thing."

Colin radioed from the van ahead that Natalie had

traced the captured kids to a GC reeducation facility on the outskirts of Des Moines. Pete pulled over and everyone got in the van.

Colin outlined the plan and everyone received their assignments. Pete would deliver the injector machines after dark that evening, while the others cut a hole in the fence outside the camp. Jim Dekker would put an order in from the fictitious Commander Blakely that all suspected Judah-ites be separated and left outside overnight. That would give the kids a chance to get their friends' attention and free them. "Plus we don't have to set foot inside the camp," Colin said.

"Any idea when they'll start the mark applications?" Conrad said.

"They can't do a thing as long as I have the goods in the back of my truck," Pete said.

"Unless they get another shipment from somewhere," Colin said, "they won't be able to start until tomorrow. That should leave us enough time to get everyone out."

"How many believers are we talking about?" Pete said.

"The official word is that thirteen Judah-ites were taken into custody," Colin said.

"We should prepare for a few more in case these kids convinced some on the inside of the truth," Pete said. "I can handle them in my truck once I deliver my load."

"Why are you destroying the guillotines but delivering the injectors?" Shelly said.

"I have to deliver *something*," Pete said. "I figure the chip injectors are bad for the people who take it, but it doesn't kill any believers. Plus it gets me inside enemy lines."

The phone rang and Colin walked outside to talk with Jim Dekker. When he came back, he had a grave look. "Jim says that site now has a guillotine. They're just waiting on the chip injectors. We'll have to go in earlier than we thought, and maybe during daylight."

"How will we get them out?" Shelly said.

Colin sighed. "We need a decoy."

Judd saw nothing from Chang throughout the morning. He logged on to the kids' Web site and read the mountain of e-mails responding to The Cube. Many reported family members and friends finally realizing the truth after seeing it.

Next, he read the latest Buck Williams report in the cyberzine *The Truth*. With his contacts around the world, Buck wrote stories that revealed Carpathia's lies without exposing believers who gave Buck information.

Judd was excited when he found a new e-mail from Tsion Ben-Judah. Tsion wrote that he was grateful for the questions he had received at his Web site because it proved many were studying and growing. He spoke of the hope of Christ's return soon and referred to a quote from the apostle Paul, who said, "Living is for Christ, and dying is even better."

The next passage disturbed Judd. Tsion wrote that the top priority of believers was not to stop Antichrist from evil.

I want to confound him, revile him, enrage him, frustrate him, and get in the way of his plans every way I know how.

But Tsion said believers should not simply try to fight Carpathia. *Isn't that what we're supposed to do?* Judd thought. The next paragraph answered Judd's question.

So, as worthy and noble a goal as it is to go on the offensive against the evil one, I believe we can do that most effectively by focusing on persuading the undecided to come to faith. Knowing that every day could be our last, that we could be found out and dragged to a mark application center, there to make our decision to die for the sake of Christ, we must be more urgent about our task than ever.

Since many had written about fearing the guillotine, Tsion wrote about his own fears.

In my flesh I am weak. I want to live. I am afraid of death but even more of dying. The very thought of having my head severed from my body repulses me as much as it does anyone. In my worst nightmare I see myself standing before the GC operatives a weakling, a quivering mass who can do nothing but plead for his life. I envision myself breaking God's heart by denying my Lord. Oh, what an awful picture!

In my most hated imagination I fail at the hour of testing and accept the mark of loyalty that we all know is the cursed mark of the beast, all because I so cherish my own life.

Judd closed his eyes and pictured himself with Global Community Peacekeepers around him, shoving him toward a guillotine. With the prospect of death, would he have the courage to say no to Carpathia? Tsion continued.

> *I have good news for you. The Bible tells us that once one is either sealed by God as a believer or accepts the mark of loyalty to Antichrist, this is a once-and-for-all choice. . . . That tells me that somehow, when we face the ultimate test, God miraculously overcomes our evil, selfish flesh and gives us the grace and courage to make the right decision in spite of ourselves. My interpretation of this is that we will be unable to deny Jesus, unable to even choose the mark that would temporarily save our lives.*

Judd smiled but was still troubled. If that's true, what happened to Chang?

Judd's computer blipped, and he quickly saved Tsion's message and vowed to read the rest later.

The e-mail was from Chang. *I need to see you. Many questions. Meet me at the gazebo tonight at dusk.*

Judd quickly replied and attached Tsion's latest letter. Though Judd had seen Chang's mark identifying him with Christ, he couldn't help wondering how Chang had Carpathia's mark and what that would do to his soul.

Lionel stood in a corner with Westin and watched the scene unfold. Z-Van and Lars emerged from the isolated room and workers clapped. Z-Van put a hand in the air and waved. "I'm not the hero here. There is one much greater than me coming."

Z-Van rocked back and forth, fidgeting and pulling his head one way and then another until his neck popped. Finally, the elevator opened. Lionel stood on tiptoes, trying to see. There was more clapping and movement, and though someone blocked Lionel's view, he sensed evil in the room. Nicolae Carpathia, the man most of the world worshiped, had arrived.

Lars hurriedly motioned his film crew to begin shooting. Cameras flashed as Carpathia shook hands with Z-Van. "It is my pleasure to welcome you as an honorary Global Community worker, and have you take the mark in the same location as my most loyal followers. Congratulations."

"You don't know what an honor this is, sir," Z-Van said.

"I can only hope the world will want to follow in your footsteps, young man." Carpathia scanned the room, nodding at the workers. "You can see we have a true representation of the world's population in this room. Every ethnic background conceivable is here."

"Very impressive, sir."

Carpathia walked to the mark application area, picked up an injector, and looked into the camera lens. "With this simple device and the application of the mark of loyalty, we will monitor every citizen on earth. Any law-abiding person would be happy to use this technology if it means an outbreak of unparalleled peace, which it does." Carpathia looked at Z-Van. "And I am pleased that a person of your stature and talent wants to show his fans such a moment of leadership."

Z-Van seemed mesmerized by Carpathia. When Nicolae finished, Z-Van nodded and a Peacekeeper took him by the arm and led him to the machine.

Lionel wanted to scream and tell Z-Van not to take the mark, not to sell his soul to the devil, but Lionel knew he was helpless. Z-Van stood spellbound by this enemy of God.

Z-Van sat in a plush chair and scooted against the back. Nicolae smiled and leaned back, allowing the camera to focus on the technician about to apply the mark. The woman looked Filipino and wore gloves. She asked Z-Van a few questions and typed the information into the computer. Since Z-Van was from the United North American States, she set the region code, brushed the hair from Z-Van's forehead, and dabbed at it with a tiny, wet cloth.

With the implanter set, she pressed the device to Z-Van's skin. People around Lionel leaned forward to get a better look. Lionel heard a loud click, then a whoosh.

"Is that it?" Z-Van said.

The woman smiled and nodded. "Now all you need is the identifying mark."

"Give me the number here," Z-Van said, pointing to his forehead.

Carpathia shook the man's hand. "I trust this will make your music even more enjoyable."

A camera flashed and people around the room

clapped. Lionel looked at Westin and shook his head. The procedure had taken only a few seconds and seemed innocent. A person simply received the embedded chip under the skin and a GC number or symbol on the forehead. But those few seconds sealed Z-Van's fate for eternity.

Carpathia held out his hands to the group, looked into the camera, and smiled. "Now, who will be next?"

5

JUDD listened to Lionel's story about Z-Van and shuddered. If they had ever hoped he would become a believer, that hope was gone now.

"We got out of there fast," Lionel said. "You think it's safe traveling with a guy who's taken Carpathia's mark?"

"I don't know that the mark means he's under any special mind control. He's just made his final decision."

Westin sighed. "Maybe it's time we all got out. We could get a flight back to the States."

"We still have time," Judd said. "And I really want to be in Israel when Carpathia comes to the Jewish temple."

Near dusk, Judd set out alone for his meeting with Chang. Along the street he saw televisions through shopwindows tuned to the Global Community Network News. He paused long enough to see footage of Z-Van taking Carpathia's mark. The anchor reported that an anonymous worker inside the Global Community provided the video.

I'll bet Carpathia had someone shoot that himself, Judd thought.

Judd rubbed sweaty palms along his pants as he approached the gazebo. A few uniformed officers strolled the grounds, and several couples talked and laughed on nearby benches. He was in the gazebo only a few minutes when Chang approached, still wearing the red baseball cap.

Chang's face looked tight, and he appeared skittish. Judd reached out to shake his hand, but Chang reached for his cap instead. "You want to see what they did to me?"

Chang whipped off his cap and stared at Judd. The mark of the believer—a cross—was clear. Over it, a small, black tattoo simply read *30*. Beside the number was a half-inch pink scar.

"They say the scar will heal in a few days, but that won't make me look any less like a freak!"

Judd put a hand on Chang's shoulder and led him to a bench. "Don't talk like that."

Chang put a hand to his eyes. "I'm sorry. I should have listened to you and got out when I could."

"What happened?"

Chang put his hat on and Judd was relieved. He couldn't stop staring at the dual marks.

"My father and one of Carpathia's top men did it. I don't remember much about what happened."

"We saw your father and Moon take you out of the elevator."

"I had another big fight with my father before all this happened. I screamed at him."

"Did you tell him the truth?"

"He and Moon both thought I was upset about getting a shot. They laughed and made fun of me because I was afraid of the needle. I have no idea what I said or did on the way to get the mark. You're looking at the newest hire for the Global Community."

Judd took a breath. "What does the *30* mean?"

"There are ten different regions or subpotentateships, as Carpathia likes to call them. Dr. Ben-Judah calls them kingdoms like it says in the Bible. There are ten different prefixes, all related to Carpathia, that people will get around the world. I get a *30* because I'm from the United Asian States."

When Chang put his head back, Judd couldn't help staring at the two marks. He had never seen anything so bizarre.

"I'm so confused," Chang said. "I met with Director Hassid, the believer."

"What did he say?"

"I was still woozy when they took me to him. I tried to act cool, like I was sure of myself, but I really wasn't."

"What aren't you sure about?"

"The Bible says nothing can separate us from the love of Christ. God says we're hidden in the hollow of his hand and that no one can pluck us out. But it also says those who take the mark will be separated from God forever."

"But you didn't choose it—they forced it on you."

"True, but I have doubts. Maybe I'm some kind of freak, like a werewolf. Maybe when the moon's full, I'll follow Carpathia and rat on all my friends."

"You know you won't do that."

Chang leaned forward and put his elbows on his knees. "It's not just my spiritual health. I'm worried about this new position too."

"What do you mean?"

"The believers on the inside of the Global Community have to get out. They want me to come with them—"

"You have to go," Judd interrupted.

"Not if I have this," Chang said, pointing to his forehead. "Carpathia loyalists can't see the mark of the believer. They just see the 30. That means I can live freely among them, buy and sell, and even work here without the slightest suspicion that I'm anything but true-blue GC. Mr. Hassid called it being bi-loyal."

"So you could stay and do what Mr. Hassid has been doing."

"He said I'd never get his job. I'm too young to be a director. But if he teaches me everything he's done inside—listening in on Carpathia, his staff, and warning believers—I could be a big help to the Tribulation Force."

"Sounds like a lot of pressure."

"It won't be very long before Christ comes back. I want to do something worthwhile, even if there's danger."

Judd smiled. He felt the same way, and he was sure others in the Young Tribulation Force did too.

"Mr. Hassid wants me to keep playing things cool until I'm offered the job in his department."

"That way they won't suspect you when he shows up missing, right?"

Chang nodded.

"How are they going to escape?"

"I can't tell you that. It's not that I don't trust you. I just have to keep their secret."

"Understood. It must be exciting thinking about being alone in your own place. I assume your parents are going back to China."

Chang nodded again.

"Have they taken the mark yet?"

"No, and it's curious. I saw Z-Van was allowed to take it. I thought my father would have pulled a few strings to get him and my mother inside to get theirs as well."

"Maybe you can convince them not to do it," Judd said.

"I pray every hour that they will not take the mark."

After much debate about whether the GC would recognize Vicki, she convinced the others to allow her to be the decoy inside the reeducation facility. She changed clothes and rode with Colin and the others in the van. Colin had asked Jim Dekker and Natalie Bishop to send immediate orders to Iowa, and Dekker gave them phone numbers and names for the leaders there. "I'll have everyone pray for you," Jim Dekker had said.

They were a few miles away when Mark and Pete pulled the van and the truck to the roadside. Everyone got out, joined hands, and prayed that God would show them what to do.

When they were finished, Colin looked at Vicki. "I'm not comfortable taking you inside the facility. I'll go in alone as Commander Blakely and take my chances."

Vicki shook her head. "I can get inside, identify all the believers, and get out. Plus I can tell them what's going on. It'll lend credibility to your story."

"If something goes wrong . . ."

"You won't be able to get me out. But it's the same for you. I don't want to have to go back to Wisconsin and tell your wife we let you die here."

Pete held up a hand and put an arm around Colin. "You haven't known these kids as long as I have. They're about as fearless as anybody I've ever known."

Vicki smiled.

"And they're reckless and irresponsible at times," Pete added.

"Why would you say a thing like that?" Shelly said.

"Because it's true." Pete looked at Colin again. "But I know one thing. God's working through them. I've seen it happen before, and I don't doubt that he's going to work through them again."

Colin pursed his lips and nodded. "Okay. Keep your radio on."

Pete drove ahead of them, making sure he had his papers for the injection devices. Mark drove to within a few hundred yards of the entrance to the facility, which was ringed with chain-link fencing and barbed wire around the top.

The kids waited while Pete made his delivery. Colin talked with Jim Dekker and verified that the transfer order for Judah-ite prisoners had been sent from the Des Plaines office.

As Pete's truck pulled away from the facility, he radioed the van. "Package delivered and ready. He is risen."

Colin dialed the number of the Iowa facility and identified himself as Commander Blakely. "You should have received a transfer request for a few of your prisoners. We've captured a suspected Judah-ite, and she's given us information about others in this area. . . . Yes, they're real squealers when you threaten them with the right punishment. . . . No, we'll be taking them with us—"

Colin frowned and closed his eyes. "Let me remind you that you're speaking to a superior officer. I say we're taking them with us. We're pulling up to your facility now, and I expect complete compliance."

Colin hung up the phone. "I hope this works."

Shelly found a pair of handcuffs Jim Dekker had included with their stash of uniforms and equipment. Vicki put her hands behind her, and Shelly quickly locked the cuffs around her wrists. "It's not too uncomfortable, is it?"

Vicki smiled. "You're supposed to be GC. You don't care how it makes me feel."

Mark got past the front gate guard by showing their fake papers. Though the road to the buildings wasn't paved, the main facility looked new. It was two stories and shaped like a U.

Mark parked the van in front and Colin turned to Vicki. "What I say or do to you in there is for your protection. Understand?"

Vicki nodded. "You're the commander, sir. I'm the prisoner."

Colin looked at the others. "The rest of you stay outside the van and wait for me. I'll signal if there's a problem. And if there is, get out of here as fast as you can."

Colin pulled Vicki out roughly, and she nearly fell on the concrete stairs that led to the main building. A man in a deputy commander's uniform walked out quickly and saluted Colin. Vicki kept her head down.

"Like I said on the phone, sir," the deputy commander said, "we're ready to process the prisoners—"

"Then I'm glad we got here in time. If you'll show me where you're holding the prisoners, we'll let this one identify her friends and be on our way."

"Sir, we've been waiting all day to begin—"

"Have I not made myself clear, Deputy Commander?" Colin said forcefully. "We have reason to believe some of your prisoners will choose the blade instead of the mark of loyalty."

"All the better," the man said. "We'll be done with them."

"Have you ever heard of Tsion Ben-Judah? Have you not been briefed on the Tribulation Force? One of your prisoners may know the location of the Judah-ites' main hideout. If my superiors or anyone in New Babylon finds out that you've hindered the process—"

"I'm sorry, sir. I understand. Right this way."

Colin took Vicki's arm and rushed her up the stairs, following the deputy commander closely. GC guards stood at the doorway with guns. As she entered, she glanced back at her friends. Shelly gave her a nod as Colin pushed Vicki into the enemy's lair.

6

VICKI felt the eyes of the GC guards on her as soon as she walked into the building. There was a sense of evil about the place. These were people who had given their lives to the Global Community, pledged their service to Nicolae Carpathia, and would no doubt kill believers without a second thought.

"It's a shame these prisoners get to take the mark of loyalty first," the deputy commander said. "I've got a whole staff here anxious to go."

Colin bristled and spoke softly to the man. "Those orders are from New Babylon, and I'll caution you not to spread dissension among your workers."

"I only meant that—"

"I know what you meant, and I commend you for wanting to show your devotion. But a subtle complaint like that can infect those around you and cause people to question the ultimate authority of the potentate."

The deputy commander stopped. "I would never want that, sir. Please forgive my lapse in judgment."

Colin nodded and put out a hand. "Proceed."

The deputy commander gleefully reported that they had received information from around the country and the world of many successful mark applications. "We haven't heard one story of applicators failing."

"Any news about those who wouldn't take the mark?"

"There have been a few pockets of resistance. We raided an underground meeting in Arizona and found Judah-ites. Every one of them chose the blade instead of—"

"Please refer to it as a loyalty enforcement facilitator," Colin corrected.

"Of course. Sorry, sir. There have been Judah-ite . . . uh, deaths in the south and northeast as well. North Carolina. Maryland. Pennsylvania. I suppose you saw the communiqué from New Babylon about this."

"I haven't yet. What did it say?"

They walked through a series of doors, and Vicki felt a whoosh of air as she walked inside one of the long buildings attached to the main one. The farther they went, the more scared Vicki became. *What if they find out Colin's not GC?*

"The report listed the number of uses of the loyalty enforcement facilitators. They seemed to be concentrated in the United Asian States and, believe it or not, in the United Carpathian States."

"How could that be?" Colin said. "I had heard the UCS had the lowest concentration of rebels than any other region."

"You would think so," the deputy commander said. "But they rounded up a large contingent in Ptolemaïs, in the country formerly known as Greece."

"And took care of the problem?"

The deputy commander ran a finger across his neck. "With one chop."

The man opened a final door that led into the holding area. "I assumed you wanted to go to the women's facility first."

Colin scratched his chin. "That's fine."

"How did you catch this one?"

"She was helping a group of Judah-ites store food and medical supplies. She has agreed to identify the rebels in this group in exchange for leniency in her sentence."

"Is that right?" the deputy commander sneered.

Colin leaned over to the man and whispered something.

The man laughed. "A Judah-ite rat, eh? If you ask me, they're all like rats, spreading betrayal to the potentate like a disease."

Colin unlocked her handcuffs and leaned toward Vicki. "Find as many of them as you can and do it quickly, Judah-ite."

Vicki glared at Colin as the deputy commander shoved her inside. "Find them or it's the blade for you."

Vicki walked inside the open area of the women's division. A thin carpet, marked in places with colored tape, covered the floor. She guessed this was where prisoners lined up each morning.

The room was lit with natural light from several skylights. Bars covered doors and windows along the walls. Vicki noticed several cameras overhead focusing on different parts of the building.

Vicki guessed there were a few hundred women in the long room. Many were teenagers or in their early twenties who had somehow run afoul of the Global Community. Some had hardened faces, while others seemed lost, frightened, and confused. Though this building was larger, it reminded her of her stay in the Northside Detention Center.

Women milled about the room in clusters, talking and laughing. Some lay on the floor while others exercised, power-walking the length of the room.

A hush fell over the crowd when they saw Vicki. A woman motioned for her to come closer. "You got any smokes?"

Vicki shook her head and walked through the crowd, looking for anyone with the mark of the believer. As she passed, she overheard a few women talking about the mark. "Those kids said if we let the GC put that chip in and give us the tattoo, we can't get into heaven."

"You don't have to worry about getting into heaven," another laughed. "You'd never make it anyway."

Several women laughed.

"Excuse me," Vicki said. "What girls were talking about not taking the mark?"

A tall blonde woman stepped forward. "Did we invite you into this conversation?"

"I'm just looking for—"

"I don't care who you're looking for. Don't interrupt!"

Vicki glanced back and saw Colin and the deputy commander moving into another room. She knew she didn't have much time, but in a group this large, it could take a while to find all of the believers.

As Vicki moved forward, a woman took her arm and whispered, "Don't be afraid of Donna. The girls you're looking for are in the back corner."

Vicki found two groups of believers surrounded by a cluster of inmates. The girls saw the mark on her forehead and rushed to her. Vicki quickly explained she had met them at the college and was here to help. A few women without the mark inched closer.

"I don't have much time. They're going to start processing people for the mark in a little while."

One girl shook her head. "They wheeled the guillotine through this morning. I thought we were goners."

"You kids aren't thinking of refusing the mark, are you?" a woman at the edge said.

A dark-haired girl spoke up. "We've been trying to tell you, if you take Carpathia's mark, you've sealed your fate for eternity."

The woman rolled her eyes and shook her head. "Religious crazies," she muttered.

"I need to identify all the believers for the GC," Vicki said. "How many are there?"

"Three guys and ten girls as far as we know," the dark-haired girl said.

"What about Cheryl?" another girl said.

"Who's Cheryl?" Vicki said.

"In the corner with her back to us," the dark-haired girl said. "We've held meetings to try and tell people the truth. Cheryl seems really interested, but she hasn't made up her mind yet."

"She'd better hurry," Vicki said.

Another believer talked with Cheryl about the Bible but seemed frustrated. Then Vicki approached, sat, and took Cheryl's hand. "My name's Vicki Byrne. Someone said you're pretty interested in what these girls have been saying."

Cheryl nodded. She was small framed, had blonde hair, and wore a sweater. Vicki guessed she was about sixteen. The girl's eyes were puffy and red.

Cheryl wiped away a tear. "I want to believe what they say, but I don't think God could love me."

Vicki stared at the girl, bit her lip, and began. "I never rush people into a decision like this, but we're in a big hurry. The Global Community wants you to take a mark of loyalty to Carpathia, and if you do that, you won't be able to accept God's truth."

"I've been really bad."

"I understand. I was no angel before I found out about God. But it doesn't matter how bad or good you are, because all it takes is one sin to separate us from God. That's why he sent his Son to die in our place and take the punishment for our sins."

"You mean, Jesus?"

"Right. In the Bible it says that anyone who receives him has eternal life. But the people who reject him, reject God himself."

"But that's not what the Global Community wants us to believe."

Someone blew a whistle at the other end of the room and Vicki stood. She looked through the masses of women and girls and saw Colin with the deputy commander.

Vicki knelt by Cheryl. "I'm going to pray a prayer because I have to go. If you want, you can say it with me or have one of the other girls pray with you. This is how you receive God's gift."

The whistle blew again, and the deputy commander yelled for everyone to sit on the floor.

"God in heaven, I know that I have sinned against you and I deserve to be punished," Vicki whispered. "I want to turn from my sin right now and receive the gift you're offering me. I believe Jesus came to die for my sins so that I could be forgiven, and that he was raised again so that I might spend eternity with you. Right now I want to reach out to you and ask you to be the Lord of my life. Forgive me. Save me. In Jesus' name, amen."

Vicki glanced at Cheryl's forehead, but there was no mark of the believer. "You still have questions?"

"How did you know?"

Vicki smiled. "It's written on your face."

Vicki glanced toward the center of the room and saw Colin and the deputy commander moving through the crowd of women. "I have to go. Please pray that prayer. And no matter what you do, don't take the mark of Carpathia."

Colin grabbed Vicki by the arm and pulled her to a standing position. "Have you found them?" he screamed.

Vicki nodded. "I don't know all their names, but I can show you which ones they are."

"She's a traitor!" the tall blonde woman yelled.

The deputy commander turned and called for silence. "There will be none of that." He looked at Vicki. "Point out the Judah-ites."

Vicki looked at Colin and gave a harried glance toward Cheryl and the dark-haired girl, who were still talking in the corner.

"Let's come back here after she's seen the males," Colin said.

Natalie Bishop was double-checking the progress at the Iowa reeducation facility to make sure the order she had sent had gone through. She had used Deputy Commander Henderson's computer while he was out earlier and had typed in Colin's fake name, Commander Blakely, as the ordering officer.

As the afternoon had worn on and she hadn't heard from Vicki or the others, she had become worried. What if she had led them into a trap? What if the deputy commander in Iowa hadn't gotten the release order for the Judah-ites?

Just settle down and stay calm, Natalie told herself.

When Henderson left and told his secretary he wouldn't be returning for the day, the woman gathered her things and walked out the door. Natalie waited, then returned to the office, got on the computer, and pulled up information about the Iowa facility.

She had just called up the release order when Deputy Commander Henderson walked into the office.

"What are you doing?" Henderson said.

Vicki wasn't allowed into the men's section of the prison. Instead, she stood at a window while men filed past. As Vicki pointed out the three believers, GC guards separated them from the other prisoners and led them to a holding room, where they were handcuffed and their names recorded.

One of the younger boys thought he was being led to the mark application site, and the guards had to restrain him. When a guard said he was being turned over to a commander, the boy stared at Colin.

Colin leaned forward and said, "Tell me the truth. Are you a Judah-ite?"

The boy nodded. "How did you know?"

Colin smiled. "Your friends have given you up. But if you will tell us what we want to know, you will live."

Colin gave the order to lead the three males outside to the van. Vicki was taken back to the women's building, and the females were paraded past her like the men had been. When the girls she had known from the abandoned college walked past, she pointed and they were taken into another holding room.

Vicki couldn't help thinking that she was somehow controlling the destinies of these women. If she chose them, they would be safe from the Global Community. If she let them pass, they would be forced to take the mark of Carpathia. She only chose the believers, of course, but she still felt bad for the women who had rejected God's love.

As the line dwindled, Vicki scanned the crowd for the dark-haired girl she had seen when she first arrived. Finally, when the last few women passed, Vicki spotted her and pointed.

The last girl in line was Cheryl. She had pulled the hood of her sweater over her head. When she passed Vicki, she threw the hood off and Vicki gasped. On Cheryl's forehead was the mark of the true believer.

7

NATALIE quickly clicked Deputy Commander Henderson's computer off and moved away from his desk.

"I said, what are you doing in here?"

"I'm sorry, sir . . . your computer is so much faster—"

"You have no right." Henderson clicked the computer back on.

"Sir, I was just composing a message to . . . a friend of mine, and I didn't want anybody to see it."

"A love interest?" Henderson said.

Natalie looked away.

Henderson studied the screen. "Let me ask you again, and this time don't lie—"

"I was helping a friend," Natalie interrupted.

"But why were you using *my* computer? Unless . . ." Henderson pulled up the last document in the computer, and Natalie closed her eyes. If he found the entry about Commander Blakely, the kids were dead.

She fell to the floor and grabbed at her throat, pretending to choke. She glanced at the wall and found the computer's power cord. Before she could reach it, Henderson's foot came down hard on her arm, grinding it into the floor. Natalie cried out, but Henderson kept his eyes on the computer.

"I've had my suspicions about you." He grabbed her arm and pulled her into a chair. "No one can see your computer from your desk. Why would you use mine?"

Natalie rubbed her arm and stared at the man. Before she could speak, he opened the order sent to the Iowa reeducation facility. The name *Commander Blakely* appeared on the screen.

Henderson turned wildly. "Did you send this order from my computer?"

Natalie put her head down and prayed that God would somehow intervene on her behalf.

Henderson pulled out his service revolver and pointed it at Natalie. With the other hand he picked up the phone and dialed. "Send two guards to my office at once." He stared at his computer, then looked hard at Natalie. "If you sent this order, then you must have been behind the escape of that teenage boy. . . ."

Natalie sat still, trying to come up with a verse about feeling peaceful in a time of great stress. All she could think of was a passage from Isaiah Jim Dekker had included with his last e-mail: *"But Lord, be merciful to us, for we have waited for you. Be our strength each day and our salvation in times of trouble."*

Natalie had wondered how it would feel to be caught.

There was a chance she could still talk her way out of this
or come up with some kind of explanation, but the more
Henderson questioned her, the more her hopes faded.
She had helped the Shairtons, Maggie, and the new
believer, Manny, escape from the Global Community's
snare. She had also helped Vicki, Darrion, and other
Young Tribulation Force members. If the plan in Iowa
went through, more lives would be saved. *Not bad for a
lowly Morale Monitor,* she thought.

The elevator dinged.

Henderson seemed deep in thought. Then he said, "If
you sent this order, then Commander Blakely is phony.
And if that's true, those four people he took from here are
loose." He slammed his hand on the desk. "How could I
have been so stupid!"

"If that's true and you report it, you admit your
incompetence," Natalie said. "Those orders were placed
from your computer. How will anyone know it wasn't
you who made Blakely up?"

Two guards rushed into the room and saluted.
Henderson set his jaw firmly. "This Morale Monitor is to
be held in a private cell until we can interrogate her
further."

"What's the charge, sir?" one guard said as he snapped
handcuffs on Natalie.

"Treason," Henderson snapped. "And I suspect her to
be a Judah-ite."

As they led Natalie to the elevator, she heard
Henderson on the phone with someone at the Iowa facility. She prayed that Vicki and the others were already out.

Vicki and the group of believers were led through a side door into an outside holding area. She looked past several GC guards to the van in front of the building. Mark walked toward her and nodded. His eyes widened as the believers were herded through the door. They both knew the van would only hold fifteen people. Counting Colin and the others, there were nineteen. Mark went back to the van and said something into his radio.

The deputy commander and Colin walked outside to count heads. "I don't think you have enough room in your vehicle for these, Commander."

"I'm not interested in their comfort during the ride," Colin said sharply. "We'll manage. Now, if you'll open the gate, we'll be on our way."

Vicki sidled up to the dark-haired girl. "The Morale Monitors at the van are believers too," she whispered. "Tell the others to act like you're upset that I ratted you out."

The girl whispered the message to the others, and it spread through the group.

The deputy commander nodded toward a guard by the chain-link fence, and the man unlocked the gate and slid it back.

Vicki pushed her way to the front, and one by one the kids walked to the van. "You said you'd take me separately!" Vicki yelled.

Conrad shoved Vicki hard. She lost her balance and went down in the gravel.

"Leave her!" the deputy commander said.

The others piled into the van, some grumbling about Vicki, others complaining about how packed the van was. A few had to sit on the floor to fit inside.

"Why don't you leave her here?" the deputy commander said to Colin. "We would be glad to take care of her for you."

Colin picked Vicki up by one arm, and she screamed in mock pain. "You're not putting me in there with those people. They'll kill me!"

Colin shoved Vicki toward the van and she climbed inside. "She may be able to tell us more."

A guard yelled that the deputy commander had a phone call. The man shook hands with Colin and went inside the building.

Colin closed the door and turned to Mark. "Get us to the main road as quickly as you can."

Mark pulled out, the tires spinning in the gravel. A boy behind Vicki said, "I want to thank you guys for helping us get out of there, but next time I'd like to order a bus."

A few laughed nervously. Colin said, "Keep it down. We're not out of this yet."

"That guy is running toward us!" someone yelled from the back of the van.

Vicki glanced in a side mirror and saw the deputy commander waving his hands, yelling at the guards, and pointing toward the van.

"What do you want me to do?" Mark said, taking his foot from the gas pedal.

"The guards have their guns out!" a girl yelled.

"Step on it!" Colin yelled. "Everybody get down!"

As the van sped toward the front gate, a shot shattered the back window. Kids screamed and Colin told them to stay calm.

"What if they shoot at the gas tank and make it explode?" Shelly screamed.

"That only happens in the movies," Mark said.

The guards at the front scrambled to action, activating a large gate that slowly blocked the entrance.

"Pete, we need some help!" Mark yelled into the radio.

"I'm on my way."

The guards flew inside the guardhouse as the van careened around the closing gate, sending sparks flying. When Mark turned onto the main road, Vicki felt the van tip slightly, and she thought they were going over. Mark swerved and the van righted itself.

"GC cruisers are following us!" someone shouted.

"Okay, here comes Pete," Mark said, slowing.

"What are you doing?" Colin yelled. "Keep going."

Mark stopped the van as Pete's truck neared the entrance. Vicki craned her neck and saw the two guards in front raise their rifles and fire at the truck, then run away. Pete's trailer slid sideways, crashing into the guardhouse and blocking the entrance. The trailer tipped but didn't turn over. GC cruisers raced after them.

Mark put the van in reverse and zoomed toward Pete. The man had a huge gash over one eye and a bruise was forming on his forehead, but he had managed to limp to the middle of the road. Vicki threw open the van door when Mark slowed enough for Pete to climb inside.

Pop-pop-pop went the rifle fire as Vicki slammed the

door. Two of the side windows shattered as Mark floored the accelerator and sped away.

"Stay down!" Colin said.

"I don't know where this road comes out," Mark yelled. "We came in the other way."

"Keep going," Pete gasped. "When you come to the next road, turn right."

"Are you all right?" Vicki said.

Pete was on the floor, wedged between a seat and the door. He was holding his right arm and for a moment let go. A dark, red stain covered his shirtsleeve.

"He's bleeding!" Vicki gasped.

One of the kids ripped a piece of cloth from his shirt and tied it around Pete's arm. The man looked pale and was having a hard time catching his breath.

"Will they be able to trace your truck?" Colin said.

Pete shook his head. "It's under a different name."

"What happened back there?" Shelly yelled.

"I knew that phone call wasn't a good sign," Colin said. "Somebody finally figured out we're not who we said we are."

"You could have fooled us, sir," a boy in the back of the van said.

Colin smiled. He dialed Jim Dekker in Illinois to update him and see if he knew how the GC had discovered them.

Vicki leaned over and put a hand on Pete's forehead. He was breathing easier now, and some of the color had come back to his face. "You hang on until we can get you some help."

Pete smiled. Someone in the back folded a uniform and passed it forward. Vicki placed it under Pete's head, and the big man closed his eyes.

Colin hung up and shook his head. "Jim has no idea how the GC found out about us. He's been trying to get in touch with Natalie, but he can't reach her at her apartment, the jail, or by e-mail."

"You don't think . . . ," Vicki said.

Colin kicked the dashboard with a foot. "I knew she should have gotten out of there."

"We have to go back for her," Vicki said.

"We have to get out of here first," Mark said.

Colin remained silent. "We'll go back and help her, right?"

When no one responded, Vicki slumped onto the floor. She felt helpless, useless.

"Maybe Natalie ran," Shelly said. "She's smart. Maybe she's on her way to Wisconsin right now."

Vicki closed her eyes and prayed that Shelly was right. But something inside her said she wasn't.

Natalie sat on the bunk in her cell, her head in her hands. By now she was sure they had found the e-mails she had sent from Deputy Commander Henderson's computer as well as from Peacekeeper Vesario's machine. Her prayer was that Vicki and the others had gotten away safely.

Natalie leaned against the concrete wall. She had longed to be away from the Global Community, on the outside with Vicki and the others, but she believed God could use her best inside. She had felt a sense of mission, working against the GC, and now her mission was complete.

Natalie regretted not being able to talk to Vicki about her story. She had imagined them sitting on a couch in front of a fire with mugs of hot chocolate steaming in their hands. Vicki would first fill in all the missing places of her story, and then she would listen to Natalie's.

But that wouldn't happen now. Natalie would never have the chance to tell Vicki about the woman who had taught her Sunday school class, who had prayed for Natalie and her family. After the disappearances, Natalie had rushed to the woman's house. When there was no answer at the door, she went inside. The woman's prayer journal was open on the kitchen table, and Natalie found her name. She also found Christian books and literature that she shoved into a garbage bag and dragged home.

Natalie smiled as she thought about how hungry she was for information in those days. She nearly inhaled the books and stayed up all hours of the night reading her Bible and asking God to show her his plan.

"Thank you, God, for using me to help others," she prayed softly.

Natalie suddenly sat up straight, realizing that someone else needed to hear the message. She banged on her cell and yelled for the guard.

8

VICKI and the others in the van raced through the back roads of Iowa, knowing their chances of escaping the GC dragnet were slim if they didn't get help.

Colin dialed Jim Dekker's phone and reached him at the satellite operations center. "They've gotten a request to track us," Colin told the kids a few minutes later.

"Then Jim can help us," Vicki said.

Colin shook his head. "An operator is trying to track us now. Jim doesn't think he can help without revealing himself."

"What about the girl who wrote us, Kelly Bradshaw?" Vicki said. "Maybe she has a place we can hide."

Vicki dialed the Wisconsin safe house and Darrion answered. "No time to talk. We need to get in touch with Kelly Bradshaw."

"I just got an e-mail from her about an hour ago," Darrion said.

"Did she leave a number?"

Darrion pulled up the message and gave Vicki a phone number. "She wants you guys to call her no matter what happens."

Vicki immediately dialed Kelly. The girl was overjoyed to hear they had gotten their friends out safely. Vicki explained the situation and told her they were coming near a more populated area.

Kelly covered the phone and spoke with someone else in the room.

"Tell her we don't have much time," Mark said. "They'll probably have helicopters out soon."

"Hide the van and we'll come get you," Kelly said.

"Where could we hide a big van like this?"

"There!" Colin yelled.

Vicki saw a long, white building with what looked like several hundred garages. On top was a sign that said U-Store It.

Mark pulled into the parking lot, and Colin told everyone to stay down while he went inside. Vicki gave Kelly the address of the building, and Kelly said they would be there as soon as possible.

"What about Pete?" Shelly said. "We need to get him to a doctor."

"I just need to rest," Pete said. "I think the bleeding's stopped."

Colin motioned for Mark to drive the van around back. He opened one of the large bay doors, and the van barely fit inside. As the others got out and stretched, Vicki covered Pete with some spare uniforms.

Several kids knelt in prayer in the darkened storage room, thanking God for delivering them from sure death at the hands of the GC. They all prayed for Pete and that they would be able to escape the oncoming GC manhunt.

"What did you tell the guy at the front desk?" Vicki asked Colin.

"I told him the truth. The GC is looking for some escapees from a reeducation facility not far from here and to keep his eyes open. I deputized him and told him to—"

Colin stopped as noise filled the storage facility. It grew so loud that the door shook.

"Helicopter," Mark said.

Natalie waited in her cell, praying that her request would be granted. She had promised to tell the GC everything about herself if she could meet with her roommate. She imagined Deputy Commander Henderson mulling over the request, thinking of some way to salvage his career.

An hour passed before a guard handcuffed her and led her to an upstairs interrogation room. "Please, God," she prayed, "I just want to tell Claudia the truth. I know she's been pro-Carpathia ever since we've been room-mates, but I've never told her what I really believe. Give me the chance today."

Claudia Zander was tall, blonde, and caught the eye of every male Morale Monitor in the building. Natalie had noticed a slight change in the girl's behavior in the past week. She seemed moody, and the two had talked late one night. Natalie had asked questions but didn't offer any information about her own beliefs.

Natalie heard a door close in the observation room behind her as Claudia walked in. No doubt Henderson and his crew were back there listening. She would give them an earful.

"Thanks for coming," Natalie said.

"I couldn't believe it when I heard. They say you're a Judah-ite and you helped people escape."

"I knew they'd ask you about me, and I wanted to make sure they don't suspect you."

Claudia scooted back from the table. "You can't be serious. You're really working with the enemy?"

"Let me explain." Natalie began at the disappearances and told Claudia how she had come to know the truth about God. When the kids in the Young Tribulation Force had gotten into trouble, she helped.

Natalie leaned forward and whispered, "I want you to know how to begin a relationship with God. All you have to do is pray and ask him to forgive—"

"Shut up!" Claudia looked at the mirror behind Natalie. "I want out of here. She's not telling me anything about the ones who escaped."

Natalie wished she could touch the girl or give some gesture of kindness, but her hands were cuffed behind her. "At least look up the Young Trib Force Web site."

Claudia shook her head and scowled. "You're crazy. I don't know how you could betray all of us like this, but you'll pay."

A guard opened the door and Claudia ran out. Deputy

Commander Henderson walked in, smiling. "We have your little group cornered in Iowa. It won't be long now. And since you're being charged with a crime against the Global Community, you're now a prisoner. You know what that means."

Natalie stared at the man. "Sir, I want you to know I'm sorry I misled you. I've lied to you in order to make sure my friends stayed free. But I'm finally ready to tell the truth."

Henderson pulled the chair around and straddled it. "I'm listening."

"God loves you so much, he was willing to die for you. . . ."

When the helicopter passed overhead, Vicki and the others gathered around Colin. "Jim was able to shut the power down at the satellite building briefly so we were able to hide before they located the van. That's the good news. Of course, they're still looking."

"If we don't show up on the satellite, they'll figure we're hiding," a girl said. "Won't they check here at some point?"

Colin nodded. "That's why we need to get this van back on the road. I'll take it and leave you—"

"No way," Vicki interrupted. "You have a wife back in Wisconsin."

"I'm also the senior member of this group."

"Which is another reason you shouldn't go," Mark said.

"They're right," Conrad said. "One of us should do it."

Colin shook his head. "What if we convince the guy at the front desk to drive it somewhere?"

"The GC will be all over him," Vicki said.

"But he's a Carpathia lover. You should have seen his face light up when he saw my uniform."

Vicki bit her lip. She and Darrion had tricked a man in Des Plaines and it still haunted her. "I don't like getting others mixed up in our problems. What if he has a change of heart and wants to trust God? He'll remember how we treated him."

Mark took off his watch. "What if we give him The Cube and tell him not to look at it until he gets to his destination?"

Vicki scowled. "Sounds like a cop-out."

"All right, you have a better idea?" Mark said.

Vicki shook her head.

"Then it's settled," Colin said. "Write the note."

Vicki mingled with the new kids, asking their names and where they were from. The newest believer, Cheryl Tifanne, was from Des Moines. Global Community Peacekeepers had arrested her for stealing food from a grocery store. "I've been so hungry lately. Sometimes I can find a place in line at one of the shelters, but recently I haven't had much luck."

"We'll make sure you get enough to eat," Vicki said.

Vicki phoned Darrion in Wisconsin and asked if she had heard anything from Natalie. Darrion said she hadn't but that she'd watch the Web.

The phone rang a few moments later, and Kelly said

they were an hour away. "We just heard about you guys on the radio. Better make sure the people at that storage place aren't listening."

Vicki volunteered to talk with the man at the front. She walked around the building and approached from the other side.

The lobby had two plastic chairs and an old candy dispenser. The carpet looked like it had been through a couple of floods. Paneling covered the walls and every few feet Vicki noticed cobwebs. There was no TV in the office, but the man behind the counter was listening to the radio.

"How's it going?" Vicki said.

The man took his feet off the desk and nearly fell backward. "You scared me. What can I do for you?"

"What's going on with the helicopter and everything?"

"It's a Global Community thing. I can't really say."

"You heard it on the radio?"

"No. I just know, that's all."

Vicki saw a few tapes scattered across the desk. "Do you like country? I sure do."

"Yeah, I got quite a collection here."

"Mind if I listen to one? I'm waiting for some friends to pick me up."

"Sure," the man said. "Take your pick."

Vicki picked up a cassette and popped it in the player. The man said it was one of his favorites. As the music played, Vicki asked more questions and found out the man lived with his wife and small baby a few miles away. The more she learned, the worse she felt about the plan to let him drive the van.

She excused herself, saying she wanted to check on her ride, and walked back to the storage room. "I've got a bad feeling about this. He's really sweet, and he has a wife and baby. What if the GC hurt him?"

Colin sighed. "I don't want anything to happen to him, but if we're caught, we're dead."

Colin's cell phone rang. It was Kelly calling to say they were only a few minutes away.

Natalie sat stone-faced, looking at Deputy Commander Henderson. She had answered all of his questions except ones about other members of the Young Tribulation Force and where the four escaped prisoners were hiding. The truth was, she didn't know for sure. She had purposefully not asked anyone for the information so she wouldn't have to lie.

Henderson berated her, accused her of treason and blasphemy against Potentate Carpathia.

"I don't argue with any charge except the last one. You can't blaspheme someone who's not God."

Henderson seethed, pointing a finger and asking about the location of the Tribulation Force's safe house. "You know where this Ben-Judah is hiding, don't you?"

"I don't, sir, and even if I did, I wouldn't tell you."

Someone knocked on the door and Henderson slipped outside. Natalie wondered if these were her last moments. Perhaps they would question her more or try to torture information out of her.

She closed her eyes and thought of Zeke Sr. He had

faced Henderson and the others with such courage. She wondered how he could possibly do it, but now, instead of feeling anxious and nervous about what was going to happen, she felt calm. She knew there was a Bible verse for this, but she couldn't remember the exact wording. It was something about Jesus giving peace to everyone who trusts in him.

Natalie sat back, relaxed her arms, and let her head rest on the back of the chair. She had never felt so focused and alive. Though others had the power to take her life, she knew God truly held her destiny in his hands.

"If you rescue me from this, I'll praise you," Natalie whispered. "And if you don't, I'll praise you in heaven. I'm yours, God."

Vicki heard a loud click from the van as Colin raised the door to the storage room. Conrad tried to get in one of the side doors but couldn't. "It's locked!"

The van started and Vicki ran to the front. Pete sat in the driver's seat, his window rolled down a couple of inches.

"Pete, get out of there!" Vicki screamed.

"I agree with what you said about that guy in the front," Pete said, carefully backing out through the open door.

Vicki ran after him but Colin grabbed her. "It's okay. He knows what he's doing."

"You can't let him go! The GC will catch him."

Pete tossed a piece of paper out the window and waved at the group. Out of the parking lot, he turned left and headed back the way they had come.

Vicki sobbed, tears streaming down her cheeks. "Why did he do that?"

"Because he cares more about us than he does about himself," Mark said. "And he cares about the guy in the office."

Vicki shook her head and prayed that somehow she would be able to see Pete again.

One of the kids handed her the piece of paper from the ground. Her name was scrawled on the front. Vicki stashed the note in her pocket.

9

VICKI watched Pete drive out of sight. More vehicles approached from the other direction.

Mark ran toward the office with the note the kids had written. "I'm going to give this to the guy up front!"

A green minivan and two other cars pulled to the back of the storage facility. Vicki recognized Kelly when she got out of the van and hugged her.

"No time for reunions," Colin said. "Everybody get in. Keep some distance between cars and keep in touch with the radios."

Mark hurried out and jumped in the minivan with Vicki, Shelly, Conrad, and several others. The rest filled the cars.

"Did you give the note to him?" Vicki said.

Mark nodded. "I didn't have time to talk. I just told him that there was information he needed to read and share with his family. I gave him my watch so he could see The Cube."

"But he doesn't know how to pray," Vicki said.

"I put the Web site address on the note. He has enough information now."

As Kelly drove along the road, Vicki kept looking behind them and checking overhead. Several times she thought she heard helicopters, but none appeared.

"Who are the other drivers?" Vicki asked.

"We've known about some older believers who live a few miles from the school. I ran there this morning. Two volunteered to drive, and the rest are praying for us now."

"Where are we going?" Mark said.

"It's better if we split up to different houses," Kelly said. "Neighbors won't be suspicious."

"We'll have to go into hiding anyway," another girl said. "They'll be giving the mark to the rest of the population soon."

Vicki knew they were right, but she had hoped to get back to Wisconsin soon. Natalie needed to get away from the GC, plus it was possible Judd and Lionel were coming back. She didn't want to miss that.

Vicki pulled the bloody paper from her pocket and held it a moment. She prayed the GC wouldn't spot Pete and asked God to keep him alive. "We've lost so many already. Don't let us lose Pete."

Vicki took a breath. The bloodstains were mostly on the outside of the paper where Pete had folded it. He had scrawled the note on the back of Colin's fake GC orders for the Iowa prisoners.

Dear Vicki,

Forgive my shaky handwriting. I agree with what you said about that guy in the office. We shouldn't use others who aren't believers just to keep ourselves safe. We're here to reach out to people who don't know God.

That's why I'm leaving with the van. I don't know if I'll escape, but know this. No matter what happens, I'll be waiting for you kids on the other side.

Vicki, I want you to know, if I ever had a daughter, I'd want her to be just like you. If your parents can see you from heaven, I know they're looking on with pride. God has planned something special for you. I know that.

I'd better stop writing because the people are almost here to pick you up.

I love you, Vicki. Tell Judd, Mark, Lionel, and all the others that I feel the same about them. Stay steady. Trust God. Celebrate him with abandon every day and never stop telling the truth. Remember, God wins in the end, so we're fighting a defeated enemy.

Pete

Vicki closed her eyes and let the tears fall. Pete had been like a big brother to her. Having friends like him who cared helped her go on each day.

She shook her head. She wasn't giving up on him. Though he was hurt and vulnerable to the Global Community, she decided not to entertain the idea that she had seen him for the last time. Pete would be back.

He had to come back. She folded the paper, shoved it in her pocket, and wiped away the tears.

Mark put a hand on her shoulder and asked if she was okay.

"I'll be all right."

Judd waited for word from Chang as he sat in front of the computer. Lionel and Westin had gone to bed, but Judd couldn't sleep. Z-Van was entertaining guests, so Judd sat at the small desk in the bedroom and put on headphones as he surfed the Internet.

Judd logged on to the official GC Web site and discovered the numbers of prisoners who had been executed in different areas around the world. He checked the States first and recognized Zeke's father's name from the Des Plaines facility. He felt bad for Zeke and wondered where he was.

There were also several prisoners in Arizona, California, and Texas who had decided against taking Carpathia's mark. Judd scrolled through the different regions and, to his surprise, found that many had chosen the guillotine in the former country of Greece, now part of the United Carpathian States.

Judd was stunned when he found Anton Rudja's name on the list of prisoners who had been executed. Anton Rudja's son was Pavel, Judd's friend who had first invited him to New Babylon.

When he recovered, Judd checked back to the kids' Web site and found an e-mail from Buck Williams.

Friends,

I'm sending this quick note so you can be the first to know that there are now many martyrs for the faith in Greece. I will write further about the specifics in The Truth when I can complete the story, but know that the believers there were brave.

The underground church in Ptolemaïs, Greece, was probably the largest in the United Carpathian States. The Greek believers were careful, even though local GC Peacekeepers seemed to look the other way for a while. Sources tell me the reason for the crackdown was that Carpathia wanted the region that bore his name to have the lowest reports of Christ-followers of the ten global supercommunities. Rather than pretend the rebels didn't exist, many were rounded up from local meetings and forced to make a decision for or against Carpathia.

I cannot begin to tell you the amount of courage those believers exhibited. GC authorities tried to scare people by carting guillotines through the streets in open trucks. They're ugly contraptions, and there isn't much to them. Just wood, screws, blade, spring, and rope. They will put these at the mark application sites to make people comply, but if others act the way our brothers and sisters in Greece did, they won't back down.

When prisoners were told they would be taking the mark, people cheered and many young people started chanting and singing about Carpathia. The GC handled the mark application and the biochip injection with great efficiency. It won't surprise me if they take what they *learned here and create a fast-moving system that will get people in and out of the process in a few minutes.*

I witnessed the most inhuman treatment of the believers. One woman who knelt to pray was treated savagely by her captors. Though she was beaten and bloody, she did not obey. And as the man who led the group asked for those who would not take the mark, more stepped forward, some of their marks appearing as they raised their hands to change lines.

When the first woman knelt in front of that ugly machine, the room fell silent. This woman began to sing "My Jesus, I Love Thee" but had only finished a few words when the blade came down to end her life.

I have never seen such courage, such resolve, and such bravery. I know we will see those women again in heaven, but their deaths, so jarring, have caused me to write you.

Pray for other believers who may even now be going through the same fate.

Judd shuddered as he read the rest of Buck's eye-witness account. He wondered how Buck had managed to be inside a prison, but he knew the Tribulation Force had many contacts in many lands.

He also wondered how many in the next few weeks would unknowingly seal their eternal fate by taking Carpathia's mark. The process would be simple. Get in line, take the biochip and tattoo, and go on with your life. Little did they know that taking the mark meant eternal death, and kneeling before the bloody guillotine was the only other option.

Judd returned to a passage in Tsion Ben-Judah's latest e-mail. Tsion had suggested everyone memorize Revelation chapter 20, verse 4:

> "I saw the souls of those who had been beheaded for their testimony about Jesus, for proclaiming the word of God. And I saw the souls of those who had not worshiped the beast or his statue, nor accepted his mark on their forehead or their hands. They came to life again, and they reigned with Christ for a thousand years."
>
> Your loved ones who have been called to what the world would call a gory end shall return with Christ at his Glorious Appearing! They shall live and reign with him for a thousand years! Glory be to God the Father and his Son, Jesus the Christ!

Judd closed his eyes and wondered if he would have to experience the guillotine. The phone rang and he quickly picked it up.

It was Chang. "I need to talk. I'm downstairs in the lobby."

Judd sneaked past the guests in the suite and hurried downstairs. He found Chang sitting on a plush chair, his back to the elevators. Judd sat across from him and stared at the mark on the boy's forehead.

"Can't help yourself, can you?" Chang said.

"I'm sorry. It's just so weird to see both of those together."

Chang shook his head. "It's haunting me. I've been trying to remember what happened—if I resisted or if I just sat down and let them give me the mark. I vaguely remember arguing with my father and a camera flashing in my face, but that's about it."

"Are your parents still here?" Judd said.

Chang nodded. "They leave tomorrow morning. I've convinced them I'm okay and that working for the GC won't be as bad as I thought."

Judd inched closer. "Have they taken the mark?"

"Thankfully, no. I think my father was upset by the whole Z-Van spectacle. He wanted to take the mark while he was here, but now he says they will simply do it when they get back home."

"Are you meeting with Mr. Hassid?"

"We try to talk after hours. We'll be going over the different things he's set up via the computer system here. It looks like I'll be their only contact inside."

Someone walked past and Chang paused. He put a hand to his forehead and sighed. "I don't know if I can do it."

"Of course you can. You're as capable as anybody—"

"It's not that. I know I can do the job. What I don't know is if I can keep it all together."

"I don't understand."

Chang leaned forward and whispered, "These two marks are driving me crazy. When I look in the mirror, all I see is Carpathia's number. I'd like to burn it off or cut it out. I haven't been able to talk with anyone. If I tell Mr. Hassid, he'll think I can't handle the job. If I tell my father, he'll know I'm not loyal to Carpathia and he'll report me."

"What about your mother?"

Chang lowered his head. "I don't know if I should trust her. There are things I can't remember. I think we talked about Ming and me being followers of Ben-Judah, but I'm not sure."

"Your sister is still working inside too?"

Chang shook his head. "She has escaped to the Tribulation Force. How I wish I could be there. I would sit down and talk with Dr. Ben-Judah."

"You'll get your chance," Judd said.

Chang told Judd the inside information he had learned about Carpathia and how angry the potentate was about the Judah-ites. "What about you?" Chang said. "Do you have a safe place to hide?"

"We're not sure it's so safe, but we're going back to Israel with Z-Van's crew."

Chang frowned when Judd told him Lionel's story of Z-Van taking the mark. He looked at his watch and rose to leave.

Judd wanted to say something that would comfort and encourage the boy, but nothing came to mind. He put a hand on Chang's arm. "The only thing I know to tell you is that we'll be praying for you. God keeps his promises, and if you have his mark, he's not going to reject you."

"Are you sure about that?"

Judd watched Chang walk out of the lobby and into the darkened streets. If Chang stayed in New Babylon, he would likely be the only believer there. It would be one of the loneliest assignments of any in the Tribulation Force.

10

VICKI awoke the next morning in the basement of a strange house. She felt something crackle as she rolled to a sitting position and found Pete's letter still folded in her front pocket.

Seven kids were staying at this house. Conrad, Mark, and Shelly had joined Vicki in the green minivan after Pete had driven away. Vicki knew the name of only one of the three girls there—Cheryl, the new believer.

Someone coughed in the bathroom nearby. Whoever it was sounded ill. A few minutes later, Cheryl came out of the bathroom holding her stomach. "Must have been something I ate."

Vicki crept upstairs to find medicine for Cheryl and found a group of adults sitting around the kitchen table, all with the mark of the believer. They stopped talking when Vicki walked in. She explained what she was look- ing for, and a woman hurried to a nearby pantry.

The others stared at Vicki until a younger man standing against the kitchen counter broke the silence. He looked about twenty, was tall and thin, with dark hair. He sipped from a coffee mug and studied Vicki. "I heard we had a celebrity in the house. Aren't you the one from the satellite broadcast?"

Vicki extended a hand. "I'm Vicki Byrne."

The man smiled and shook Vicki's hand warmly. "Chad Harris. Nice to meet you."

"You saw the satellite broadcast?"

"In Des Moines. We drove some believers there to hand out copies of *The Truth*. I assume you know about Buck Williams's reporting?"

Vicki nodded.

"It was impressive what you were able to do. We saw a lot of kids actually get the mark of the believer after your presentation."

Vicki told them about the satellite truck and how Carl Meninger had risked his life in Florida to help them beam the signal to Israel and around the world.

The woman came back with some medicine and said she would go downstairs to help Cheryl.

"Is the Global Community looking for us?" Vicki said nervously.

Chad laughed. "I'd say that's a pretty good guess."

Vicki gritted her teeth. "What I mean is, are there reports about us in the media?"

Chad sobered. "It's been pretty silent about you kids. I don't think the GC wants anybody to know they let you get away."

"What about the others?"

"We have you split up in different houses. You're all safe."

"And Pete? He's the guy who drove the van—"

An older man at the table sat forward. "Haven't heard anything about him yet. We'll let you know if we do. Right now, you need to get back downstairs and relax. We'll take care of you."

Vicki thanked them, and Chad lifted his coffee mug toward her. "If you need anything, just let us know."

Vicki went downstairs to find Mark on the phone with Jim Dekker in Illinois. Mark's face showed the strain of the past two days when he hung up. "Jim was able to keep the power off in the building until the van was hidden. A couple hours later the GC spotted the van heading west and caught up to it before nightfall."

"They have Pete?" Vicki gasped.

"Jim doesn't know. He needs to talk with Natalie to get the information."

"Let's e-mail her."

"He's done that. No answer."

"If they have the van, they'll trace it to Wisconsin, right?"

"Colin took care of that a long time ago. But there's another problem." Mark sat on a couch.

The television was on in the background, and two of the girls from the reeducation facility were watching the latest news. Thousands had gathered near a statue of Nicolae Carpathia in Spain and knelt before it. The report switched to Australia, then to a city in South Africa, where more people worshiped Carpathia.

Mark turned back to Vicki and pursed his lips. "Dekker was supposed to have returned the commander's uniform that Colin's been wearing. Because of this trip, he couldn't."

"So Jim's in trouble," Vicki said, sitting next to Mark.

"They haven't accused him yet, but the operator of the cleaners in Jim's building was taken in for questioning. They must have found out Colin's Commander Blakely was fake and traced the missing uniform."

"Is the guy a believer?"

Mark shook his head. "No, but Jim says he won't let the guy hang for something that's Jim's fault. If he's not released soon, Jim may turn himself in."

Vicki put her head back on the couch and sighed. "That means they'll search Jim's house. Are the Shairtons and the others still there?"

"They were supposed to be on their way to Wisconsin overnight. I checked with Darrion and she said they hadn't made it yet."

Vicki put a hand to her forehead. "Everything's falling apart."

Cheryl came out of the bathroom with Shelly. Shelly gave Vicki a strange look.

"Feel any better?" Vicki said.

"A little. I'm going to rest some more."

When Shelly joined them, Vicki asked her what the look was for. "I'll tell you later," Shelly said.

Conrad called them over to a computer stacked on top of a pool table.

Mark told Vicki that he'd learned something about this house where they were staying. Before the Rapture the people who owned it had several children, one of whom was left behind during the global disappearances. "He opened the house to some of his uncles and cousins. They've been reading Tsion's Web site every day."

"Is Chad the son who was left behind?" Vicki said. Mark nodded.

"He's pretty cute," Shelly said playfully.

"Watch it," Conrad said. He turned the computer screen where everyone could see it. "I was doing some research too. Look at this information I found buried on the official GC Web site."

A picture showed several people standing in front of a fire, with what looked like a huge church in the background. Vicki inched closer and saw it was the Vatican.

"These are photos of Global Community officers destroying paintings, sculptures, icons, and even old Bibles," Conrad said. "The directive came from Leon Fortunato himself."

Mark shook his head. "That stuff is priceless."

"A spokesman said they destroyed everything that paid tribute to the impotent God of the Bible," Conrad said.

"Pretty soon they're going to see he's not so impotent," Vicki said.

Judd talked with Chang on the phone the next day and discovered that Chang's parents were gone. The GC had offered to let them both take the mark in New Babylon, but Mr. Wong had refused. There had been a tearful good-bye at the airport, and Chang returned to the apartment and was assigned permanent quarters. "I'm all by myself now with my own room and my own computer. I don't have to worry about my parents listening in on my conversations."

"Have you talked with Mr. Hassid about his escape?"

"Sorry, Judd, I can't tell you about that. I can tell you this though. Director Hassid and I are designing a new computer system. I should be able to do everything he did up until now from my office or from here in my new apartment."

"What will you do?"

"I'll give the Tribulation Force access to anything they want to hear or see in the palace. But first, I have to monitor the escape and keep things going in the safe house in Chicago. It's going to be a pretty complex mission."

"Who will be your new boss after Hassid leaves?"

"A guy named Aurelio Figueroa. David says he treats the people above him like kings and queens and the people below him like servants. I should be able to handle him okay."

Judd asked how Chang was doing with his feelings about the dual marks, but the boy quickly changed the subject. "Director Hassid showed me how to tap into both live and recorded conversations in the palace, and I came across something you'll be interested in. Are you ready?"

Judd heard several keyboard clicks, then the unmistakable voice of Nicolae Carpathia. "Now when I spoke the other day of a host of enforcers, I wanted you to gather that I meant the very core of my most loyal troops, the GCMM. They are already armed. I want them supported! I want them fully equipped! I want you to marry them with our munitions so their monitoring will have teeth. They should be respected and revered to the point of fear."

"You want the citizenry afraid, sir?" another man said.

"Walter! No man need fear me who loves and worships me. You know that."

"I do, sir."

"If any man, woman, young person, or child has reason to feel guilty when encountering a member of the Global Community Morale Monitoring Force, then yes, I want them shaking in their boots!"

Chang stopped the recording. "Carpathia's talking with Walter Moon, the new supreme commander. They go on about their budget, and then Carpathia says he's going to have at least one hundred thousand armed troops in Israel when he returns there."

"A hundred thousand?"

"You may want to reconsider going."

"Maybe it's time we head back to the States. It's probably a lot safer."

Vicki and the others were careful to stay inside the rest of the day. All the kids were glad when they received the news that Bo and Ginny Shairton, Maggie Carlson, and Manny Aguilara had made it safely to the hideout in

Wisconsin. They had also taken an ample supply of Jim Dekker's uniforms and Global Community gear.

But their joy quickly turned to concern when Jim Dekker phoned. Vicki answered and asked for an update.

"No change with me," Jim said, "but you need to sit down."

"What's wrong?"

"It's about Natalie."

"Is she still in Des Plaines? She should have gotten out of there a long time ago."

"I'm afraid she won't be getting out, Vicki."

"No, even if I have to go down there and—"

"She's gone, Vicki. I just received a communiqué from Des Plaines. That deputy commander over her is being—"

"What do you mean, she's gone?" Vicki interrupted.

"Let me read this release to you. It's to all United North American GC."

Vicki's heart raced as Jim Dekker slowly read the words she dreaded to hear.

> *"Deputy Commander Darryl Henderson was relieved of duty after a Judah-ite plot was discovered under his command. At least four prisoners were released in Des Plaines, and more than a dozen more in Iowa when a man posing as Commander Regis Blakely presented false papers and escorted prisoners out of custody.*
>
> *"It is believed that a female Morale Monitor, Natalie Bishop, 17, aided the impostor by sending information of the transfer via Deputy Commander Henderson's computer.*

*"The Global Community joint chiefs of the United
North American States have appointed Commander
Kruno Fulcire as head of the Rebel Apprehension
Program (RAP). Commander Fulcire will visit the subur-
ban Chicago facility, as well as the Iowa reeducation
facility where the escapes took place."*

"But it doesn't say anything about Natalie's death,"
Vicki said. "They could still want to interrogate her!"

"Let me finish," Jim said. He took a breath and
continued.

*"Commander Fulcire reported that the Morale Moni-
tor Bishop was given the opportunity to swear allegiance
to Potentate Carpathia by taking his mark of loyalty.
Upon refusal, Peacekeepers used the loyalty enforcement
facilitator."*

"No," Vicki whispered. She felt like she had been
kicked in the stomach. Shelly, Mark, and Conrad kept
asking questions, but she waved them off.

"They go on to say they think this is the first Global
Community employee to die for not taking Carpathia's
mark. Commander Fulcire says this shows the importance of administering the mark to everyone on the
planet. He has commanded complete compliance from
every Global Community employee."

"Jim, you have to get out of there right now. If you
turn yourself in for stealing the uniforms—"

"I'm not letting somebody take the fall for my

actions! Even if he is an unbeliever." Jim clicked at his computer, then gasped.

"What's wrong?"

"They've taken the guy from the cleaners to Des Plaines to give him Carpathia's mark."

"Then you have to get out."

"This is my fault," Jim said. "I have to go. I'll let you know what happens."

"Jim, listen—"

Click.

Mark, Conrad, and Shelly gathered around Vicki, and two others from the reeducation center joined them. Vicki was too overcome to speak, but the others could tell what had happened from the conversation.

"Father, we've lost another member of our team today," Mark said, his voice breaking. "We can only imagine what those last moments were like for Natalie. But you gave her the courage to be faithful to you, even until death."

"We know that one day we'll see her again," Conrad continued, "but right now we're hurting. Show us every step we need to take, and make us brave like Natalie. Amen."

11

VICKI spent a few hours alone, thinking about Natalie, how they had met, and what the girl had done for the Young Trib Force. They wouldn't have escaped the schoolhouse or gotten Charlie and the others away from the Global Community without her. Vicki cried herself to sleep and had nightmares about the guillotine.

When Vicki woke up the next morning, she didn't want to talk with anyone. Turning over in bed, she grabbed a Bible, leafed through the pages, and closed it.

"God, I don't know why you let this happen. You saved people before, you helped us get out safely, but you let Natalie die. Why? I don't understand."

Vicki buried her face in her pillow and wept. She wanted to blame someone for Natalie's death, but she couldn't shake the feeling that the girl had died because of Vicki's choices.

While Z-Van and his group went into a studio to record, Judd and Lionel went with Westin Jakes to Z-Van's plane at the New Babylon airport. Though they were able to talk at the hotel, they all felt freer on the airplane.

The three prayed about their next move, feeling strongly that they should get out of New Babylon. But they didn't know whether they would travel to Israel or the States.

"The truth is," Judd said, "you may have to get out before we do."

"Why?" Westin said.

"Z-Van has already taken the mark. His fate is sealed. But you know he's going to want everyone around him to take the mark. Working for him might be worse than being inside the GC."

Westin frowned. "Ever since I prayed to God, I've known that my days with Z-Van were short. I guess I didn't want to think about it."

"If all three of us leave together, we could fly commercial back to the States," Lionel suggested.

Westin frowned again. "Is it wrong to take an airplane like this?"

"You mean steal it?" Judd said.

Westin nodded. "We could really use this thing for the Young Trib Force."

Lionel sighed. "Maybe if we were running for our lives, but I don't like just stealing the plane because it's here. God can take care of us some other way."

Lionel brought up an e-mail he had received from

Sam Goldberg in Israel asking them to come back to Jerusalem. *You won't believe what God is doing here,* Sam wrote.

As they talked and prayed, Judd and Lionel both felt they should still go to Israel. They wanted to see the spectacle Carpathia had planned for the world firsthand.

"Why don't we stay on the plane until it's time to go?" Westin said. "We'll have the whole thing to ourselves, and we won't have to put up with the parties and head-banging music. When Z-Van starts recording, things get wild."

Judd and Lionel brought their things to the plane and settled in. They both had access to the latest computers and communication equipment.

"We should get a conference call together with the rest of the Force," Judd said.

Lionel smiled. "We'll make it a videoconference. That way you can see Vicki."

Late that evening in Iowa, Vicki was sitting up in bed, writing down a few thoughts in her journal when Shelly knocked. She came in, sat on the bed, and asked how Vicki was doing.

Vicki shared her thoughts about Natalie. Then she said, "You didn't tell me what was going on with Cheryl. Is she okay?"

"I don't know how to tell you this and not shock you." Shelly sighed. "Cheryl's going to have a baby."

Vicki's mouth dropped. "Are you sure?"

"We gave her a test and it was positive. She was as shocked as anybody."

"How far along is she?"

"Two, maybe three months."

Vicki thought about Lenore and her baby, Tolan. The child had been such a bright spot in everyone's life at the schoolhouse. But as cute and cuddly as a new baby would be, Vicki knew Cheryl was in for a rough season. "How's she taking the news?"

"She said if she didn't know that God loves her and forgave her for her sins, she'd probably have an abortion."

"I want to talk with her."

"She's resting now, but there's somebody else who says he needs a word."

"Mark?"

Shelly shook her head. "That cute guy upstairs, Chad. He asked to see if you'd meet with him. He seems really nice."

"Now?" Vicki scowled. "What's he want to talk about?"

"I think he's concerned about you."

Vicki got dressed and started upstairs. She stopped outside the door and listened to the believers gathered in the kitchen. They discussed Carpathia, the guillotines, Tsion Ben-Judah, and the kids downstairs.

"We can't keep them here indefinitely," a man said. "The GC will find out and they'll haul us all in."

"We've already had neighbors snooping around and asking questions," a woman said.

Vicki opened the door a crack and looked at the group. With the exception of Chad, they were all older.

Chad held up a hand. "I know we're all worried about what's going to happen, but let's put ourselves in their place. They came out here and risked their lives to save some brothers and sisters. What if it had been us in that GC compound? You think they would have gotten us out?"

The room fell silent as Chad continued. "Of course they would have. I think the least we can do is help them out as long as we can."

Vicki stepped through the door. Chad introduced her to the rest of the group. "Vicki is the one I told you about who was up on the screen giving kids the gospel in the middle of a Global Community education event."

Several around the room clapped and Vicki smiled. Chad took her hand and pulled her onto the back porch. "I know you've been through something terrible, but I want you to come with me."

"Where? I thought we weren't supposed to go outside."

"Trust me."

Chad grabbed a basket and took Vicki to a dirt bike parked in the garage. Vicki climbed on the back and held the basket while Chad revved the engine and drove into the moonlit night.

He drove over a narrow path that led into a burned-out thicket of trees and bushes. The cool wind felt good and the air was fresh on Vicki's face. Chad seemed to drive like he had traveled the path a thousand times before. He stopped at the edge of the charred trees and pointed to the crest of a hill. Three deer stood at the top, feeding on grass. They glanced toward the motorcycle, then continued eating.

"The plague of fire destroyed a lot of forests and homes around here, but you can still see the beauty God created if you look hard enough."

"I'd almost forgotten how pretty things can be."

Chad leaned the bike against a tree, and the two hiked to the top of the hill. The deer moved across the slope, keeping watch on the two as Chad spread a blanket on the ground. "We got off to a bad start. I didn't mean to upset you when you asked—"

"It's okay. I was stressed." Vicki lifted the lid on the basket but couldn't see inside. "Your friends back at the house don't seem too happy about us being here."

"They're a little worried about their families."

"I can understand that."

"I heard about your friend Cheryl. If there's anything we can do, let me know."

Vicki sighed. "I want her to stay with us, but I don't know how safe she'll be."

"You think she'll keep the baby?"

"I haven't talked with her yet."

Chad glanced away. "I also heard about Natalie. I'm sorry."

Vicki bit her lip and stared at the sky. It had been a long time since she had been outside at night and not on the run. "I can't get her face out of my head. The last time I saw her, I begged her to come with us, but she wouldn't. I feel responsible for her death."

"I don't think she'd feel that way."

"Why not?"

"Let's say you went into that GC compound to help your friends and the GC caught you. Would you blame the others?"

"Of course not. It was my choice to go in there."

"Then why is Natalie any different? She chose to risk her life and she got caught. She wanted to risk it for you and your friends. Don't take that away from her by punishing yourself for her death."

"I hadn't thought about it like that."

"If there's one thing I know, it's that God has a purpose for things. Everything fits together like a puzzle, but we're looking at it from a human angle. All we can see are missing pieces. He sees the big picture and knows how it all fits."

Vicki wiped away a tear. "It doesn't make her death any easier to live with."

"You'd have to be a robot for it not to hurt." Chad opened the basket and dumped the contents on the blanket. He unwrapped a hot loaf of homemade cinnamon bread and pulled off a piece. "I forgot the knife. This is how they used to do it back in Bible times."

"I'm sure they had cinnamon bread back then." Vicki laughed as she took the bread. It almost melted in her mouth. "So tell me your story."

Chad leaned back on an elbow. "It's pretty boring. My parents were Christians and took my brothers and me to church. I was the oldest and had pretty much decided I was going to have some fun before I got serious about God. I figured I had plenty of time."

"Where were you on the night of the disappearances?"

"I was out late with some guys from my baseball team. We'd have a few beers and drive to Des Moines to see a movie or go to a club that wouldn't kick us out. Our third baseman, Kyle Eastman, never drank with us, but we asked him to come along sometimes because we knew he'd be the only one sober enough to drive home."

"He was a Christian?"

Chad smiled. "We called him the hot-corner preacher. He didn't really preach at us. We just knew he didn't do the same stuff we did."

"Had you ever prayed before?"

Chad took another piece of bread. "When I was a kid, I'd go to church and listen. Every time the preacher would ask people if they wanted to pray and ask God into their lives, I'd almost do it. Sometimes they'd have you come forward, and a couple of times I almost got up and went, but something held me back. I was embarrassed and didn't want anybody to think I was weak."

"It's not weak to admit you need God."

"I know that now. I wish I could go back and change all that, but the way I look at it, if I had, I wouldn't have met you. Don't blush."

Vicki smiled. "Finish your story."

"Kyle had told his parents where he was going and when he was coming home. When a couple of the guys went off by themselves, he called home and told them he'd be late. It took a couple hours to catch up with our friends, but we finally headed home.

"I was in the front seat next to Kyle, and there were

three others in the back, asleep. Kyle started talking to me about spiritual stuff. He asked if I knew where I'd go if I died. I got paranoid and asked if he was going to drive off the road on purpose. He just grinned.

"I told him I believed all the stuff about Jesus, but I wasn't ready to leave my friends and fun yet."

"What did he say?"

"He tried to convince me that I wouldn't be giving up anything if I asked God to forgive me. He said I'd be gaining all of heaven if I just gave God control and let him do what he wanted."

"And?"

"I pretended to pass out. I didn't want to hear it. I knew what he said was true, but I didn't want to face it. As I was sitting there with my head against the seat, I heard Kyle whispering. He was praying for us, asking God to show us the truth and to use him in some way. Then he got quiet. He had the radio tuned to a Christian station and it was on really low.

"That's when the car ran off the road. I looked over and Kyle was gone. There was nothing in the seat except his clothes, his watch, and his baseball jacket."

"Did you wreck?" Vicki said.

"He had the car on cruise control. It drifted off the interstate, and we almost hit a guardrail before I jerked it back onto the road and hit the brake. The guys in back woke up and didn't believe me when I said Kyle had disappeared. They jumped out of the car and looked for him along the road. I knew what had happened and I was scared.

"We were freaking out when another car behind us plowed into the same guardrail we'd almost hit. The car was smashed really bad, and we all ran to see if we could help. The other guys got there first and started screaming. There was nobody inside."

"How long after that was it before you prayed?"

"I didn't waste any time. I prayed right there and told God I was sorry I had waited. I tried to get my friends to pray, but they were scared out of their minds. The Christian radio station Kyle was listening to played a few more songs, and then it went dead. I didn't know whether God would forgive me or if I'd missed my chance. It wasn't until I read a guy's Web site a while later that I knew the truth that God did forgive me and had made me a tribulation saint."

"Did any of your friends pray?"

"Nobody in the car that night. I found some relatives who weren't believers and told them. That's how we all came to the house."

Vicki loved hearing these kinds of stories. She told what had happened to her family and Chad listened closely. When Vicki yawned an hour later, Chad scooted closer.

"I'll get you back to the house, but I need to say something. I know I'm being bold, but the way I see it, we only have about three and a half years before Christ comes back. I'd like to get to know you better."

"I don't know what to say."

"Shelly said you had a boyfriend but that he's away."

"He's not really my boyfriend. We've known each

other since the disappearances, but I don't know where our relationship is going."

Chad packed their things in the basket, and they walked down the hill to the dirt bike. Vicki put a hand on his shoulder. "Thanks for talking about Natalie. I feel a lot better."

Chad smiled. "I don't know what you're planning, but I'd be more than glad if you guys want to stay with us."

JUDD knelt by Lionel in front of the tiny camera mounted on the computer on Z-Van's plane. They were only a couple of days away from Nicolae's appearance in Israel, and Judd knew from the Bible and Tsion Ben-Judah's writings that things would get very bad very quickly. They both smiled when Darrion appeared on the screen, wiping her eyes and yawning. Charlie sat in the background petting Phoenix.

Darrion told them what the kids had been through. Judd gasped when he heard about what had happened in Iowa. He put his head in his hands when Darrion broke the news about Natalie. Though he had never met the girl, she had been part of the Young Trib Force. Darrion told Judd that they hadn't heard any more about Jim Dekker and Pete Davidson.

Judd ran a hand through his hair. "Where are Vicki and the others?"

Darrion told him and gave him the number in Iowa. "I know they're trying to get back here, but I think they should stay where they are if they're safe."

Lionel waved at Charlie, and the boy moved to the camera. "I heard you had a pretty close shave with the GC."

Charlie smiled. "Vicki came to get me. But if it wasn't for Natalie, I'd probably be in the head chopper right now."

"Well, we're glad you didn't have to face the head chopper," Lionel said.

Darrion asked where Judd and Lionel were and Judd told her. Darrion shook her head. "At least you guys know how to ride in style."

"We're headed to Israel in the next couple of days with Z-Van and his crew," Judd said. "We're going to join Sam and Mr. Stein, watch the festivities, and try to get back home from there."

"Be careful," Darrion said. "The GC is really cracking down here. When the public starts taking the mark, things will get ugly."

Judd and Lionel prayed with Darrion and Charlie a few minutes, then said good-bye. Judd moved to the back of the plane. He knew it was still early in the Midwest, but he felt like he had to talk to Vicki.

The phone rang twice before Shelly picked up. She seemed thrilled that Judd had called and told him Vicki was still sleeping. "She had a late night with the guy we're staying with. He's really cute."

"She was on a date?" Judd yelled.

"It wasn't like that. Vicki's been torn up about Natalie

for days, and Chad took her back on his farm. She told me about it when she came in."

"Fine. I just wanted to make sure you guys were all right and hear your plan."

"We want to get back to Wisconsin, but we don't know when it will be safe. We're trying to decide if we should take some of the people we rescued from the reeducation facility."

"Why would you take them with you?"

"Well, one of them is pregnant and has just become a believer, so we thought she—"

"I don't believe this. . . ."

Shelly paused. "I thought you called because you cared about us. It sounds like you're mad that you can't boss us around."

"Let me talk with Mark."

A few seconds later Mark came to the phone. "What was that all about?"

"I can't believe what's going on back there. You guys take off halfway across the country and you don't—"

"Whoa, big boy," Mark interrupted. "Take a breath. What's wrong with you?"

"Nothing's wrong with me. I'm upset about the chances you guys are taking."

"If you were here, you'd understand. We got a distress call from Iowa and felt like it was worth the risk."

"And there's at least one believer dead, and maybe more if they catch Pete and this Dekker guy!"

"Judd, calm down. And if you can't, call me back. Do you want us to just sit on our hands until you can help us decide everything? If that's true, we would never have sent The Cube out, and that's been a success beyond our wildest dreams."

Judd took a breath. He looked in one of the many mirrors in Z-Van's plane and saw that his face had reddened. "Can I talk with Vicki?" Judd finally managed.

"If you're going to be like this, I don't think it's a good idea. Natalie's death really hit her hard. She blamed herself for not getting her out of there."

"I just . . . want to talk."

Judd waited, staring at himself in the mirror. He had known Vicki and the others for three and a half years. God had changed him in many ways, helping knock off the rough edges, but he still had a barrelful of anger inside and he had no idea why.

Vicki awoke from a sound sleep with Shelly standing over her. The girl held out the phone. "Judd's on the line for you."

Vicki tried to clear her throat, but her voice still sounded groggy when she said, "Judd, what's up?"

"Darrion told us everything that's happened. I wanted to make sure you're all right."

Judd sounded tense. Vicki scrunched her eyes and sat up. "Things could be better, but we're relatively safe. Just waiting to get back to Wisconsin."

"I should have gotten in touch with you a long time ago. So much has been going on over here."

"Any news on when you're coming back?"

Judd told her about their planned trip to Israel. "We
want to see Sam and Mr. Stein again and watch
Carpathia's next showdown." Judd paused. "Vick, about
this Chad guy . . ."

"What about him?"

Another pause. "I don't know. I guess . . ."

"What?" Vicki said warily.

"I think Z-Van and his crew are headed to the plane. I
need to go."

"Okay, be careful."

"I will. Good-bye."

Vicki clicked the Off button, and Shelly came back in
the room. The two shared notes about his call, and Shelly
said she thought Judd was way out of line.

When Vicki told her that Judd had mentioned Chad,
Shelly threw up her hands. "I thought you'd appreciate
me stirring up the competitive juices."

Vicki frowned. "I don't need anybody competing over
me. We don't have time for those games." She lay back
and put an arm over her forehead. "Do you remember
anyone named Ben or Brad?"

Shelly shook her head. "Why?"

"I went to sleep thinking about Cheryl and her baby.
Part of me thinks she should place the child with someone older who will know how to care for it."

"Like Lenore?" Shelly said.

"Lenore would be perfect. But when I woke up, those
two names came to me and I can't figure out why."

Shelly whistled. "Maybe I can make Judd jealous of
them too."

"Maybe it was too much cinnamon bread last night, but I can't help thinking it means something."

Judd and Lionel retreated to the back of the plane as Westin raced through warning that Z-Van was near. "You guys stay out of sight and they'll probably never notice you."

Judd peeked into the main cabin after they were airborne and noticed that Z-Van's manager and his band members now had the mark of Carpathia. They joked and toasted each other.

Z-Van pulled out a piece of paper and asked for quiet. "His Excellency gave me this before we left. He even has a melody picked out for it."

"He wrote this himself?" one of the band members said.

"Here's how it goes." Z-Van lifted his head and closed his eyes, as if he were uttering something sacred.

> *Hail Carpathia, our lord and risen king;*
> *Hail Carpathia, rules o'er everything.*
> *We'll worship him until we die;*
> *He's our beloved Nicolae.*
> *Hail Carpathia, our lord and risen king.*

People in the room clapped and asked Z-Van to sing it again. Soon they all joined in with an off-key version of the hymn to the Antichrist.

Lionel shook his head. "I think we made a big mistake coming with these people."

Two days later, Vicki and the others joined in the basement hideout as Mark called the kids together. He stood
at the computer with an e-mail message opened. "This
came on the Web site early this morning."

> *Dear Young Tribulation Force,*
>   *I need your help. My name is Claudia Zander. I was*
> *Natalie Bishop's roommate. Before she died, she talked*
> *with me about God. I didn't want to listen at first, but*
> *now that she's gone, I think what she said might be true.*
> *She told me not to take the mark of Carpathia, and I've*
> *only got a few more days to comply.*
>   *Please write back.*
>   *Claudia*

Mark looked at Vicki. "Did Natalie really have a
roommate?"

Vicki nodded. "Natalie said she was a rabid follower
of Carpathia."

"Then it must be a trick," Conrad said.

Vicki pursed her lips. "What if it isn't? Can we afford
to not try and help her?"

Judd and Lionel walked the streets of Tel Aviv, where the
GC planned to open the first loyalty mark application site
to the public. It was a festive atmosphere, almost like a
carnival, as people gawked at the sub-potentates' vehicles
on their way to meet with Carpathia.

Judd couldn't wait to get to Jerusalem to see Sam and
Mr. Stein, but Westin had convinced them to stay until
the whole group went there. "You don't want to miss
Z-Van's debut of his new songs, right?"

Judd had rolled his eyes. The thought of more songs
devoted to praising Carpathia turned his stomach. What
he really wanted to see was the man who would stand up
to Carpathia, as foretold in Scripture. Though Judd didn't
know for sure, he suspected it would be Tsion Ben-Judah,
and he wondered if the man might spare a few moments
with him.

The streets were packed with people from all over the
world waiting to see the risen potentate in person. People
spoke in different languages and were animated about
what would happen in Jerusalem. Some said Carpathia
would destroy the Judah-ites the same way he had the
two prophets, Eli and Moishe. Others said there were
massive protests planned by Judah-ites and Orthodox
Jews and that a special weapon was being shipped to
Jerusalem to annihilate anyone who came against the
Global Community's chosen one.

"Why do they need a weapon when they have god
himself," one woman said, "and his right-hand man, the
Most High Reverend Fortunato?"

Streets clogged with cars and pedestrians. Judd and
Lionel followed the crowds to the seashore, where an
amphitheater had been quickly constructed. One area
was overrun with people standing in line, and Judd went
for a closer look. He wasn't surprised to find it was the
site where citizens would take Carpathia's mark.

Judd and Lionel skirted the masses and stood on the shore where they could see the stage and not be hemmed in by the crowds. A few minutes later, a caravan of cars pulled up and the most powerful people in the world walked onto the platform. The crowd went wild.

Nicolae Carpathia thanked everyone for welcoming them so warmly. He talked about the improvements in the world since the Global Community had come into existence and said that he felt a renewed energy for the task ahead.

The crowd laughed when Nicolae attributed his vigor to the "three days of the best sleep I've ever had." They cheered again when the potentate said there would be a special musical presentation by the most popular entertainer in the world.

First, he introduced Leon Fortunato, head of all Carpathia worship. Leon knelt and kissed Nicolae's hand, then moved to the podium. "Allow me to teach you a new anthem that focuses on the one who died for us and now lives for us."

"Uh-oh, here it comes." Lionel sighed.

The crowd quickly picked up the lyrics to "Hail Carpathia, Our Lord and Risen King" and sang along. Judd turned when he noticed a loud droning and saw a sleek aircraft heading over the city toward the site.

"As you can tell," Carpathia said, taking the podium again, "we have another surprise for you. The plane you see in the distance carries not only the equipment needed for this site, but also a brief display of its capabilities, ably demonstrated by the pilot of my own Phoenix 216, Captain Mac McCullum. Enjoy."

With that, Carpathia stepped back and was surrounded by the other sub-potentates at the back of the stage. The jet screamed over the crowd, very low and fast, and surged toward the Mediterranean Sea.

"I guess Mac is still employed by the GC," Lionel whispered. "Wonder when he'll leave?"

The plane flew so low it looked like it skimmed the water, then turned and flew over the stage. Judd noticed that a few of the sub-potentates wanted to duck, but they kept their places, squinting to see the plane speed past.

The plane eventually flew out over the water and shot straight up. When it reached the peak of its climb, it seemed to stop in midair and drift toward the ground.

"Something's not right," Lionel said.

The nose of the plane turned and plunged toward the water at a frightening speed. People around Judd laughed and pointed, thinking this was part of the show. "Pull out, pull out," Judd whispered as the plane rocketed toward earth.

But it did not pull out. The plane, a technological marvel of the Global Community, slammed into the beach at hundreds of miles an hour. The shock of seeing the sure death of Mac McCullum and his crew, along with the explosion of the aircraft itself, sent Judd to his knees.

"Please, God, not another death among the Tribulation Force."

13

JUDD Thompson Jr. closed his eyes as a plume of smoke rose from the aircraft wreckage less than a mile away. The jet had slammed into the beach at hundreds of miles an hour, followed by a deafening explosion. Judd's ears still rang as he knelt on the beach.

Judd's friend, Mac McCullum, was piloting the plane. Judd tried to imagine the horror of those last few seconds. Chang Wong had told Judd that Mac and a few other believers who worked inside the Global Community were trying to escape. Why hadn't Mac pulled the plane out of the plunge to earth?

A siren sounded from emergency vehicles in the distance, but everyone knew they could send a thousand ambulances to the crater and it wouldn't make any difference. Lionel Washington put a hand on Judd's shoulder.

People near Judd and Lionel, as well as those who surrounded the platform, fell silent. Angry black-and-orange flames billowed from the crash site as the blaze melted the Quasi Two.

A man several feet from them turned to his wife. "I hope they have a record of passengers on that plane. They'll never find any bodies."

The man's wife covered her face. "This was supposed to be such a happy day for the potentate."

Judd looked at Lionel. "The way that thing came down, you think it was sabotage?"

"What do you mean?"

"If somebody found out about Mac and the others, the GC could have made it crash."

Lionel shook his head. "With all these people around? Plus, the plane had equipment for the mark application. They wouldn't have destroyed their own machines."

The eerie silence continued until a woman cried out, "Save them, Potentate!"

Z-Van, the singer Judd and Lionel were traveling with, stood at the back of a group of dignitaries. He leaned forward and spoke to a man in front of him as Nicolae walked to the microphone.

Carpathia held up a hand and tried to soothe the masses with his voice. "Peace be unto you. My peace I give you. Not as the world gives."

Lionel gritted his teeth. "He's ripping off Jesus again."

"Would you please quietly make your way from this place, honoring it as the sacred place of the end for four brave employees. I will ask that the loyalty mark application site be appropriately relocated, and thank you for your reverence during this tragedy."

Z-Van stepped forward, then was ushered off the stage, along with the regional potentates. Leon Fortunato, now the Most High Reverend Father of Carpathianism, stepped to the mike and spread his hands wide. The folds of his robed arms looked like great wings.

"He looks like the most high turkey," Lionel whispered.

Fortunato tried to speak comfortingly to the audience as Carpathia had done, but his voice didn't have the same tone. "Beloved," he said, "while this sadly preempts and concludes today's activities in Tel Aviv, tomorrow's agenda shall remain in place. We look forward to your presence in Jerusalem."

The crowd scattered, some hurrying to automobiles and others standing by the motorcade to get one more look at Carpathia. Bodyguards and officials flanked the man.

Judd and Lionel wandered along the beach to the crash site. The heat from the twisted metal was intense. Global Community security forces had already cordoned off the site with yellow tape. A few people passed, shaking their heads. Some took pictures.

One woman, overcome, laid a bouquet of flowers on the sand. She looked at a friend, wiped away a tear, and said, "They gave their lives in service to the potentate. Those four were heroes."

Judd turned to Lionel as the woman walked away. "Let's get back to Z-Van's plane. I want to call Chang and see if he knows anything about this."

Vicki Byrne rubbed her eyes and looked out at the dark sky. It was early morning in Iowa, and several kids were still awake discussing their next move. Mark and the others agreed that Cheryl Tifanne should accompany them to Wisconsin, but Vicki wanted to go immediately. Colin Dial arrived from one of the other safe houses and joined the discussion.

In the middle of the argument, Mark took a call from Jim Dekker, a believer working inside the Global Community. Mark turned on the speakerphone, and Jim updated them about what had happened since they last talked.

Jim said he was still at the satellite tracking center, searching for any information he could find about Pete. "I know the GC has impounded the van, but I haven't heard anything about Pete. I also know this Commander Fulcire of RAP is in Iowa."

"RAP?" Shelly said.

"The Rebel Apprehension Program," Jim said. "The United North American States have pledged to lead the world in cracking down on anti-Carpathia activity."

"Then they're mostly after believers," Vicki said.

Mark looked at Colin. "Won't they be able to trace your van, the one Pete took?"

Colin shook his head. "We altered the vehicle identification number and assigned it to the GC fleet. I'll call Becky and have her be on alert just in case."

"What about you?" Vicki said. "Why aren't you out of there?"

"I'm not leaving until I know there's nothing I can do to help Pete," Jim said. "There are rumors about us being required to take the mark later today. I want to be out before then."

Vicki asked if Jim knew anything about Claudia Zander. He didn't but said he would check. When a new report flashed on GCNN, Jim said he would call back soon and hung up.

A news reporter, April Wojekowski, stood on a dark road in Iowa, lights of squad cars flashing behind her. "GCNN has learned of a search for anti-Carpathia forces here in Iowa. We were allowed to fly in with Commander Kruno Fulcire, who wouldn't comment on a possible escape of prisoners at a nearby GC holding facility. But the commander was optimistic that an abandoned van discovered at the side of this road may yield more clues about a possible rebel conspiracy."

Natalie Bishop's picture appeared on the screen and Vicki gasped. Natalie had been accused of helping rebels by using a superior's computer.

The scene switched to April's recorded interview of Commander Fulcire on his plane. "Are there others inside the Global Community who may be helping the rebels?"

Commander Fulcire frowned. "We hope not. That's why we're administering the mark of loyalty as soon as possible to all United North American employees."

"What new measures will you take to capture anti-Carpathia forces?"

Before Fulcire could answer, GCNN switched live to April again, her hair swirling wildly below a hovering helicopter. She screamed into the microphone to be heard. "We have some activity now in the brush, a few yards from where they discovered the van."

The camera swung to the right, past the television truck, and focused on about a dozen Global Community officers walking through tall brush by the roadside.

"What do you think they found?" Shelly said.

"I just hope it's not Pete," Vicki said.

Judd and Lionel made their way through the lingering crowd in Tel Aviv. Judd had heard there would be as many as 100,000 GC troops brought into Israel, and he did notice more Morale Monitors and Peacekeepers patrolling the streets. Some rode in Jeeps and covered personnel vehicles. Others walked with guns slung over their shoulders. Judd wondered if Carpathia hoped to scare everyone in Israel into following him. If so, Nicolae had greatly misjudged followers of God.

People along the street spoke sadly about the plane crash. Some called it a shame, while others blamed Tsion Ben-Judah. "Some say the thing exploded before it even hit the ground," one man said. "I'll bet the Judah-ites planted a bomb and had it explode over Tel Aviv just to make the potentate look bad."

Some young people sat on sidewalks, dressed in shirts and hats that bore images of The Four Horsemen. They were almost as dejected as Z-Van that his appearance had been cancelled.

Westin Jakes, Z-Van's pilot, came down the stairs of

the airplane when Judd and Lionel finally made it to the airport. Westin had become a believer soon after Nicolae Carpathia's rise from the dead.

"I don't mean to spoil the party," Westin said, "but I don't advise you guys riding with us. It's not a pretty sight back there."

"What's wrong?" Lionel said.

No sooner had Lionel spoken than a guitar flew out the open door, spinning down the stairs, and smashing onto the tarmac. Z-Van screamed and cursed at someone inside.

"Who's he mad at?" Lionel said.

"Everybody," Westin said. "Join me in the cockpit."

Judd and Lionel quickly ran up the steps and slipped into the cockpit.

Z-Van screamed from the back of the plane, "We had the potentate right there! We were all ready, and because of this airplane foul-up, we have to reschedule!"

Someone spoke softly and Z-Van screamed again. "I swear, Lars, if you film any of this I'll throw the camera twice as far as I threw the guitar."

"That film guy still following Z-Van around?" Lionel whispered.

Westin nodded. "They were set to shoot the songs at the platform, but the plane crash wiped their schedule."

Judd fumed. "I can't believe he's more concerned about singing his new songs than he is about the people killed in the crash."

Westin cocked his head. "That's my boss."

Westin turned on a tiny monitor and tuned in the

GCNN station in Tel Aviv. They had been showing the live broadcast of the festivities up to the crash of the plane. Two grim-faced anchors played amateur video that showed the best moments of the fatal flight.

Westin scowled. "The way that thing came down tells me there was a major problem."

"What do you mean?" Judd said.

"You have all those acrobatic moves, all the fancy flyovers, and then everything goes blank. The pilot doesn't even try to pull out."

"Maybe he couldn't," Judd said.

A photo of Mac McCullum flashed on the screen. The news anchor said, "We now have confirmed those members of the flight crew and the two passengers. Captain Mac McCullum was said to be one of the Global Community's most experienced pilots, the person who usually flew Potentate Carpathia's plane, the Phoenix 216. He is presumed dead, along with copilot Abdullah Smith, a former Jordanian fighter pilot and first officer for the Global Community."

The news anchor paused. "We should be reminded that there are perhaps family members of these victims who are just now finding out about their loved ones' deaths, and for that we apologize.

"Also among the dead, this woman, Hannah Palemoon. Originally from the United North American States, she was a nurse by profession, so one can assume she may have been on the flight to help administer the mark of loyalty here in Tel Aviv.

"Perhaps the most shocking casualty was a director in

Potentate Carpathia's cabinet, David Hassid. We understand he was one of the technical geniuses who helped behind the scenes in New Babylon. I'm sure His Excellency will miss the input of these colleagues, and again, our hearts go out to those who are family members and those who knew the deceased."

Z-Van threw open the cockpit door and rushed inside. "Get me back to Jerusalem!" He eyed Judd and Lionel and cursed again. "And get these two off my plane."

Westin started his preflight procedures and said, "Sir, we promised them—"

"I don't care what you or I or anybody else promised. I want them off and I don't want them back on. Understood?"

"Yes, sir," Westin said.

Vicki and the others sat engrossed in the GCNN coverage of the situation in Iowa. Periodically the news switched to Israel to report on the plane crash that had taken four lives. Vicki whimpered when Mac McCullum's picture appeared. The kids knew Mac was a member of the Tribulation Force.

The phone rang and Mark picked up as the kids continued to monitor the news. His eyes darted around the room. When he hung up he looked at Vicki. "If we're getting out of here, we should do it now. Jim said the GC is converging. He sent an urgent message that a small convoy was fleeing south toward Kansas City. He thinks that'll give us enough time to get on the road back to Wisconsin."

"Is he getting out?" Vicki said.

"As soon as he knows we're safe," Mark said.

"Let's go," Colin Dial said, grabbing a few of their belongings.

"Wait," Shelly said. "The van's gone."

"Take my family's minivan," Chad Harris said from the shadows.

Vicki turned to the young man and smiled. Chad had helped her deal with Natalie's death. She put a hand on his arm. "Thank you for being here when we needed you."

Chad nodded. "I hate to see you go, but you'll always have a place here if you need it." He took Vicki's hand, then hugged her.

Conrad yelled and the kids rushed back to the television. The reporter was excitedly announcing that after an exhaustive search, Global Community authorities had found something about a hundred yards from the road. The camera zoomed into the darkness where two uniformed officers dragged someone through the brush.

"It appears to be a large man," April Wojekowski said.

Vicki put a hand to her mouth as the group approached. Between the two GC officers was her friend Pete.

14

VICKI looked closely at the television, trying to see Pete. As the GC officers dragged him past squad cars, she noticed how pale he was. A large, red stain spread through Pete's shirt.

Commander Fulcire moved in front of the camera and barked orders. The officers dragged Pete toward the chopper.

The reporter, April, touched the commander's shoulder. "Sir, how did you make this arrest?"

"The chopper can see anything on the ground giving off heat," Fulcire said. "Without the chopper, we'd have never found him in that clump of bushes."

The camera focused on Pete, and the commander waved April through. It was clear they had worked out an agreement about this exclusive story.

"We have to go," Colin said from the top of the stairs.

"Let Vicki watch," Mark said.

Vicki knelt in front of the television, too stunned to cry. She had met Pete after the great wrath of the Lamb earthquake, as the kids were trying to escape from another GC commander. Pete had always been kind to Vicki, willing to listen or help. She knew God had changed him drastically, and it was difficult watching his arrest.

Vicki had hoped Pete would find a way out with another trucker, or perhaps locate a motorcycle or another vehicle. Now, as the officers trudged past a squad car, she knew her friend was in deep trouble.

The reporter thrust a microphone in front of Pete and yelled, "Sir, do you have anything to say?"

"Yeah, I sure do." The camera zoomed in on Pete's face. His hair was matted and filled with grass, his face streaked with mud. Vicki guessed Pete had tried to camouflage himself in the underbrush. She could only imagine what had gone through his mind as he lay bleeding, wet, and cold, watching the lights of the oncoming GC.

Pete caught his breath and looked into the camera. "Everybody watching needs to know that if they take Carpathia's mark, they'll regret it for eternity."

April pulled the microphone away, but Pete grabbed it. "Jesus Christ is the true potentate. Ask him to forgive you!"

The officers wrestled the microphone from Pete and threw him on the ground. Pete yelled out the address to Tsion Ben-Judah's Web site as they restrained him.

The reporter composed herself. "Well, that's not a surprising response from an avowed Judah-ite. As we've been told, these fanatics will stop at nothing to push their beliefs on others."

Pete was led to the chopper and shoved inside.

Mark touched Vicki's shoulder. "We should leave."

Vicki nodded. It wasn't until she was in the van, driving away, that the tears finally came.

Judd stood and motioned Lionel to follow as Z-Van left the cockpit.

Westin shook his head. "I can't let him treat you guys like this."

"It's okay," Judd said. "We'll find a ride to Jerusalem."

"But I have to leave him sooner or later. Why not now?"

Judd stared at Westin. "When the time's right, you'll know."

Westin handed Judd a wad of cash. "You can pay me back later. Look me up at Ben Gurion airport. I promised you a ride back to the States and I'm going to keep my word, no matter what he says."

Westin grabbed a cell phone from a compartment behind him and handed it to Judd. "It's solar powered. My number is the first one on the list. Call me if you have any problems."

Judd and Lionel shook hands with Westin and headed for the stairs. When they were halfway down, Z-Van yelled at them from the doorway. His eyes seemed on fire and his face was tight with anger. "I'm going to tell them about you."

Judd nodded. "I figured you would."

"I could have given you up in New Babylon if I wanted."

"Why didn't you?"

Z-Van smirked. "I thought I could get you two to see the truth. I was going to make you GC poster children, you know, two kids who were once Judah-ites who did a 180. I was going to prove to everybody that people like you could be rehabilitated."

"I guess there's just no hope for us," Judd said.

Z-Van clenched his teeth. "You'll regret not turning. You'll see how powerful His Excellency is in Jerusalem. I know what he's going to do, and it'll prove once and for all how wrong you are."

Judd took another step down the stairs. "We know what he's going to do too, and all it's going to prove is that Nicolae is the enemy of the true God."

Z-Van waved a hand, dismissing them, and went back inside.

When Judd and Lionel reached the terminal, the jet engines fired. The cell phone in Judd's pocket rang and he answered it.

"I just heard Z-Van on the phone with airport security," Westin said. "Get out of there as fast as you can."

Judd quickly told Lionel what Westin had said. Since there was a fence around the runway, they had to go through the terminal. They rushed inside to the baggage claim area and ducked into a men's room.

Judd checked the stalls and made sure they were alone. "They'll be looking for two of us. Let's split up and meet out front."

"I wonder what Z-Van told them we did," Lionel said.

"He's probably ticked that we don't worship Carpathia like he does."

"Yeah, his album sales would go in the tank if everybody was a believer."

Lionel walked out first and went to the right. Moments later, Judd walked out and turned left. He noticed a security guard standing watch by the door leading to the tarmac. Judd stared straight ahead and kept walking.

Judd spied three airport officials with walkie-talkies at the escalator leading upstairs to the street level. He turned into a hallway and found a wall of vending machines. As he put in a few coins, a radio crackled.

"Yes, we heard you," a man said, "one black, one white, and they're together. Do you have a description of their clothing?"

A candy bar fell with a clunk to the bottom of the machine, and Judd heard a noise down the hall. A cleaning woman exited a service elevator pushing a cart.

Judd raced toward her and managed to slip inside before the door closed. *I hope Lionel made it out okay,* he thought.

Judd pushed the button for the main floor, but nothing happened. He pushed other buttons, but the lights remained unlit. He was about to hit the Door Open button when the car shook and slowly moved upward. When it reached the main floor, Judd slid to the side and waited as another cleaning person walked inside.

Judd darted out the door and was down the hall before the man stuck his head out and said, "Hey, you're not supposed to use this."

Judd turned the corner and walked into the crowded terminal. Directly ahead was a row of exits, each with a security guard poised and watching. Several young men had been pulled out of line, so Judd kept moving, hoping he wouldn't see Lionel in custody.

When he reached the end of the concourse, he glanced outside and noticed Lionel beside a small car, looking anxiously toward the terminal. Judd checked the exits again and spotted an emergency door at the far side of the room that led directly outside. Judd figured he would have no problem reaching Lionel before the guards realized what was happening, so he moved toward it, reading the sign on the lever that said, "Attention: Alarm Will Sound If Door Is Opened."

Judd took a breath and hit the door running. Alarms rang throughout the concourse and a red light he hadn't noticed swirled overhead. Whistles sounded behind him as Judd sprinted toward Lionel.

Lionel jumped in the back of the small car, pulled Judd in with him, and yelled, "Go!"

The driver was a short, Middle Eastern man, with graying hair and glasses. He turned to Judd and stuck out his hand as he pulled into heavy traffic. Judd shook it quickly, startled at the speed of the oncoming cars. Airport officials ran toward the street, but the car blended into traffic before they could reach it.

"I didn't mean to scare you," the driver said. Judd noticed the mark of the believer on his forehead. "My name is Sabir. It is nice to meet you, believer Judd. I will drive you to Jerusalem."

Vicki sat in the backseat of the van with Cheryl. The only sound during the first few minutes of the drive was the sniffling of the kids. Mark rode with Colin in front, checking their route with Jim Dekker by phone. Shelly had her head on Conrad's shoulder in the middle seat, wiping away tears.

As the sun slowly appeared over the horizon, everyone relaxed a little and ate sandwiches their friends in Iowa had made.

"What will happen to the other kids who came from the reeducation facility?" Cheryl said.

"They're safe in people's homes if they stay put," Colin said. "I was staying at a place with a secret subbasement where the guys stayed. Even if the GC did house-to-house searches, I doubt they'd find them."

Conrad checked the latest on the Web from the laptop. News of the plane crash in Tel Aviv was the top story. The world awaited the special ceremony in Israel the following day.

Cheryl put a hand on Vicki's shoulder. "I'm really sorry about your friend. What's going to happen?"

"They'll probably question him, and when they're done, they'll offer him the mark of Carpathia."

"But you said people shouldn't take it."

"Pete won't. And he won't tell them anything about us, no matter what they do."

"He did that for us, just like Jesus gave himself," Cheryl said, looking out the window at the passing landscape. "You know, I was really upset about being caught by the GC, but the way I see it now, it's probably the best thing that's ever happened to me."

Vicki smiled. "When we get to Wisconsin, we'll see if Colin's wife can find you some prenatal vitamins."

"What are those?"

"You take them so your baby will be strong and healthy."

Cheryl gave her a pained smile and glanced out the window again.

"You want to talk about it?" Vicki said.

"There's not much to tell. I grew up in an orphanage. I never knew my mother and father, but I always felt like they didn't want me. I was sixteen when the disappearances happened. We woke up and most of the workers were gone. Little kids too.

"Later, I moved into an apartment with three girl-friends who were older and going to school. That's when I met Thomas. He was a student at the university, and I loved him." She frowned. "I thought he loved me."

"What happened?"

"A month ago, I was out looking for work. I had lost my job. I went to his apartment and it was empty. He had left a note with one of my roommates saying that he was moving back in with his family, and that I shouldn't look for him. I felt so alone and betrayed."

Cheryl put her head in her hands. "My roommates laughed at me for believing Thomas could love me. I laughed along with them at first, but I couldn't take it anymore and decided to leave."

"Where did you go?"

"I lived on the streets for a while. Ate in soup kitchens and GC shelters. A few days ago I wandered into this grocery store without any money, which was a mistake. I smelled the fresh-baked bread and I had to have a bagel or something. I stuffed a couple in my pockets and I guess somebody saw me. They caught me outside and the GC brought me to that reeducation place. I was glad to have something to eat, but it wasn't much fun.

"That's when those girls started talking about God. I was drawn to them because they seemed to have so much love. Then I wondered if I was believing for the wrong reasons. You know, that I just wanted a family and somebody to love me so much that I'd fall for anything. But when you told me those verses and how God loved me, something happened I can't explain. I knew what you were saying was true."

Vicki smiled. "When I prayed with you and saw you didn't have the mark, I was really scared. I'm glad you're part of our family now."

"I want to learn as much as I can and help other people know the truth," Cheryl said. She paused.

"What is it?"

"I don't want to be a bad influence on your friends."

"You mean the baby?" Vicki said.

Cheryl nodded.

"We've all made mistakes. Big ones. God loves each of us, and he loves your child too."

Vicki scooted closer. She had been thinking about Cheryl's baby since she had heard the girl was pregnant.

"Have you thought of what you're going to do after the child is born?"

Cheryl winced. "It's all so new. . . ."

Vicki wanted to tell Cheryl about the two boys she had been thinking of, but she had no idea why the names *Ben* and *Brad* had stuck in her head. "If there were someone who might want to take care of your baby, would you consider it?"

"Who?"

Vicki frowned. "Honestly, I don't know. But would you be open to an adoption?"

Cheryl smiled. "If you think it's a good idea, I'll consider it."

As the minivan rumbled through the back roads of Iowa, Vicki racked her brain thinking about the two boys. She ran through the faces of everyone she had met in the past few years. From Chloe Williams to Hattie Durham to her teachers at Nicolae High, she could think of no one with those names.

15

JUDD kept watch behind them for signs of Global Community officers, but Sabir knew the roads well and was soon traveling through parts of Israel neither Judd nor Lionel had seen before.

"How did you get out of the airport?" Judd said to Lionel.

"I saw an African-American couple and started up a conversation. I went through the front doors with them, and I hoped security would think I was with them. They weren't checking families."

Judd explained how he had found the service elevator and eluded the guards. "I don't know what Z-Van said, but they sure seemed anxious to get us."

"You were with Z-Van?" Sabir said. "The one who screams and calls it music?"

Judd smiled and looked at the man's eyes in the rear-view mirror. He seemed kind and good-humored, and

141

Judd wondered what he had gone through in the past three and a half years. "If you think Z-Van's music is bad, wait until you hear the new tune Leon Fortunato wants you to sing."

"You mean 'Hail Carpathia'? I've already heard it and have a different version."

Lionel chuckled. "You came up with new lyrics?"

In his soft voice, Sabir sang the melody to "Hail Carpathia" with a mocking twist.

Hey, Carpathia, you're not the risen king;
Hey, Carpathia, you don't rule anything.
We'll worship God until we die
And fight against you, Nicolae.
Hey, Carpathia, you're not the risen king.

Judd laughed. As Sabir sang again, Judd thought about some of his old high school friends and how they had laughed together at television programs and movies. With the death and destruction in the world, that carefree spirit was gone. In fact, Judd couldn't remember when he had laughed this hard. It wasn't the humor in the words, but the tone of Sabir's voice, his perfect imitation of Leon Fortunato, and the way he waved his arm over the steering wheel like he was leading a thousand-voice choir.

One of Judd's favorite phrases, that always angered his father, was "Lighten up!" Judd recalled times when his father's business wasn't going well and his dad appeared weighed down with responsibilities. Now, Judd felt that same weight. He knew there would be a time when he could laugh freely again, and this brief chuckle was a taste of what was to come.

When Sabir finished his concert, Judd asked why he was going to Jerusalem.

The man shrugged. "To take you there, of course."

"Why were you at the airport?"

Sabir smiled. "I live not far from there. Sometimes I feel God tells me to go there. Other times I park and pray for the people I see and try to find a believer or two and encourage them."

"What about today?" Lionel said. "Did God tell you to come there?"

Sabir shook his head. "I was listening to coverage of Carpathia's arrival on the radio. It grieved me that so many were going to take his mark of loyalty, and I wanted to pray for them. I drove around the site asking God to show people the truth and wound up at the airport."

"So you're making a special trip just for us?" Judd said.

"You would do the same for me if I had come to your country, would you not?"

Judd nodded. "I hope I would."

Sabir pointed out some of the ancient sites as they passed, and Judd was amazed at the history of the country. Finally, he asked how Sabir had become a believer in Jesus Christ.

Sabir winced. "For that story, I have to tell you some terrible things about myself."

Vicki listened to more of Cheryl's story. The girl seemed hungry to learn about the Bible, and Vicki gave a quick overview of the Scriptures. Cheryl asked Conrad and Shelly to tell their stories, and the two joined the discussion.

When it was Vicki's turn, she described meeting Judd and the others in the Young Tribulation Force after the disappearances. She told Cheryl that it was a pastor, Bruce Barnes, who had explained the truth to her and the other kids.

"Now that I understand what God did for me, I want to tell other people," Cheryl said. "Did that happen to you?"

Vicki smiled. "Absolutely. I couldn't believe people at Nicolae High couldn't see the truth. One of the first people I talked to about God was . . ." Vicki stopped and stared off.

"What is it?" Cheryl said.

"I just remembered something. A woman whose husband was a police officer wanted to know why all the children had disappeared."

Now Vicki had Conrad's attention. "What are you talking about?"

"Fogarty. Josey Fogarty was her name. Her husband was Tom. Judd and I helped him catch a couple of crooks."

"Did Josey become a believer?" Cheryl said.

Vicki nodded. "I remember I wished Bruce would come and talk with her, but she wanted to pray with me."

"What about her?" Shelly said.

"She told me she had been into all kinds of religions and some weird stuff when she got divorced from her first husband. She lost custody of her two kids."

"But why is she important—?"

Vicki put a hand on Shelly's shoulder. "She had two sons who disappeared. Their names were Ben and Brad."

Judd sat riveted to Sabir's story as they drove toward Jerusalem. Sabir said that before the disappearances, he had been a terrorist.

"I grew up in a community that hates all Jewish people, just like Carpathia. He hates Jews even though he signed the peace treaty with them. Our religious leaders believed that God would reward us for actions against Israelis, and so we plotted terrible acts."

"You tried to kill them?" Lionel said.

"Yes. Looking back, I can't believe I did some of those things. I actually taught people, some younger than you, how to use explosives and blow themselves up in buses, on sidewalks, or other crowded places. The goal was to kill as many people as possible, and we did it in the name of God."

Judd had read the history of violence in the Middle East, particularly in Israel. During the time before the Rapture, there had been many attempts at peace, some of which seemed like real breakthroughs, but no sooner was a treaty signed than the violence broke out again and people were killed. But the peace treaty signed by Carpathia brought a new era to the world. Judd knew it was only the lull before the storm of Carpathia's wrath against Jewish people.

"Why did you stop the bombing and violence?" Lionel said.

"Because I learned the truth about God. I love my family and my culture, but I discovered the God who created me is a God of love, and the Jewish people have a special place in his kingdom. Now I love them with all my heart, and I pray that they will turn to their Messiah."

"How did you go from wanting to blow them up to loving them?" Judd said.

Sabir smiled. "That is a question many in my family continue to ask. Though I have tried to explain, they do not understand."

Sabir merged with traffic and found the main route between Tel Aviv and Jerusalem. "I had never questioned whether I was doing the right thing when I helped plan killings. I was taught to hate from the time I was a boy. We learned songs that glorified violence, we thought God was on our side, and that we would gain special favors in heaven for sacrificing ourselves."

"You actually planned the killings?" Lionel said.

"I trained many young assassins and helped build explosive devices." Sabir ran a hand through his hair. "My own son, not much older than you, died in a terrible explosion I planned. Sometimes I have nightmares about him and the others I sent to their deaths."

"But didn't you feel bad about the people you killed?" Judd said.

"A terrorist cannot afford sympathy. It is the same as being a coward. That's how we were trained."

"If you were convinced you were right, what changed your mind?" Judd said. "It must have been miraculous."

Sabir nodded and smiled. "It was about three years ago and I had been having trouble sleeping. My wife—I wish you could meet her—had been reading everything about the disappearances she could find. There were magazine articles and, of course, theories by the Global Community. She was interested in the possibility that God had taken his people to heaven. I told her it was a foolish idea. We were still on earth and we were God's faithful.

"One night, I tossed and turned on my bed, unable to sleep. I went to the roof of our home and sat outside, looking at the stars. I must have dozed off, but I suddenly saw a man in a white robe standing on the other side of a body of water. He motioned for me to come to him and said my religion did not follow the truth.

"Understand, I'm not saying God spoke directly to me. Some people have based their faith on some kind of vision and have been very wrong. This message caused me to investigate Jesus and do something I had never done before—read the Bible."

"What did your wife think?" Judd said.

"I woke her and told her what had happened. We found a Web site that talked of Jesus. I found a Bible on-line and read the prophecies he fulfilled. We both knelt by our computer and asked God to forgive us. As you can see by the mark on my forehead, he did."

"What did your friends say?"

Sabir pulled the collar of his shirt down, revealing an ugly scar. "They nearly killed me. My wife and I put everything we owned in this car and drove to the Old City. I had plotted against the lives of so many Jewish people, and I was going into that city looking for help. That's when another great miracle occurred."

Vicki told the others more about Josey Fogarty. Cheryl asked if Josey's husband had become a believer.

Vicki pursed her lips. "I'm not sure. One of his friends on the police force died and Judd tried to convince him of the truth, but I never heard what happened."

"And you think this woman would take care of my baby?"

"All I can tell you is that those two little boys' names came to mind when I heard about your situation. I think Josey would be a great mom, but we'd have to find her and ask."

Vicki dialed the safe house in Wisconsin and spoke with Colin's wife, Becky. When Darrion came on the line, Vicki gave her all the information about Josey she could think of and asked Darrion to do a search for her.

"I'll give it my best shot," Darrion said.

"What happened in Jerusalem?" Judd said, scooting forward so he could hear Sabir better.

The man put both hands on the wheel and stretched.

"When I think of it now, I see it as a great answer to prayer and a sign from a loving God that he cares for his children. My wife and I drove through the streets late that night. But what were we looking for? Someone, anyone, who believed in Jesus as Messiah. And how would we find such a person? The Orthodox Jews hate even the mention of his name."

Judd tried to put himself in the man's place. Sabir and his wife had turned their backs on everything they had followed their whole lives.

"I pulled to a stop at the side of a narrow street and my wife and I prayed that God would show us where to go. A man walked by and I asked if there was a church nearby. I figured I might find a believer there.

"The man laughed at me and said there were plenty of churches, but that no one would be at any of them that time of night. He pointed out the Church of the Holy Sepulchre. I had no idea of the history of that place. I simply needed help.

"We parked and walked there. The man was correct— the church was locked tight, so we sat outside near the front, our heads in our hands, and prayed."

Sabir wiped his eyes and continued. "A few moments later we heard footsteps, and someone came out of the dark and stood only a few feet from us. He said, 'Have you come to find the way?' I asked him what way he was talking about. The man, his name was Ezra, knelt before us and said, 'He is risen.' I knew then that he was a believer in the true Christ.

"But I felt like the man should know who he was helping. I told him what I have told you, that I had plotted to kill Jews and that I was guilty of many deaths. With tears in his eyes he said, 'Have you asked God to forgive you, and have you accepted the forgiveness he offers in the Lord Jesus?' I broke down and told him we both had."

Sabir's shoulders shook, and Judd thought the man was going to run off the road. When he had composed himself, Judd said, "What did the man do?"

"He told me that his wife and two children had been killed in an attack in Ramallah a few years earlier. It was one I had planned."

"Did you tell him that?" Judd said.

"I had to. I told him how sorry I was, but he stopped me, grabbed my hand, raised me to my feet, and hugged me. 'You have been forgiven by God and you are now my brother in Christ.' From that day on we have lived and prayed and eaten meals with Jewish believers. I have committed my life, not to killing, but to saving as many lives as I can from the evil one. That is why I have given you this ride. I do it in the name of Jesus."

A sign posted the number of kilometers to Jerusalem. Judd could barely see the writing.

AS THE car neared the outskirts of Jerusalem, Judd saw the preparations for Nicolae's return. Banners and signs welcomed the potentate and all visitors. Trees and shrubbery had been planted to spruce up the city's appearance.

"What about the site of the earthquake?" Lionel said.

Sabir shook his head. "The 10 percent that was ravaged by the quake is still a disaster area. Some of the dead still haven't been found."

Judd hadn't seen this much excitement on the streets since the opening of the Gala before Nicolae's assassination. Overnight it seemed Carpathia had created jobs for hundreds of vendors selling trinkets and souvenirs. Some sold palm branches to wave at the potentate or lay in his path, a gesture of worship. Others peddled floppy hats, sandals, sunglasses, and even buttons with Nicolae's picture on the front. People could have their picture taken beside a life-size cutout of Carpathia, and one kiosk offered to record a person singing 'Hail Carpathia' and digitally add the person to the video from the day before in Tel Aviv.

Morale Monitors and Peacekeepers clogged streets with military vehicles. They were prepared for any kind of uprising.

Judd told Sabir the address for Sam and Mr. Stein, then called Chang. He expected to find Chang upset about Mac and the others, but Chang sounded upbeat.

"I'm sorry about what happened," Judd said. "Lionel and I were on the beach in Tel Aviv."

"I heard it came a lot closer to the spectators than it was supposed to," Chang said.

"Than it was supposed to? You mean they planned to crash?"

Chang chuckled. "I'm sorry. I forgot you didn't know."

"Know what?"

"Mac, David, Hannah, and Abdullah are fine. They weren't on the plane."

"Now I'm really confused," Judd said. "We saw them fly over and do acrobatic stunts before the crash."

"Mac used a remote control to fly the plane. He had already programmed the craft to do those fancy maneuvers."

"But wouldn't he have to talk with people over the plane's radio?"

"Again, by remote control. They thought of every-thing."

Judd relayed the good news to Lionel and Sabir, and they both cheered. Judd asked, "But won't the GC know there was no one on the plane?"

"They intended to crash in the middle of the Mediterranean, but smashing on the beach was just as good. The GC haven't found any bodies and believe they must have been vaporized."

"But when they search their rooms, won't they be suspicious that all their stuff is gone?"

"That is the beauty of Ms. Palemoon's suggestion. She told them to pack like they were only going on a short trip. They left change on their dressers, and Mac even made a doctor's appointment for when he was scheduled to return."

"Perfect," Judd said.

"David scheduled staff meetings for next week as well. They even got into a fight with one of the cargo people about how much weight the plane was carrying. I'm sure they're blaming Mac or Director Hassid for overloading the aircraft. I'm telling you, no one suspects anything."

"So you're alone?"

"Yes, but I have much to keep me occupied. The Tribulation Force is converging on the Middle East, and it's my job to make sure Operation Eagle goes as planned."

"Back up. What are you talking about?"

"Because of what Dr. Ben-Judah believes is about to happen in Jerusalem, they have prepared for an evacuation. I will monitor the escape and stay tied in with the computers at the safe house in Illinois, keeping everyone up-to-date on how the mission is going."

"Who are they evacuating?"

"Anyone who wants to get away from Carpathia, but mostly the Jews and believers in Christ."

Chang told Judd the Tribulation Force's plans and how they had constructed a remote airstrip and refueling center right under the Global Community's nose in the Negev Desert. "They're going to airlift people there and then take them to Petra."

"Petra?" Judd said.

Chang's phone beeped. Judd wanted to hear more and ask Chang how he was coping with his dual marks, but Chang told Judd he would explain later.

Sabir slowed as they turned onto a familiar street. Judd told the story of meeting General Solomon Zimmerman at a meeting led by Mr. Stein. They passed Dr. Chaim Rosenzweig's estate, which had been burned to the ground.

Lionel gasped and pointed. General Zimmerman's home lay in charred ruins.

As Vicki and the others continued toward the Wisconsin hideout, she thought about the changes of the past few days. Her late-night discussion with Chad had helped her deal with her guilty feelings about Natalie's death. She still ached for the girl, but she knew Natalie would want her to keep going and helping as many as she could.

Thoughts of Natalie reminded Vicki of the e-mail that had caused such a stir among the kids. Vicki wanted to believe Claudia and talk with her about Natalie's last moments alive. Vicki pulled out a wrinkled copy of the e-mail and reread it.

Dear Young Tribulation Force,
  I need your help. My name is Claudia Zander. I was
Natalie Bishop's roommate. Before she died, she talked
with me about God. I didn't want to listen at first, but
now that she's gone, I think what she said might be true.
She told me not to take the mark of Carpathia, and I've
only got a few more days to comply. Please write back.
  Claudia

Vicki sighed and closed her eyes. She had long ago
decided to take every opportunity to talk to others about
God, no matter what the risk. She had done a study of
some of the major characters in the Bible—from Abraham to David to Jonah to Paul—and discovered that God
had taken them to dangerous places.

Before she had become a believer, Vicki took chances
and lived on the edge. Now, with so many bad things
happening and the Glorious Appearing a few years away,
Vicki felt more alive than ever. She believed God had
chosen to involve her in his great plan and was calling
her to dangerous places. At times, that meant taking
risks. Other times it meant admitting she was wrong
or revealing her feelings to people around her. Deep
inside, Vicki ached to make a difference. She saw people
blindly following Carpathia and hoping he had the
answers.

She had written in her journal, *There is a spot in my
heart God has touched that simply longs to follow. No matter
where he sends me, no matter what he asks, I want to go.*

But as Vicki studied Claudia's note, something didn't

feel right. The words felt calculated, like the girl had tried too hard to say the right thing or not to say the wrong thing. Dismissing Claudia's plea as a trick of the Global Community could be a mistake that would ruin Claudia's life for eternity. But meeting her face-to-face and falling for a trap would be equally wrong.

"How do I know the right thing to do when the choices aren't clear?" Vicki whispered. "How do I follow my heart when my heart doesn't know what to do?"

Vicki scribbled a note on a piece of paper. Before she was finished, she had scratched out words, written on the margins, and turned the paper over and started again.

> *Dear Claudia,*
>
> *Natalie mentioned you in some of our conversations. She said you were true-blue GC. I'm sorry to be hard on you, but I'm having trouble believing you would stop being faithful to Carpathia.*
>
> *If you want to know more about becoming a believer, look on our Web site. You'll find information and even a prayer. Whatever you do, don't take Carpathia's mark. You'll regret it forever.*

Vicki showed the note to Conrad and Shelly to get their input and the phone rang.

It was Darrion. "Melinda and I have tried all the leads you gave, but we haven't been able to find anything about Josey Fogarty. We did come up with some pretty bad news about her husband though."

"Tom?" Vicki said. "Did he die?"

"No," Darrion said. "He's working for the Global Community."

Lionel walked to the front of General Zimmerman's home. Judd had wanted to keep moving, but Lionel felt a deep sadness at seeing the beautiful house destroyed.

Judd shook his head. "The GC sure seems to like starting fires to get rid of people."

Sabir joined them. "I would hate to think someone found out about the band of believers you have described."

"How can we find out if they survived?" Judd said.

"What about Yitzhak?" Lionel said.

"Great idea," Judd said.

As they wove their way through the narrow streets to Yitzhak's home, Lionel explained how they had met the man and what he had done for them. He held his breath as they turned onto Yitzhak's street, afraid his home might have been torched as well. Lionel sighed when he saw it was still there.

Sabir followed Lionel and Judd up the front steps and Judd knocked on the door. Nothing. Judd knocked again and said, "Hello? Anybody home?"

"Just a moment," someone said. "Who is there?"

"Friends," Judd said.

A curtain opened and a man studied the three.

"We're looking for Yitzhak," Judd said. "Does he still live here?"

"What do you want with him?"

"We're friends."

The man opened the door and looked up and down the street. "Come in quickly."

Lionel followed Judd and Sabir into the home and the door closed behind them. "I see you have the mark of the believer. We have to be very careful. Global Community Morale Monitors have been active in this area."

Lionel couldn't believe the number of people in the room when they reached the bottom of the stairs. They crowded so tightly that when Sam and Mr. Stein saw Judd and Lionel, it took them nearly a minute to move past the others to greet them.

"We have been praying for you since you left," Mr. Stein said as he hugged Judd. "I have just been going over our action plan for the next few days. Share what has happened to you since we last met."

"In front of everyone?" Judd said.

Mr. Stein smiled. "We are all anxious to hear."

Lionel held up both hands and smiled when Judd looked at him. "He asked you, not me."

Judd told the group what had happened with Z-Van in New Babylon. When he described Nicolae's funeral, everyone groaned. Judd asked Lionel to tell about Z-Van's pilot, Westin Jakes, and how he had prayed after Nicolae's resurrection. Several people said, "Praise God" and "Hallelujah," when Lionel finished.

Judd asked people to pray for their friend who was still working inside the Global Community and who had both the mark of the believer and Carpathia's mark.

The room fell silent. Then several people spoke up,

not understanding how a person could have both marks. Judd tried to explain that his friend had been forced to take the mark of Carpathia against his will, but still the room grew louder.

Finally, Mr. Stein held up a hand and said it was time to end. After he led in prayer, people left in small groups through different doors so no one in the neighborhood would become suspicious.

Lionel moved to the back of the room as several people questioned Judd about the Global Community's plans in Israel. Sabir excused himself, hugged Lionel and Judd, and slipped into the night.

When the room was nearly empty, Mr. Stein took Judd and Lionel aside. "We have so much to tell you, so much to prepare you for, and so little time."

"What do you think will happen tomorrow?" Judd said.

"The evil one wants to defile the temple of God, but we are praying that it will actually bring people to the truth."

17

VICKI reeled from the news that Tom Fogarty was now working for the Global Community. If Josey was a believer, how could the two live in the same house? Was Tom a secret believer behind enemy lines? Could Josey have died or moved away?

"What do you want me to do?" Darrion said.

"I need time to think. First, let me dictate a message to you that I've written to Natalie's roommate, Claudia." Vicki read the message and asked Darrion to send the response quickly.

"If it's a trap, she's probably going to ask for information about the group or to meet you," Darrion said.

"Exactly," Vicki said. "Let me call you back about the Fogartys."

Vicki spotted a sign welcoming travelers to Wisconsin. They only had a few hours of driving ahead, and she wanted to talk with Mark about the plan she was forming. She knelt on the floor by Mark's side and explained her idea about Cheryl and the baby going to live with Josey.

"Sounds complicated," Mark said. "If the husband is GC, you won't really know until you've talked with Josey."

"And we can't get in touch with her without going through her husband."

Colin held up a hand. "I have an idea. Pull over."

Mark found a rest area for travelers and pulled into the parking lot. The kids got out and stretched their legs as Vicki followed Colin inside.

Colin dialed information and got the number to the Global Community personnel department outside of Chicago. There he was told that Thomas Fogarty had been assigned to a new GC facility in Rockford, Illinois.

"That's not far from the Wisconsin line," Colin said, putting more money into the phone. He dialed the number for the Rockford station and asked to speak with Fogarty. "Do you know when he'll be back? . . . I see. Well, I have a friend who used to know him from his days in Chicago and wants to check in with him. Is there a good time to call back? . . . Okay. Oh, one more question. This is kind of awkward. Do you know if he and Josey are still together? . . . Right, I understand. Thanks a lot."

"What did they say?" Vicki said.

"She said she can't give out personal information."

Colin dialed another number and asked for a telephone listing for Thomas Fogarty in Rockford. He frowned and hung up. "Unlisted."

When they were back on the road, Jim Dekker phoned and asked about their progress. Colin told him where they were, and Jim said they shouldn't have any more trouble from the GC.

Vicki asked for the phone. "Jim, I hope you're getting out of there before they make you take the mark."

"I'm two steps ahead of you," Jim said. "I've packed everything I'll need for a few days and it's in my car. I'm hoping to see you guys in Wisconsin in a few hours."

Vicki gave him Tom Fogarty's name and asked if he could get a home number for him before he left.

"I'll do my best," Jim said.

Judd felt exhausted, and when he heard what was planned for the following day, he wanted to make sure he was rested. But when Sam and Mr. Stein began explaining what had happened since they had last seen them, and what they suspected from reading the Scriptures, Judd felt energized.

"First, we have to remember the truth about our enemy," Mr. Stein said. "Satan is much more powerful than any human, but he is still a created being. He will deceive many in the coming days and even scare people into following him, but we must remember that our God is still in control. He will only allow this pretender to continue his charade for a limited time."

"What does Carpathia have in mind this time?"

Sam started to speak, then stopped.

Mr. Stein smiled and waved a hand. "Go ahead."

"Well, Carpathia's true nature is about to be revealed," Sam said. "From the beginning of time, Satan has been against those whom God loved. He delighted in deceiving the man and woman in the Garden, and he has always been against God's chosen people, the Jews."

"But our God always has a plan," Mr. Stein said, picking up the story. "He has a place of refuge for his people."

"Petra?"

Mr. Stein scratched his beard. "We do not know the exact place, but that is an interesting possibility."

Judd told them what he had heard from Chang. Sam became animated. "My father took me there when I was younger. It is one of the most unreachable places on earth."

"I've never heard of it," Lionel said.

"Petra is a city known for its red rock walls and its isolation," Sam said. "The only way to get inside is through the Siq, a mile-long path with cliffs on either side. There is a temple carved out of the rock 150 feet high. Inside the city are tombs and theaters and dwellings carved right out of the rock by ancient people. I think Petra would be a perfect place of refuge."

"Back up," Judd said. "As I understand it, Carpathia's going to defile the temple in some way and someone's going to stand up against him."

Mr. Stein nodded. "God has prepared the right person for the right time, but we have no idea who it will be."

"What about Tsion?" Judd said.

"Perhaps," Mr. Stein said. "We simply do not know."

"Well, it's clear from the reports that people in Jerusa-

lem haven't been exactly anxious to put up a statue of
Carpathia," Judd said.

Mr. Stein smiled. "Of course, believers would never
want such a thing, but the Orthodox Jews and others
have refused to even begin to build a replica statue. I
believe the time is ripe for God to show his people the
truth. Carpathia believes he is coming here to stamp out
any opposition, but I believe God has something else in
mind."

Sam sat forward. "We have heard some distressing
things about Carpathia's schedule, so you must not be
alarmed at what might happen. Don't be surprised if
Carpathia does some sickening things."

"Like what?"

"Like mocking Jesus by walking down the Via
Dolorosa, the same path of Christ's suffering just before
his crucifixion."

"How are the Orthodox Jews and the Christ followers
getting along?" Judd said.

"We are unified in our stand against Carpathia," Mr.
Stein said. "On spiritual matters we are far apart. But I am
trusting in the God who is able to open blind eyes. We
pray they will see that Jesus is truly their Messiah."

Vicki couldn't wait to get to Colin's home and sleep. The
kids had been on the run for so long that a long night's
sleep was a luxury. For the past three and a half years,
Vicki had learned to nap scrunched in a car, outside
under the stars, or in some dark hideout. She longed to

feel safe again, to have a place she could call her own, to simply sit and watch television without fear of being caught by the Global Community.

But the truth was, Vicki wouldn't trade her life now for what she had known before the disappearances. Her fears back then were that her parents would discover her sneaking out at night, or that she'd be grounded for flunking a class in school. A couple of her teachers had given her the line she always hated, "You have so much potential." Now, Vicki knew what they meant. If she studied and worked hard, God could use her to accomplish great things.

The phone rang and Colin handed it to her. "It's Jim."

Jim Dekker had escaped from the Global Community satellite operations center just before authorities came to apply the mark of Carpathia. "Before I left, I got an update on Pete in Iowa."

Vicki held her breath.

"He's still alive, and they're saying on the news that he's talking about Judah-ite groups around the country, that some young people have a hideout in Missouri. They're even saying he's talking about the location of Tsion Ben-Judah."

"Pete doesn't know where Tsion is. Nobody does."

"I know that, but reporters are saying Pete's spilling his guts about everything."

"Which means he's not giving them anything," Vicki said.

"You know they'll make him take the mark or choose the blade."

"Yeah. I know. Where are you?"

"Headed back to the house for a few things. As soon
as they figure I've flown the coop, they'll come looking,
and I don't want them to find my stash of uniforms and
stuff. Should be a nice night for a bonfire. Too bad I can't
stay around to roast marshmallows."

"Any luck with Mrs. Fogarty?"

"Almost forgot. I have the address and phone number
right here."

Vicki repeated the address and phone number to
make sure she had it right and told Jim to be careful.
When she hung up, Colin turned and pointed to a map.
"The address you mentioned is right across the state line,
here. We're probably about fifteen to twenty minutes
from there."

Vicki studied the map. "Should I call her?"

While Mr. Stein found a place for Judd to sleep, Lionel
went with Sam. The boy seemed excited to have someone
his age to talk with. "I want to show you what has
angered so many."

Sam led Lionel to the familiar holy sites of the Old
City. They passed the Wailing Wall where several Global
Community guards stood watch. No one was allowed to
worship or pray to anyone or anything other than
Carpathia without permission.

When they neared the Temple Mount, Lionel heard
construction and wondered who was still working at that
time of night. They went around a corner and saw a huge

staging area where the mark application would begin. It looked to Lionel like the staging area could hold several thousand. People would no doubt be herded toward the front, kept busy watching huge video screens.

"What are they going to play on that, a karaoke of 'Hail Carpathia'?" Lionel said.

Sam frowned. "Worse. Earlier I saw them playing clips of Fortunato and Carpathia speeches. They show a segment with Fortunato calling fire down from heaven."

"I'll bet they have old Nicolae rising from the dead too."

"Of course," Sam said.

A few people had camped out by the crowd-control barriers to be first in line. When the monitors flickered and Carpathia came forth from his Plexiglas coffin on the huge screen, several cheered.

"So not all in Jerusalem are against Nicolae," Lionel said.

"Sadly, no. Mr. Stein says he believes some will be caught up in Carpathia's theatrics in the next few days and will be fooled or scared into taking his mark."

Lionel watched as a truck backed up to the area and unloaded a heavy box. Workers uncrated wooden parts and a sharp, metal object. Lionel realized it was a guillotine. "I've only seen pictures of them."

"Ugly, aren't they?"

Lionel shook his head. "What I can't believe is that people would willingly follow a man who would cut people's heads off simply because they believe in the true God."

Sam pawed at the dust with his foot. "I have a feeling this ground will be stained with the blood of some very brave people in the days to come."

A man walked toward them and Sam's face lit up. "Daniel!"

Daniel Yossef smiled and shook hands with Lionel as Sam introduced them. "I showed The Cube to Daniel three days ago and he still hasn't made up his mind."

Daniel smiled and nudged Lionel. "These young people come up with new ideas. I have to at least hear him out."

"What is holding you back from believing the truth?" Sam said.

Daniel waved a hand. "Let us not talk of things that divide us on this important night. Tomorrow your so-called evil ruler will visit. I have never seen him in person. If what you say about him is true, I will believe."

"Do not put off your decision," Sam said. "Carpathia deceives. It is his nature to—"

"You told me yourself that you cannot make this decision for me. Do you see a mark on my forehead or my hand? Let me investigate what you have said, see the man in action, and decide."

Sam shook his head. "I do not know what else you need to see. He has come against the people of God."

"He signed a treaty of peace, but you Judah-ites won't stop accusing him." Daniel smiled and patted Sam on the back. "Let me do this my way. If you're right, I'll be the first to admit it."

"All right," Sam said. "I will be praying for you."

As Sam and Lionel walked back to Yitzhak's house, Sam talked about Daniel and how they had met only three days earlier. "Perhaps it's that he looks so much like my father, but I have a deep concern for the man."

"Has Mr. Stein talked to him?" Lionel said.

"No. I hope to get them together soon."

"How are you coping with your father's death?"

Sam sighed. "Sometimes I wonder what would have happened if I had tried to explain my faith in some other way. I picture my father and I telling others the truth about God, speaking to anyone who will listen. But that is only a dream."

Sam put a hand on Lionel's shoulder. "Reality is that I now have a heavenly Father and brothers and sisters in the faith who care about me."

Vicki's hands shook as she dialed Josey Fogarty's home phone. She wondered what would happen if Tom answered. Were they making a mistake to bring Josey into their problem?

After four rings, the answering machine picked up. Tom's gruff voice said, "You've reached the Fogartys. As you can tell, we're not able to answer your call. Leave a message. He is risen."

The last phrase startled Vicki for a moment and she realized her stuttering was being recorded. "Uh, Josey? I don't know if you'll remember me or not, but I really need to talk. I'll try back in about—"

The phone picked up and a woman said, "Hello? Who is this?"

"Is this Josey?" Vicki managed.

Vicki could tell the woman had been crying. "Yes, it's me. Go ahead and come for me. I don't care anymore."

"I don't understand—," Vicki said.

"Yes, you do. Well, I don't care what you do to me!"

"Josey, it's Vicki Byrne."

The woman sniffed and caught her breath. "Vicki? I don't believe it."

"I'm only a few minutes from your house. Do you mind if I come see you?"

The woman sobbed. Finally she said, "Yes, I would love to see you again."

18

IT WAS after midnight when Lionel found a place to sleep. He was grateful that God had led them to Yitzhak's house and that they had reconnected with their friends. Before Sam left, Lionel asked about General Zimmerman, the man who had opened his home up to so many believers.

Sam looked at the floor and whispered, "We were speaking openly in the streets with some of the undecided when a band of Global Community officers approached and asked the General to follow them. He looked at us, not knowing what to do. Finally, when he saw things might get violent if he refused, he went with them.

"Mr. Stein and I came here to begin a time of intense prayer. The next night, one of the General's servants who had become a believer rushed to tell us that the GC had surrounded his home. We believe everyone got out before they set it on fire."

Lionel shook his head. "Have you heard anything from him since?"

Sam nodded. "We continued to pray that God would protect him and have him released. However, when the GC began marking their prisoners, the newspaper carried the story of General Zimmerman's choice of the blade."

Lionel bit his lip. "You know, we were responsible for putting him in that situation."

Sam smiled. "You and the others helped him see the truth, and today, though it pains us to lose him in such a terrible way, he is with God."

Lionel went to bed with thoughts of Carpathia and what would happen the next day. Would he and Judd be treated the same way as General Zimmerman? As Lionel fell asleep, he was praying for Vicki and his friends back home.

As they drove closer to Josey's home, Vicki studied the countryside west of Rockford. Some areas still showed the effects of the great earthquake. Trees and grass had been scorched by the plague of fire, and residents had done their best to try and bring back some of the beauty of the city.

Mark continued his protest of the plan, though he admitted some curiosity about seeing Josey and finding out what had happened to her. He had talked with Judd many times about the sting operation against Cornelius Grey and LeRoy Banks, two bad guys the kids had helped catch. Mark's main concern was that they not be anywhere near Global Community officers who were sure to be on alert.

Vicki felt a tingle down her spine as they came closer. She had often thought of Josey and hoped to one day meet again.

"Turn left here," Colin said.

Josey's street seemed similar to Judd's in Mount Prospect. The houses were nice, with big, fenced-in backyards, but the place seemed deserted. *All this space and no children*, Vicki thought.

Mark drove past the house and turned around, making sure everything looked okay. He parked on the street and the kids unbuckled.

"Let Vicki go first and talk with Mrs. Fogarty," Colin said. Everyone agreed and Colin gave Vicki one of the handheld radios from their operation in Iowa. "If anything goes wrong, call us. We'll be waiting."

Josey opened the door before Vicki could knock. Vicki recalled first meeting the woman and being blown away by her simple beauty. Though Josey didn't wear makeup, not even lipstick, her pale blue eyes, sandy blonde hair, trim figure, and huge, easy smile were striking. Now, only three years later, Josey appeared to have aged ten years. Her hair was tinged with gray, her face, cutely freckled before, was wrinkled. Her eyes were bloodshot and puffy. The woman was still trim, and Vicki couldn't help thinking she looked gaunt.

"Come in, Vicki," Josey said in her familiar husky voice.

Vicki hugged her. "It's been a long time."

"Too long. Are you with friends?"

Vicki nodded. "They thought it would be best for us to talk alone first."

Josey showed her into the living room and brought her a hot cup of tea. She wiped away a tear and sat next to Vicki. Vicki wanted to tell her everything, but she sensed the woman needed to talk.

"I need to ask first about your husband," Vicki said quietly.

"I understand. He's not a believer, if that's what you mean."

Vicki scooted forward. "And he works for the Global Community?"

Josey nodded.

"Has he taken Carpathia's mark?"

Josey sighed. "The Global Community came in and took over. If he was going to stay in law enforcement, he had to go with them."

Vicki put a hand on her arm. "I need to know if he's taken the mark."

Josey hung her head and sighed. "Not yet. But with all that's going on around the country, this new commander, Fulcire, is pressuring employees to take it quickly."

Vicki took the woman by the shoulders. "You have to convince him not to take it."

"He'd have to leave the GC."

"Exactly."

"He's not going to do that."

Vicki asked more questions, but the woman broke down. When she stopped crying, Vicki asked what had happened after they last saw each other.

"Tom went back to work and pushed God aside. I started reading the Bible and studying, trying to understand what would happen next. I didn't want to beat Tom over the head with my beliefs, so I was careful to not come on too strong. But at times, I couldn't help it. I'd find a passage that really helped, and I'd want to share it."

"Did it drive him away?"

"At first he thought it was just a phase I was going through," Josey said. "I'd been into crystals, channeling, astrology, and angels. You name it, I'd tried it. I'd hop from one to another as fast as some people switch channels on their TV. I think he figured my belief in Jesus would change sooner or later too."

"But it didn't?"

For the first time since Vicki walked in, Josey showed a hint of a smile. "I can't say that I've been perfect in following him, but I still believe in God. It's just that I've had no one to talk with. The first time I saw someone with the mark of the believer, I nearly fainted."

"We're going to have to get you plugged into an online group."

"I didn't want to offend Tom, and I know how much the GC hate underground groups, so I backed off. Then the earthquake came and we moved here and I've been sort of stagnant."

"What happened when the locusts came?"

"Tom was stung the first day and suffered for months. He couldn't believe they didn't sting me, and I told him it was because I was protected by God. He wouldn't listen."

"So you've seen no change in him?"

"At times he seems open. I even saw him cry once when I started talking about my boys, but most of the time he just seems mad at God."

"And you've been alone, so it's been hard to grow."

Josey nodded. "I've read your Web site, and Tsion's of course, but I've been so worried about Tom that I'm afraid I haven't been much good to the cause."

"Don't say that," Vicki said. "God gives everybody a gift and—"

"That's why I feel so guilty. I could be doing something, using my hospitality to have people in and tell them the truth, but here I sit, paralyzed with fear that my husband is going to come home with the mark of Carpathia on his forehead and ask me to do the same. That's who I thought you were on the phone, the GC coming to take me away."

"You don't have to worry about taking the mark," Vicki said. "God will give you the strength to resist it."

Josey wiped her eyes. Vicki didn't want to bring up Cheryl's situation until the time was right.

"Do you think there's still hope for Tom?" Josey said.

"I have to admit, if he's known the truth this long and has still waited—"

"He sees through Carpathia," Josey interrupted. "He knows the guy isn't what he seems."

"Then why is he working for the GC?"

Josey shook her head.

"Does he know that you won't take the mark?"

"We've talked about it. He says he'll keep my secret, and no one needs to know, but I'm scared."

"You should be." Vicki looked at her watch and keyed the microphone on the walkie-talkie. "Mark, where are you?"

"End of the street. You want us to come?"

Someone moved behind Vicki, and Josey put a hand to her mouth and gasped. Vicki turned and saw Tom Fogarty staring at her.

"How long have you been here, hon?" Josey said.

"Vicki, you want us to come over there?" Mark said.

"No, stay where you are," Vicki said, returning Fogarty's stare.

"So, Vicki Byrne, Vicki B., Jackie Browne, or whoever you're calling yourself these days," Tom said, "I've been following your little rebellion against the Global Community."

"Tom, Vicki was one of the kids who helped you—"

"I know what she did, and I know her friends on the other end of that radio are probably the ones wanted in Iowa. Am I right?"

Vicki stared at the man and stayed silent. She had wanted to help Cheryl so much that she hadn't counted on this. Now she was trapped.

"You just going to sit there, or are you going to try and save my soul too?" Tom said.

"Vicki, is something wrong in there?" Mark said on the walkie-talkie. "Conrad said he thought he saw someone walk through the backyard a moment ago."

Vicki keyed the microphone. "Just stay where you are. I'm okay for now."

"Why don't you tell your friends I can have ten squad

cars and a couple of choppers here in five minutes?" Tom said.

"Tom, you won't," Josey said.

"You don't know what this girl and her friends have been up to. Stealing satellite trucks. Breaking into international video hookups. I was there at that schoolhouse after you kids left."

"Did you burn it down?" Vicki said coolly.

"Whatever she's done, it's been for a good reason," Josey said.

"Ends justify the means, huh? I thought Jesus followers were supposed to be good, law-abiding citizens. Instead, you break people out of jail and defy every rule the Global Community has made."

As she listened, Vicki thought about the others in the van. Fogarty could have already called in a team of GC officers before he walked into the room. She stood and faced him. "You used to be a cop, and a good one from what Judd told me. You shot straight with people, even perps, and they respected you."

Fogarty pursed his lips and lifted his hands. "What's your point?"

"Well, I'll shoot straight with you. I assume since you're telling me all this that you haven't talked about me and my friends to your superiors. You've been following us on your own, wondering when we'd make a mistake."

"Keep going."

"And if you're willing to keep quiet about us, there must be some reason. You must agree with what we're doing, or at least are willing to look the other way."

"I feel sorry for people who are misguided, that's all."

"Well, here's the story. I met this girl in Iowa. She's pregnant. Two, maybe three months along. She's had a hard life and the baby will have an even harder time if I don't do something about it."

Vicki looked at Josey. "I was thinking about her situation, and for some reason the names of your two boys popped into my head. I don't know why."

Josey put a hand over her mouth and shook. Tom's mouth dropped as he sat on the edge of a chair.

"She's not prepared to care for a child, and I asked how she would feel if we found someone to adopt it. Maybe take care of her while she was having it. Someone with experience."

"What did she say?" Josey said, her eyes wide and filled with tears.

"She wants the baby to have the right family. That's why I'm here."

"Praise God," Josey said, and she broke down. Tom fell back onto the chair and stared at the ceiling.

Vicki knew something was going on with Tom and Josey, but she didn't know what.

Finally, Josey spoke. "I didn't tell you this, Vicki, but the doctors told me I would never have children again. A few weeks ago Tom and I were talking and I was trying to tell him how good God is, that he wants to help us. Tom brought up Ben and Brad—he always loved them even though they didn't live with us—and said God was selfish and mean to take them."

Josey fought the tears. "I asked what it would take to

get him to believe God was there and wanted a relationship."

Vicki looked at Tom. "What did you say?"

Tom Fogarty, former Chicago policeman and now
Global Community tough guy, shook in his chair, overcome with emotion. When he could finally speak he said,
"I told her . . . I would believe in God . . . when he gave
us a baby."

19

VICKI didn't know what to say or do, other than put an arm around Josey and hug her.

Tom had moved to the window and stared out at the street. "Your friends out there?"

Vicki nodded. "What are you going to do?"

"I'd be the GC hero of the day if I brought you guys in."

"But you're not going to?"

Tom turned. "In the morning everyone will be talking about Carpathia and what a great god he is."

"And you?"

Tom shook his head.

Josey reached for him and said, "This is a perfect time to give your life to the true God. You know everything I've been telling you is true. And our prayers have been answered."

Tom looked at Vicki. "You think this girl would let us care for the baby if I'm working for the GC?"

"I think that puts her and Josey in too much danger," Vicki said.

"So you think I'm going to just give in and get religion?"

Josey said, "It's not religion—"

"I know, it's a relationship. I've heard that about a million times." Tom paced in front of the window, gesturing wildly. "I've lived my entire life without God. I've never tried to use religion as a crutch—"

"And you think that's what *we're* doing?" Josey said.

"I didn't say that—"

"It takes a lot bigger man to admit he needs help than one who says he can do it himself," Josey said. "You've arrested enough people in your career who have done it their own way and paid the price."

"I'm not going to say I believe this just to make you guys happy, or to make sure we get that baby."

"I'm glad," Josey said, "because we'd know you were faking it."

Tom rolled his eyes. "Oh yeah, the thing on the forehead."

Vicki stepped forward. "Mr. Fogarty, the Bible talks about people being blinded to the truth at this time of history. I don't know how it works, but it's clear there's something supernatural going on that keeps people from believing what's obvious."

"So I've been blinded by little demons running around? Or maybe by Satan himself? You expect me to buy that?"

Vicki put out her hand to stop him from pacing. "I'm

not asking that you buy anything. Just stop and ask God to take the blinders off. If he's real, he'll help you understand the truth. Are you willing?"

Tom stopped and folded his arms. "All right, but I feel stupid."

"It's okay," Vicki said. "You want me to pray with you?"

"No, I can handle it." Tom cleared his throat and took a deep breath. "God, I know that my wife and this girl care about me, and they've said if I pray, you'll open my eyes. So if you're there, I pray you'd show me where I'm wrong and what I need to do about it. Amen."

The radio crackled with Mark's voice. "Vicki, we need some direction here. There's a car pulling up to the house."

Tom pulled the curtain back, looked out the window, and cursed. "It's my partner. Tell your guys to get out of the neighborhood. Vicki, you go upstairs with Josey."

"Is this a trap?" Vicki said.

Tom scowled. "Just go upstairs. He's coming up the sidewalk."

As she followed Josey upstairs, Vicki told Mark she needed more time. "We've got GC company, so move the van out of sight and maintain silence until I get back to you."

Josey left the door open a crack as Tom's partner knocked downstairs. Vicki strained to hear as the men laughed and walked into the kitchen.

"His partner's name is Cal Trachsel. They've been together since we moved here."

"Is Cal 100 percent GC?"

Josey shook her head and closed the door. "I think he knows there are problems just like Tom. He's pretty level-headed."

"Have you ever talked to him about God?"

"No. I've only met him face-to-face twice. He calls for Tom a lot and we chat, but that's about it."

The front door closed and Josey walked to the stairs. "Tom?"

When he didn't answer, Josey went to the window and made sure Cal was leaving. Vicki followed the woman downstairs to the kitchen and found Tom sitting at the table, his head in his hands.

"What's the matter?" Josey said.

"That's the first time I've ever lied to my partner. A relationship like that is built on trust. Now I've violated it."

"What did he want?" Josey said.

"He wanted to make sure I was okay, and that I understood what would happen if I didn't comply."

"Comply with what?"

"His new tattoo. He got it on the back of his hand."

"Oh no," Vicki said.

"Memo came down saying we had to take the mark this afternoon."

"Is that why you came here?"

"I felt a little conflicted, yes. My wife tells me I'll be selling my soul and flushing my eternal existence if I do this, and the Global Community tells me they'll chop my head off if I don't comply."

"What did you tell Cal?"

Vicki felt like an intruder on the conversation, but she stood in the background and listened.

Tom's face twisted and turned red the more he talked about his situation. "I told him you haven't been feeling well and I wanted to make sure you were all right."

"Why did you lie?"

Tom stood and pushed his chair back. "Maybe I was scared of losing you. Maybe I was scared of losing myself, and I came back here to . . ."

"To what?" Vicki said.

Josey sat forward. "You don't want to take that mark, do you?"

"I don't know," Tom said, running a hand through his hair. "I had it all planned. I was going to convince you to take the mark and we'd be okay. I figured you'd leave this Christian thing behind, but it's clear you're serious."

Vicki went to the living room and found Josey's computer. As she logged on to www.theunderground-online.com, Vicki contacted Mark and briefly explained the situation.

"Would it help if Colin talked to Mr. Fogarty?" Mark said.

"Give him a few more minutes," Vicki said. "But be ready."

"Vicki, we need to get moving," Colin said.

"Just a few more minutes."

Vicki noticed an e-mail from Claudia, but she didn't dare open it at such a critical time. A war was raging in Tom's mind, and the only question now was who would win, the true God or Nicolae? Vicki asked to see Tom in the living room.

"One of the things we wanted to do with our Web site was lay out the truth of the Bible so anyone could understand it."

"I've seen this," Tom said. "We read your Web site and Tsion Ben-Judah's to look for clues."

"But you haven't looked at it since you asked God to open your eyes, right?"

Tom nodded and sat. Vicki pulled up different Old Testament prophecies that pointed to Jesus Christ. As she explained, she noticed Tom trying to concentrate, rubbing his forehead, and perspiring.

"I understand what you're saying," Tom said when Vicki was through. "I understood it when Josey explained it a long time ago. I'm just not sure I can believe in something just because it gets me to heaven. I don't want to face any more of the judgments you talk about, but I don't want you to scare me into a decision."

"The point isn't escaping judgments or not getting stung by some evil creature, it's choosing to follow the true God. You have to decide whether you're going to follow the one who gave his life to save you, or the one who threatens to cut off your head if you don't follow him."

Tom scratched his head. "I hadn't thought about it that way."

Vicki pulled up an Old Testament verse Tsion Ben-Judah had used on his Web site. "At a crucial time for Israel," she said, "a leader named Joshua challenged people to follow the true God instead of the fake ones they had worshiped. He wanted to make sure they understood how important their decision was."

Tom read the verse aloud. " 'So honor the Lord and serve him wholeheartedly. . . . But if you are unwilling to serve the Lord, then choose today whom you will serve. . . . But as for me and my family, we will serve the Lord.' "

Vicki prayed silently. She had given Tom the truth, backing up her beliefs with the Bible. Josey had lived the truth before him the past few years. Now it was Tom's decision.

The phone rang and Josey looked at the caller ID. "It's from work."

When it stopped ringing, Tom took a breath. "So what happens if I decide like you want me to? We go on the run? Try to hide for the rest of our lives?"

"Honey, if you choose him, God will take care of us."

Tom nodded. "I asked him to take off the blinders. I can see this is the only sane decision I can make, but I feel like I'm choosing more *against* Carpathia than *for* God."

A car pulled up in front of the house. Josey ran to the window and gasped. "It's a GC squad car."

"Cal said they're sending officers to pick up off-duty people to give the mark."

"No," Josey said, "tell them you're not going."

A car door slammed.

"You need to pray," Vicki said. "Just ask God to forgive—"

"I have to stall them. Josey, pack some things."

"Don't put this off," Vicki pleaded.

Someone knocked on the door.

Tom lowered his voice. "Do your people have enough room for two more in their van?"

"We'll make room," Vicki whispered.

"Go upstairs, get on your radio, and have your people drive to the end of the cul-de-sac—"

Thump, thump. "Officer Fogarty? Global Community Peacekeeper. Open up, please."

"Don't let them go down this street," Fogarty said. "Have them park on the next street, just west of us, in the same part of the block."

Vicki sprinted to a room at the top of the stairs. She pushed the door almost closed as Tom opened the front door. Out of breath, Vicki listened to the man outside.

"Officer Fogarty, we've been instructed to bring all Global Community personnel to the station for the loyalty mark application."

"Yeah, I know. I was headed back that way as soon as I checked on my wife. I told my partner she's not feeling well—"

"You'll need to come with me, sir."

From the next room came a shriek and a sob that sent chills down Vicki's spine. "Tom, I need you!" Josey wailed. "Hurry!"

Vicki peeked through the crack in the door. As Tom started toward the stairs, the officer grabbed Fogarty's arm. "I'm sorry, sir. I have orders."

"And I have a wife in pain! Surely the Global

Community has enough compassion to let a man comfort his wife."

"Your wife can come with us if she—"

Josey wailed again and Tom shook free of the man. "She's in no condition to be moved." He pushed past the officer and ran upstairs.

"I'll give you five minutes," the officer said, stepping outside.

Vicki pressed the Talk button of the walkie-talkie and whispered instructions for Mark. Mark clicked his radio twice, the signal that they had heard and were on their way.

Vicki joined Tom and Josey in the next room and quietly locked the door. Tom had the window open and a duffel bag filled with clothes lay on the bed. He threw the bag out the window, and Josey climbed onto the lattice that ran to the bottom of the wall.

"Quickly," Tom whispered.

As Josey carefully climbed down, Vicki helped push a dresser in front of the door. Then Tom helped her through the window and onto the lattice. It felt rickety, and Vicki wondered if it would hold her weight.

When she was almost to the bottom, a voice yelled from inside the house. "Officer Fogarty, it's time. Come down immediately or I'll come up there and get you."

191

20

VICKI and Josey hopped over a fence and ran between two houses toward the next street. Vicki glanced behind them as Tom dropped to the ground and picked up the duffel bag.

Vicki spotted the van about three houses away. She put a hand to the front gate when Tom whispered, "Get down!"

Vicki fell behind a bush, breathing hard. She glanced at the Fogartys' house and saw the GC officer at a window. "The window's open and I think he's making a run for it, sir!" the officer said into his radio. When he moved away, Tom raced forward.

"I see him now, sir," the officer said. "He's running toward the next street. I'm giving chase."

Vicki opened the gate and waved wildly at Mark. The van pulled forward and Vicki, Josey, and Tom jumped in as Mark floored the accelerator. Colin grabbed the duffel bag as Tom struggled to get the door closed.

"Take a right at the stop sign," Tom said.

"Was that officer alone?" Josey said.

"I think so, and he followed us on foot, so we've got a chance."

Mark turned right and Tom directed him to an unpaved road that cut across a field. A few minutes later, with Tom's help, they were headed north to the Wisconsin border.

Josey stared out the window, holding a scrape on her arm from the lattice. "I can't believe we've just left everything behind. I only had a few minutes to decide what to take and what to leave."

Mark glanced at Tom, then glared at Vicki in the rearview mirror. "What were you thinking?" he mouthed.

Vicki put a finger to her lips. She introduced Mark and Colin, then turned to Shelly and Conrad. Finally, Cheryl leaned forward and held Josey's hand. "I'm very glad to meet you, ma'am."

Josey teared up, turned in the seat, and hugged the girl. "And I'm glad to meet you."

Tom listened to his GC radio and watched for any activity. When they reached the Wisconsin border, he seemed to relax.

"What would they have done with you if you stayed?" Mark said.

"I guess they would have made me choose. Everybody was required to take the mark at some point today."

"And why didn't you?" Mark said.

Tom sighed. "The truth is, I've been having second thoughts all along. I didn't want my wife to know it, but the whole GC system was bugging me. I kept hoping things would get better, but they didn't."

"So you want to pray now?" Vicki said.

Tom looked around the car at the others. "I guess this is as good a place as any." He put his hands together and leaned forward against the back of the seat in front of him.

Josey put a hand on his back and asked if he needed help. He nodded. "Just tell God that you're sorry about your sin and that you want to receive his forgiveness. You believe that Jesus died on the cross and paid the penalty for what you've done. You also believe that God raised Jesus from the dead and wants to give that new life to you. You receive his gift right now, and you want him to guide your life from this day on."

Tom nodded again and began. To Vicki's surprise, he prayed aloud. "God, you know what a mess I've made of my life and how long I've rejected you. I've done some bad things, things even Josey doesn't know about. So I'm asking you right now to forgive me. I want to receive that gift you're offering. I do believe you died for me, and that you rose from the dead. Give me a new life, and change me."

"Amen," Josey said softly.

When Tom looked up, Josey touched his face and smiled. Tom looked at her, then at Vicki and the others in astonishment. "I don't believe it. You guys were serious about God giving you a mark."

After everyone had congratulated Tom, Josey pulled out a tattered photo album from the duffel bag. "When you have to pack in five minutes, you realize what's most important."

Josey flipped through pages of photos, memories, ticket stubs, and important events. She showed Vicki the last pictures she had taken of her two boys, Ben and Brad, before the disappearances.

Mark turned the van east, toward the kids' new hideout, with a brand-new believer, Tom Fogarty.

Judd awoke early after a good night's sleep and joined the others in the basement for breakfast. Lionel had come in late, so Judd tried to keep quiet and let him sleep.

Yitzhak and Mr. Stein were leading the others in prayer for the events of the day. Though Mr. Stein said he knew what Nicolae's ultimate plan was, he confessed he did not know exactly how things would take place.

"You must remember that Nicolae wants to set himself up as a divine being. He is intent on the destruction of all of God's creation, both human and otherwise. From my reading of Scripture, his persecution of the Jewish people will begin soon."

"Many people do not want to take Carpathia's mark," one man said, "but they do not believe that Jesus is the Messiah. How can we persuade them?"

Mr. Stein nodded. "We must continue to pray that God will reveal himself and convince them. The fact that they do not recognize Carpathia as a god is very encouraging. But simply seeing the truth about evil is not enough. They must believe the truth about Jesus."

Though Judd knew what would happen would probably disgust him, he still felt a sense of excitement about the day and prayed God would protect him. He prayed for the others in the Young Trib Force and decided to check with Chang before he left.

Chang answered the phone and explained that he was at his computer in the palace, monitoring the complex number of pilots, planes, drivers, and vehicles that would help with the mass departure of people from Jerusalem.

"I still don't understand how they're going to slip by the GC," Judd said.

"As long as the GC believes what the Trib Force is doing is one of their own exercises, Operation Eagle will continue."

"How did they come up with that name?"

"It comes from a passage in Revelation 12. 'She was given two wings like those of a great eagle. This allowed her to fly to a place prepared for her in the wilderness, where she would be cared for and protected from the dragon for a time, times, and half a time.' Tsion believes the woman represents God's chosen people. The two wings are land and air, and her place is Petra."

"How long are people supposed to stay there?"

"Dr. Ben-Judah teaches that 'a time' is one year, so 'a time, times, and half a time' would be three and a half years of protection."

"And the dragon is Nicolae?"

"Yes, Antichrist."

"Any news about the GC finding anything in the plane crash?"

"They are still combing the wreckage. The four are presumed dead, but there's no final report."

Something in Chang's voice bothered Judd and he asked if the boy was all right. When Chang paused, Judd said, "I know you're under a lot of pressure, but I might be able to help."

"I have talked with Dr. Ben-Judah this morning about . . . my problem."

"The dual marks?"

"Yes. He understands how alone I feel, and he tried to help me, but I still can't look in the mirror. This mark of Carpathia mocks me."

"What did Tsion say?"

"He assured me that I have the seal of God and that I did not voluntarily receive the mark. But in Dr. Ben-Judah's own writings, he says the mark of the beast condemns me."

"The Bible says you can't *take* both marks. You didn't *take* it—they forced it on you."

"Which is exactly what he said. But I keep thinking about the brave ones who stayed faithful to the end. God gave them the ability to face the blade without fear. What did I do?"

"You've stayed in the den of the lion," Judd said. "Don't tell me you're chicken. You're in the most dangerous place on the face of the earth."

Chang was silent a moment. "I appreciate you trying to encourage me, but even Dr. Ben-Judah admits my problem puzzles him. The only thing I can do is stay at my post and fulfill my duties until he contacts me again."

Vicki and the others were given a hero's welcome when they arrived safely in Wisconsin. Becky Dial greeted her husband warmly, and Phoenix went wild when he saw Vicki. Charlie had to put him in another room so they could hear the story of what happened.

Janie hugged Vicki and told her she'd been praying for her. The kids all welcomed Josey and Tom Fogarty, but with all of the new people added, Vicki wondered if there would be enough room.

Darrion pulled Vicki aside a few minutes after she arrived. "I know you have to be tired, but I'd like you to look at Claudia's response."

Vicki nodded. "I saw that she'd written, but I haven't had time to look at it."

Darrion pulled up the response, which had Vicki's message pasted at the front of the e-mail. Claudia wrote underneath:

> *Dear Young Trib Force,*
> *I totally understand how you might think this is a trap. You probably get that a lot. I have visited your Web site many times and I decided to pray the prayer, but nothing happened. I don't see a mark on my forehead or on anyone else's. We only have another day to comply with taking Carpathia's mark. What should I do?*
> *Claudia*

Vicki took a breath and sighed. "It's not what I expected."

"What did you think she'd do, write some nasty note admitting she was a Carpathia follower?" Darrion said.

Vicki looked hard at Darrion. "What if she's telling the truth? What if she's really a believer and we just let her hang down there? I thought she'd ask for a face-to-face meeting, but she didn't."

"If she's a true believer, don't you think she'd have the sense to get out?"

Vicki squeezed her forehead with a hand and pulled her hair back. "I'm too tired to think straight."

"Then do this," Darrion said. "Write her back and tell her to get out of there as fast as she can. When she's a safe distance away, write us again and we'll try to help."

"Sounds good."

While Darrion worked on the return e-mail, Vicki talked with Jim Dekker and the other new arrivals. Ginny and Bo Shairton nearly cried when they saw Vicki, and Maggie Carlson wept as she talked about Natalie's sacrifice for them.

Vicki found Manny Aguilara a shy young man, with multiple tattoos on his neck and arms. He said he felt out of place but very welcomed.

"I would like to tell you my story when you are rested," Manny said.

"I'd love to hear it," Vicki said.

Vicki found a cot in one of the girls' rooms and listened to the conversation through the thin walls. Tom Fogarty asked questions, Josey talked with Charlie about his family, and Shelly told Janie and Melinda about Chad Harris, the good-looking guy they had met in Iowa.

When she was almost asleep, Vicki was startled by
something moving against her cot. She leaned over and
saw Phoenix wagging his tail. She patted the covers and
the dog jumped onto the cot and slept at her feet the
entire night.

The sun was coming up as Judd finished talking with
Chang. Judd told him he would be praying for him
throughout the day.

"Thank you," Chang said, "but don't forget to pray for
Dr. Rosenzweig as well."

"Where is he?"

"You don't know? Dr. Rosenzweig is the one who will
stand up to Carpathia."

"What?" Judd said. "I thought it was going to be
Tsion."

"Dr. Rosenzweig has been studying with Dr. Ben-
Judah, and for some reason he is going to be the main
person to challenge Nicolae."

Judd thought it through. Chaim was Jewish, a believer
in Jesus as Messiah, but he didn't fit the profile of a
prophet. He had heard the man speak before, and his
voice wasn't strong and commanding like Tsion's had
been. Still, if Chaim was God's chosen, God could give
him the strength he needed.

Judd told Chang he would check with him later and
he went to wake Lionel. This was going to be a day no
one alive would forget.

21

JUDD met with Lionel and Sam and discovered from one of the Jewish believers that Carpathia was supposed to appear in the Old City at 11 A.M.

"That will give me time to show you some of what's happened since you left," Sam said.

Sam showed them several meeting places used since the fire at General Zimmerman's home. A few were secluded, where people could secretly ask questions without fear of Global Community crackdown. Others were out in the open.

"And the GC never stopped you or arrested you?" Lionel said.

"A few people have been arrested," Sam said, "but God has protected us and allowed us to talk with hundreds. Plus, we've been using this." Sam pulled out a handheld computer and activated the screen, showing The Cube, a high-tech presentation of the gospel.

"I hope we get to meet the guy who developed that someday," Lionel said.

Sam took them through a major street as they moved toward the Old City. People swarmed out of hotels looking for transportation. Lionel nudged Judd and pointed at a convoy of Global Community troops. "I thought this guy was for peace. Are those just toy guns and missiles?"

Judd shook his head. Convoys of tanks, fighters, and bombers rolled by, and people cheered when they saw the show of military might.

They reached the Via Dolorosa before 9 A.M. and were surrounded by masses looking for a spot to view Carpathia. Judd's parents had taken him to parades in Chicago and the suburbs, but they were nothing like this. Men and women elbowed their way to the best spots. Global Community Peacekeepers and Morale Monitors moved through the crowds in small groups.

GC sharpshooters prowled tops of buildings. It was clear this event would not be marred by another assassination attempt.

Vendors had run out of real palm branches, so they sold plastic ones to toss before the potentate. People who supported Carpathia talked about his "triumphal entry" and Judd could hardly stand it. Hawkers walked up and down the streets selling paintings of Nicolae coming back to life, pictures of Carpathia standing on his glass coffin, and even commemorative coins featuring numbers from the different regions of the world. Judd couldn't believe that one man was selling replicas of guillotines. He called them "Judah-ite Eliminators" and had sold hundreds.

Sam pointed out many who were Orthodox Jews. These men scowled and sneered at the vendors.

There were fewer Peacekeepers and Morale Monitors inside the Old City. Some shopwindows and businesses were boarded up, still feeling the effects of the Jerusalem earthquake. A man with a handheld television near Judd called for quiet as Reverend Father Leon Fortunato's face appeared on a newscast. The news anchor spoke of Fortunato in glowing terms, saying the man was bringing the world together through his efforts to bring peace and healing to a hurting world.

Lionel rolled his eyes as the news showed yet another replay of the airplane crash in Tel Aviv. Security and Intelligence Director Suhail Akbar appeared at a press conference held earlier that morning.

"Unfortunately," Akbar said, "while the investigation continues, we have been unable to confirm the evidence of any human remains. It is, of course, possible that four loyal patriots of the Global Community were vaporized upon impact in this tragedy. Medical personnel tell us they would have died without pain. Once we have confirmed the deaths, prayers will go to the risen potentate on behalf of their eternal souls, and we will extend our sympathies to their families and loved ones."

"We have learned from sources inside the investigation," the news anchor said, "that the crash may have been caused by pilot error. GCNN has learned that the flight crew was warned before takeoff of a cargo weight-

and-balance problem. We'll have more on that story as it develops."

"Sounds like the GC took the bait," Lionel whispered to Judd.

"Let's hope they don't catch on."

Judd's phone blipped and it was Chang. He asked where Judd was and Judd told him.

"I have big news. Mr. Hassid just had me patch into the Phoenix 216 and listen in on Carpathia."

"What's going on?"

"Fortunato is itching and scratching. He acts like something bit him. Even Carpathia is laughing about it."

Judd scratched his head. "I can't remember, is there some kind of plague of mosquitoes or something on its way?"

"I'm not sure either, but watch out for Carpathia's grand entrance."

"What else is going on?"

"They've got a new guy, Loren Hut. I think he's the new head of Morale Monitors. He says every one of them is carrying a weapon there in Israel, and all the rest will be armed around the world by the end of next week. And get this, Nicolae is expecting opposition."

"He'd better," Judd said. "There's plenty of it. And not just from Christ followers."

"This guy gets more evil every time I hear him. He's telling his head guys how to kill anyone who opposes him. He wants people to suffer before they die. And even after they've been killed, he wants them beheaded as an example to others."

"Are they headed this way?"

"Yes, they will be leaving within ten minutes. They have been going over the schedule, changing things."

"Changing what?" Judd said.

"Believe it or not, they are planning a mockery of the last steps of Jesus to Golgotha."

"I believe it."

"Carpathia cut out half of the stuff they had planned. He said it never happened. The others protested, said it was part of tradition, but Carpathia just cut it."

A chill went down Judd's spine. Carpathia was claiming to have been present when Jesus was mocked, spit on, and nailed to a cross. Judd knew Jesus would win the final victory. He would crush Satan and all of his followers in three and a half years. That was one triumphal entry Judd hoped he would live to see.

Darrion had slept a few hours off and on during the kids' ordeal in Iowa. With help from Melinda, Janie, and Becky Dial, they had monitored incoming e-mails, news from the Global Community's Web site, and any other information they could find.

Now, with everyone asleep in the underground shelter in Wisconsin, Darrion wandered into the media room. She was encouraged about the safe return of the kids and the escape from the Iowa GC facility. Jim Dekker was safe, and The Cube had reached many around the world.

But there were also problems and question marks. How would the kids survive for three and a half years without taking the mark? How many believers would lose their lives standing up to Carpathia?

Darrion recognized Commander Kruno Fulcire on Global Community Network News. An anchor had broken into the live coverage in Israel to highlight something happening in the States. Mark walked in and Darrion asked him to record the interview.

"And when did this occur?" the news anchor said.

"We finished the interrogation about an hour ago and gave the prisoner an opportunity to obey international law," Fulcire said. "He refused, so we immediately implemented punishment."

"The guillotine?"

"The loyalty enforcement facilitator, yes."

"What kind of information did you get from this Pete Davidson?"

Darrion gasped.

"It's surprising how much this truck driver knew," Commander Fulcire said. "He gave us names of Judah-ites, locations of hideouts and storage facilities. He even told us where Judah-ites are hiding weapons of mass destruction."

"The guy's lying," Mark said.

"How do you know?"

"First, Pete would never have talked, and second, since when do the Judah-ites have weapons of mass destruction?"

The news anchor continued his questioning. "So the Judah-ites plan actions against the Global Community?"

"Of course. It's what they live for. They want to

disrupt the peace and harmony the Global Community
has tried to create. Davidson was one of their low-level
operators, with a very small intellect. You see, these
people are easy to lead. They're brainwashed by these religious crazies and they choose death over taking the mark
of loyalty."

The screen switched to a live shot of crowds in
Jerusalem.

"Before we continue with our live coverage from
Israel, sir, just one more question. We've heard of a
Global Community Morale Monitor deciding not to take
the loyalty mark. Is there any truth that there are more
Judah-ites working inside the Global Community?"

Fulcire hesitated. "We do have some reports which
haven't been confirmed yet that I can't go into. One that I
can mention is the case of Morale Monitor Claudia
Zander. She is missing from her post in Des Plaines."

A photo of Claudia flashed on the screen along with a
special hot-line number.

"We are in the early stages of developing rewards for
those we suspect of being Judah-ites," Fulcire continued,
"but now we simply want to talk with this Morale Monitor and make sure she hasn't fallen into the wrong
hands."

"Think we should wake the others?" Darrion said.

Mark shook his head. "Pete's dead. They'll find out in
the morning. I'm worried about this Zander girl. We all
assumed she was faking being interested in the message.
Have you checked e-mail lately?"

Darrion had been concentrating so hard on the broadcast that she had forgotten the Web site. There were at least a hundred more messages since she had checked it.

"There," Mark said, pointing to an e-mail with the subject line, *Help!*

Darrion opened it quickly and saw the message was from Claudia.

> *Dear Young Trib Force,*
>
> *They were going to make me take the mark, so I ran like you suggested. I grabbed a few things from the apartment, and I took Natalie's Bible. I guess that was okay since she's gone.*
>
> *I need a place to hide until I figure out what to do next. This new commander is really intense. I don't know if you heard, but the guy in Iowa chose the blade. I don't think I could ever stand up like that, but I guess God could give me the courage.*
>
> *I'm sorry for rambling. Please e-mail or call me as soon as you can. I'll put my number at the bottom of this message.*
>
> *And one more thing. I still can't see the mark Dr. Ben-Judah wrote about. Does that mean I'm not a true Judah-ite?*

Darrion scribbled Claudia's phone number on a scrap of paper and saved the message. "Do you think we should wake Vicki?"

Mark looked at his watch. It was almost time for Carpathia to make his grand entrance in Jerusalem. "She needs to know about Claudia. Wake her."

Judd dialed Chang and apologized for bothering him. "It's no bother," Chang said. "I'm a multitasker. Mr. Hassid has me back on track."

"What did he say?"

"He chewed me out and said I don't have time to focus on my dual marks. He even threatened to destroy the setup he and I worked so long to build, so I'm going to concentrate. When I have time, I'm going back to find video recordings of what really happened when I got Carpathia's mark."

"Let me know as soon as you do," Judd said. "Things are heating up here. There's more excitement down the street."

"Nicolae is on his way. I've heard the image of Carpathia is being moved to the Temple Mount. People are gathering there to worship it and take the mark of loyalty."

"It's time for a showdown," Judd said.

"Just keep away from the cross fire," Chang said. "And keep praying that the undecided choose Christ!"

22

JUDD walked through one of the ancient gates of Jerusalem and nearly lost sight of Lionel and Sam, all three pushed by the huge crowds bustling toward the city. Judd watched for Chaim Rosenzweig and Buck Williams, but the place looked like a human sea. Lionel and Sam caught up with Judd, and the three prepared for Carpathia's arrival.

Thousands cheered in anticipation. Toddlers were held high on shoulders, waving real palm branches. Teenagers wearing Z-Van's style of clothes danced through the streets, forming a human chain. Many of them already had the mark of Carpathia and celebrated by shouting slogans and singing songs.

"I wonder if Z-Van is going to make an appearance at this," Lionel said.

"You can bet he's ticked if he doesn't get to," Judd said.

Judd's heart leapt when a loudspeaker truck moved through the street announcing that all citizens were expected to display the mark of loyalty to Carpathia. "Why not take care of this painless and thrilling obligation while His Excellency is here?"

A teen in the line of dancers shouted, "Come on, we're going to the Temple Mount now to get our mark!" Several people followed, but most stayed, not wanting to miss a glimpse of Carpathia.

Lionel glanced at Judd, his eyes wide. "You think they're going to check and see if we have the mark?"

"Relax," Judd said. "Those application facilities have to be packed."

People sang an off-key song a block away. Judd finally realized it was "Hail Carpathia." Hundreds broke into wild applause, thinking Nicolae had appeared. A GC tank topped with revolving blue, red, and orange lights rolled past. Behind that was a motorcade of three black vehicles, followed by more tanks. The crowd cheered and Judd hustled for a better view.

When the convoy stopped, another cheer rose. The first black vehicle held local and regional dignitaries. They exited, quickly followed by the Most High Reverend Father Leon Fortunato. Leon straightened his long robe, then slowly scratched at his hip.

Judd explained what Chang had overheard about Leon's pain. Sam wondered if this was part of the next plague sent by God. Global Community officials Suhail Akbar and Walter Moon stepped from the second car, but the biggest ovation yet came when a woman dressed in blue stepped from the vehicle. Her white hair stood out among all the men dressed in dark suits. Though she was short, she carried herself regally, her head held high and her back straight. She moved to a podium and held up both hands. The crowd hushed as she leaned toward the microphone.

"Who's that?" Lionel said.

"Isn't she a relative of Nicolae?" Judd whispered.

"It's Viv Ivins," a woman behind them said. "She's a member of the potentate's inner cabinet." The woman eyed the three boys. "Why haven't you taken the mark of loyalty?"

Judd smiled and moved a few steps away. "Guess we have to be more careful."

Viv Ivins welcomed the participants and introduced honored guests. When she welcomed "our spiritual leader of international Carpathianism, the Reverend Fortunato," the crowd went wild. Judd noticed that Leon was still scratching his backside.

Judd recalled Sabir's imitation of "Hail Carpathia" as Leon led the crowd, directing with his right hand and scratching with his left. Voices echoed off buildings, and people had a difficult time staying in sync with each other.

As Leon urged the throng to "sing it once more as we welcome the object of our worship," an official opened a door and Nicolae Carpathia bounded out alone and bowed deeply. The crowd gasped, then roared in approval as they saw Carpathia's gold sandals, glistening white robe, and glowing, silver belt. Nicolae stretched out his hands toward the crowd, as if he were ready to embrace them all, as a group of bodyguards dressed in black suits formed a half circle behind him.

A military truck pulled up and Judd noticed a strange smell. Looking closely at the trailer hitched to the truck, Judd saw a dangling rope and two enormous eyes.

Sam drew close to Judd and whispered, "Here it comes. The moment I have been dreading."

It took Vicki a few minutes to awaken from her dead sleep. She hobbled into the meeting room groggy and half awake, but one glimpse of the scene on television and her eyes were open.

Nicolae Carpathia looked like some kind of Greek god with bad jewelry. If the scene wasn't such a shake of the fist at God, it would have looked funny. The camera showed a trailer ramp lowering and two Peacekeepers leapt inside. Another angle caught them pulling and pushing something off the truck.

"Is that what I think it is?" Vicki said.

The two Peacekeepers struggled with a massive pig, trying to pull it onto the street. The camera angle switched and showed Nicolae Carpathia gazing at the enormous animal.

"Look at the size of that thing!" Darrion said.

"I don't think I can watch," Vicki said.

Mark flipped a switch to record the scene and turned. "We need to tell you about Claudia."

Judd watched in fascination and revulsion as the pig walked a few more steps and stopped. A leather saddle was fastened around its middle, complete with stirrups. The animal seemed woozy, unaware of the crowd's whooping and yelling. Though GC handlers had scrubbed the pig clean, the stench almost took Judd's breath away.

"They must have drugged it," Sam said, "but why?"

They soon found out. Carpathia waved at the crowd, pointed at the pig, and laughed. When he reached it, he cupped the pig's face in his hands and draped a noose around its neck.

"He's going to ride it?" Lionel said.

"That's why they drugged it," Judd said. "Under normal conditions that pig would never let anyone on its back."

Carpathia grabbed his robe, pulled it up to his knee, and got onto the pig's back. The crowd laughed and hooted as Carpathia jammed his feet in the stirrups and yanked on the rope, ordering the pig down the street.

"Why wouldn't they use a horse?" Lionel said.

"He's putting all religions in their place," Sam said, "especially Jewish and Christian religions."

"That's right. Jews don't eat pigs," Lionel said.

"And since Christianity comes out of the Jewish faith, Carpathia offends two groups with one ride."

Judd looked back at the gathering of dignitaries near the microphone and noticed that Leon Fortunato was still scratching.

Vicki ran a hand through her hair and checked the clock. It was a little after three in the morning. Making life-threatening decisions with this little sleep was dangerous, but if Claudia was telling the truth, they had to help.

"Driving back there could be suicide," Mark said.

"What if we find out where she is," Darrion said, "and let someone who doesn't know her go in?"

Vicki heard someone move behind her and turned. Manny Aguilara waved sheepishly and said, "I'm sorry. I woke up and couldn't help hearing. Let me do it. Claudia doesn't know me."

Vicki looked at Mark. "Let's talk. And, Darrion, write Claudia and ask her exactly where she is."

As Darrion typed, Vicki took a breath and prayed for wisdom.

Judd followed Carpathia and was joined by Sam, Lionel, and thousands of spectators lining the Via Dolorosa. People sang and cheered Nicolae as the pig carried him along. Suddenly, the drugged animal pitched forward, its front legs buckling, and a few aides helped the potentate off.

The crowd became too thick to move through, and Sam suggested they go another route to Calvary. "I think he'll eventually go there."

They arrived at the traditional site of Jesus' crucifixion and took their place at the base of the hill. Carpathia arrived a few minutes later, climbed to the edge of the Mount, and threw his arms out.

Leon Fortunato stepped beside Nicolae and imitated him, still scratching his rear. "Behold the lamb who takes away the sins of the world!" Fortunato roared.

Suddenly, the sky blackened and Judd felt a gust of wind. People murmured and looked for shelter, but Fortunato seemed to anticipate their movement. "You need not move if you are loyal to your risen ruler! I have been imbued with power from on high to call down fire on the enemies of the king of this world. Let the loyalists declare themselves!"

Thousands screamed and waved in support of Carpathia. Judd looked around for any other believers, wondering if Chaim Rosenzweig would stand to challenge the evil one.

The sky was black as night and Judd could only see Fortunato when lightning flashed. "Today you shall have opportunity to worship the image of your god! But now you have opportunity to praise him in person! All glory to the lover of your souls!"

People around Judd knelt and raised their arms in praise to Nicolae. Judd recognized what a dangerous position he and his friends were in. They were not about to bow the knee to Carpathia or his statue. Would they be struck dead?

"You think we ought to get out of here?" Judd whispered to Lionel and Sam.

Before either could answer, Fortunato yelled, "How many of you will receive the mark of loyalty even this day at the Temple Mount?"

The crowd rose as one to wave and cheer. Fortunato

responded with, "My lord, the very god of this world, has granted me the power to know your hearts!"

"Is that true?" Lionel whispered.

Judd shook his head. "That's not what Tsion teaches. He says Satan doesn't know what we think. How could he tell Fortunato if he doesn't know himself?"

Lightning flashed and claps of thunder overwhelmed the crowd. "I know if your heart is deceitful!" Fortunato yelled. "You shall not be able to stand against the all-seeing eye of your god or his servant!"

People began singing "Hail Carpathia" as Fortunato looked at the crowd with piercing eyes.

Suddenly, everyone fell deathly still as a woman a few yards from Judd screeched and pointed at Carpathia and Fortunato. "Liars!" she screamed. "Blasphemers! Antichrist! False Prophet!"

The people around her moved away quickly, and the woman was left alone. As Judd listened, he thought her voice sounded familiar.

"Woe unto you who would take the place of Jesus Christ of Nazareth, the Lamb of God who takes away the sin of the world!" the woman continued. "You shall not prevail against the God of heaven!"

Lightning flashed and Lionel grabbed Judd's arm. "That's Hattie Durham!"

Lionel was right. It *was* Hattie! Judd had first seen the woman on an airplane over the Atlantic the night of the disappearances. Though she had spent some time working for Nicolae, she was now a member of the Tribulation Force.

"I have spoken!" Fortunato spat back.

"Yours is the empty, vain tongue of the condemned!" Hattie yelled. She pointed to heaven and said, "As he is my witness, there is one God and one mediator between God and men, the man Christ Jesus!"

Judd was so captivated by Hattie's words that he didn't see Fortunato's movements. He heard a ghastly sound behind him and instinctively ducked as a ball of fire roared from the sky, lighting the whole area.

Hattie Durham didn't have time to react. She burst into flames and Judd fell to the ground, shaking, screaming, scared out of his mind. Sam and Lionel huddled close, their eyes covered. Judd wondered if they would be next.

Judd peeked at Hattie once more and saw fire engulfing her body. She seemed to melt in the white-hot heat, her body shrinking to the ground. The sun appeared again, chasing the darkness. A soft breeze blew Hattie over, and Judd noticed her shadow imprinted on the ground.

The crowd focused on Fortunato. "Marvel not that I say unto you, all power has been given to me in heaven and on the earth!" he said.

Carpathia slowly led the procession away from the area. Some people in the crowd kicked at Hattie's ashes or spit on her remains. When most of the crowd was gone, Judd knelt beside Hattie and thanked God for a courageous woman who dared stand up to the most evil ruler the world had ever seen.

23

JUDD caught his breath and told Sam how he had met Hattie. He wished there was something he could do for her.

"Do you want to go back to Yitzhak's house?" Sam said.

Judd nodded. "I think I'd better. Seeing that happen to someone you know . . ."

Lionel put a hand on his shoulder. "We understand. We'll give you a full report when we get back."

As Judd walked through the oncoming crowd, he wondered about Operation Eagle and when Rayford Steele and the other pilots would airlift believers and Jews out of Jerusalem. What a massive job that had to be. And with an enemy like Carpathia, it was vital that they get these people out before Carpathia killed them.

Lionel and Sam moved with the crowd toward the Garden Tomb. By the time they arrived, Supreme Commander Walter Moon was speaking.

"Oh, he's better than all right, judging by his performance at Golgotha," Moon said.

"Who's he talking about?" Lionel said.

"Shhh," an older woman in front of Lionel said. "Reverend Father Fortunato has gone ahead for preparations. Please be quiet."

Sam looked at Lionel and frowned. "Everything's ready at the Temple Mount. Why would he leave?"

Vicki explained Claudia's situation to Manny and he perked up. "I might be able to help."

"How?" Vicki said.

"There may be someone in the gang who could do this for us, but you have to understand that the people we're dealing with don't think like you. We'll have to motivate them."

"Give them something?" Vicki said.

"Exactly."

Vicki looked at Darrion. "How much money do we have left?"

"A few hundred Nicks," Darrion said.

"Is there anybody inside the gang who owes you?" Mark said.

Manny bit his lip. "There is one person. His name is Hector."

"Call him as soon as we hear where Claudia is," Mark said.

Judd sat heavily on a couch in Yitzhak's basement. Mr. Stein and the other witnesses were spread out in Jerusalem. The images of Hattie Durham flashed through Judd's mind. He dialed Chang, but there was no answer.

A few minutes later Chang called back. "I was on another call, and you will not believe what I have found."

"You won't believe what I've just seen," Judd said. He detailed the episode at Calvary and what had happened to Hattie.

Chang said he had seen the event on the live GC feed. "I was on the phone with Mr. Williams. He is there in Jerusalem with Chaim. We've just discovered top secret information about Fortunato. He is being treated by one of the palace doctors for some kind of rash. They report that it looks like boils erupting from his skin."

"That would explain why he's scratching so much," Judd said. "Was that why you were so excited when I called earlier?"

"I have more good news, but let me share it with you later."

Lionel and Sam moved for a better view of the Garden Tomb. The afternoon sun was hot, and Lionel was glad when Nicolae stepped from behind a curtain. The crowd before him didn't cheer or sing. They seemed afraid and many had chosen to go straight to get their mark instead of watching Carpathia's evil spectacle.

"I was never entombed!" Carpathia began. "I lay in state for three days for the world to see. Someone was said to have risen from this spot, but where is he? Did you ever see him? If he was God, why is he not still here? Some would have you believe it was he behind the disappearances that so crippled our world. What kind of a God would do that?"

Lionel glanced at Sam and whispered, "This whole show is supposed to mock Jesus."

"I stand here among you, god on earth, having taken my rightful place," Carpathia said. "I accept your allegiance." He bowed and the crowd applauded.

Walter Moon stepped forward and bent toward the microphone. "He is risen!"

"He is risen indeed," the crowd replied, less than enthusiastic.

Moon chided them and the crowd responded a little louder. "We are providing you with the opportunity to worship your potentate and his image at the Temple Mount, and there you may express your eternal devotion by accepting the mark of loyalty. Do not delay. Do not put this off. Be able to tell your descendants that His Excellency personally was there the day you made your pledge concrete."

Moon lowered his voice and added, "And please remember that neither the mark of loyalty nor the worshiping of the image is optional."

The wind whipped up as a helicopter landed to take

Carpathia and other dignitaries to the Temple Mount. Lionel saw many with the mark heading for the holy site, while others rushed to get in line for their mark.

While Vicki waited for Claudia's response, the kids watched the live coverage in Jerusalem. Darrion called the others over when she found an e-mail from Tsion Ben-Judah. Vicki could tell by the way he composed the message that the man's heart was heavy.

> *I received a message from our sister in Christ, Hattie Durham, composed two days ago. As she was praying in her hotel room in Tel Aviv, God sent the angel Michael to minister to her. He said he had come in answer to her prayers.*
>
> *Michael encouraged her to be strong and said, "Those who turn many to righteousness shall shine like the stars forever and ever. Many shall be purified, and made white and refined, but the wicked shall do wickedly; and none of the wicked shall understand, but the wise shall understand."*
>
> *Hattie believed she should speak out against the lies of the Antichrist. She knew there were others who had been believers longer and asked why she should be chosen to confront the evil one. In her note she said, "Maybe this is all silly and will not happen. If I chicken out, it will not have been of God and I will intercept this before it gets to you. But if you receive it, I assume I will not see you until you are in heaven. I love you and all the others, in Christ. Your sister, Hattie Durham."*

Hattie was the one who spoke against Carpathia and his False Prophet Leon Fortunato. She was consumed by fire, but we will see this dear sister again.

Vicki sat stunned. She remembered her conversation with Hattie years before, trying to convince her that the Bible was true and giving her life to God was the only choice. Now Hattie was dead, another casualty in the war between good and evil. Vicki wondered when all the dying would end. She put her head in her hands and wept.

Lionel and Sam moved cautiously toward the loyalty application facility and the brewing chaos. Hundreds of military vehicles were parked outside the Old City. Sam wanted to avoid them, but Lionel noticed only a few Peacekeepers tending the vehicles. When they came near the Temple Mount, Lionel saw why. Global Community personnel were in line to take the mark themselves. Citizens who rushed to be processed grew angry that they had to wait in the back of the line.

Sam led Lionel to the Wailing Wall where many Orthodox Jews were praying. "These men, even if they are not believers in Messiah, will oppose the defiling of the new temple."

As Peacekeepers and Morale Monitors took the mark, Lionel and Sam moved to the east-facing steps of the new temple. It sparkled in the sunlight, a replica of Solomon's original temple. As they approached, Sam pointed out the image of Carpathia, an exact replica of the man. People fell to their knees when they first glimpsed the golden statue, some crying or singing softly. Then they quickly moved on and dozens more fell to their knees.

A dark cloud covered the sun and the temperature dropped suddenly. The huge crowd fell silent as the golden statue seemed to rock back and forth. Then a deep voice boomed from the image. "This assemblage is not unanimous in its dedication to me! I am the maker of heaven and earth, the god of all creation. I was and was not and am again! Bow before your lord!"

Lionel froze. If the image shot fire like Fortunato, he and Sam were dead. He didn't want to kneel before the image, but his legs felt shaky.

"Don't look at it," Sam whispered. "Just move away slowly."

Lionel kept his head down, but the voice again blasted behind him. With every word he expected a bolt of lightning or an explosion of fire to engulf him.

"The choice you make this day is between life and death! Beware, you who would resist the revelation of your true and living god, who resurrected himself from the dead! You who are foolish enough to cling to your outdated, impotent mythologies, cast off the chains of the past or you shall surely die! Your risen ruler and king has spoken!"

Lionel had made it to the outer edge of the crowd and was glad to be alive. He turned and looked at those in line for the mark. More and more pilgrims took their place behind GC personnel.

"Carpathia's right," Sam whispered. "This is life or death, but those people have no idea they're choosing death."

Lionel had seen enough. He and Sam quickly made their way through the streets back to Yitzhak's house.

———————————

Vicki watched in horror as GCNN covered Nicolae's appearance at the temple. Carpathia announced he would be watching all night until every citizen of Jerusalem had received the mark of loyalty and worshiped his image. "And tomorrow at noon, I will ascend to *my* throne in *my* new house."

Darrion yelped and said they had a new message from Claudia. Vicki turned from the scene of Nicolae waving farewell to the crowd and studied the e-mail.

> *I'm sorry it took me so long to get back to you. If you'll tell me when to expect you, I can arrange to be at a nearby restaurant, if you'd like. I'm at a hotel, but I only have enough money to stay one more night. Please call me or come get me.*
> *Claudia*

Vicki looked at Mark. "What do you think?"

"She gave us a phone number and location. That's a good sign."

"She seems sincere," Darrion said, "but it could still be an act."

"We can't afford to not take her seriously," Vicki said.

Manny called his friend Hector. After a few minutes of conversation, Manny hung up.

"What did he say?" Vicki said.

Manny hesitated. "Hector said he would help us find out if Claudia is telling the truth. We should go now."

24

VICKI called a meeting of the Young Trib Force in Wisconsin. The underground hideout was overcrowded with new arrivals, and everyone knew some would eventually have to move to another hiding place. Vicki explained the situation with Claudia and, though there was intense discussion, they agreed that Mark and Vicki would accompany Manny back to Des Plaines in hopes of bringing Claudia to safety.

Vicki stressed the importance of prayer, and everyone agreed there would be someone in a designated room praying while they were gone.

"We've received another message from Dr. Ben-Judah," Vicki said.

"Nobody else has died, have they?" Charlie said.

"No. This is a message he wants everyone to hear. I'll leave it for you to read, but I want to stress a couple of his points.

"Tsion says Nicolae has scheduled what the Bible calls the desecration of the temple." Vicki pulled an Old Testament text onto the huge screen. "Daniel prophesied that the king of this time period in history will 'exalt and magnify himself above every god' and 'shall speak blasphemies against the God of gods.' "

"What are blastomys?" Charlie said.

Vicki smiled. "A blasphemy is making fun of God. It means you take what is holy, and make it unholy. It's like riding a pig down the Via Dolorosa just to make fun of Jesus."

Charlie nodded. "That Carpathia's a really bad guy."

"Tsion writes about why people don't believe the truth of God. There is a danger that the people we're trying to reach have hardened their hearts. People who do this won't be able to change their minds."

"But we don't know who those people are," Darrion said.

"Exactly," Vicki said, "so we need to keep giving the message and looking for as many opportunities as possible."

When she was through, Mark, Manny, and Vicki knelt in the middle of the room. Jim Dekker and Colin Dial prayed first, putting their hands on them. The others prayed and asked God to protect them when they began their travels later that night.

Judd awoke wondering if it would be his last morning on earth. It was clear Carpathia and Fortunato had the power

to kill believers, and with all the GC Peacekeepers and
Morale Monitors in Jerusalem, Judd knew he had to be
careful.

He walked with Mr. Stein toward the Temple Mount.
Sam and Lionel followed a few minutes behind. Military
vehicles lined the streets leading to the Old City, but
there were few Peacekeepers or Morale Monitors.

Mr. Stein smiled. "The Global Community workers
are experiencing the truth of the Bible."

"I don't get it," Judd said.

"Revelation 16:2 says, 'So the first angel left the
Temple and poured out his bowl over the earth, and
horrible, malignant sores broke out on everyone who had
the mark of the beast and who worshiped his statue.' "

"A plague of boils?"

"Yes."

One of Mr. Stein's friends rushed to them. "It's
happening. The prophet of God has come!"

"Where?" Mr. Stein said.

"At the Temple Mount. He just spoke and demanded
an audience with the evil one. He warned Carpathia not
to touch the remnant of Israel, believers in Jesus of Nazareth! He calls himself Micah. And when Global Community guards tried to shoot him, they became paralyzed.
Now one of the GC leaders is questioning Micah."

Judd and Mr. Stein rushed toward the Temple Mount,
finally spotting a ring of GC Peacekeepers around an old
man dressed in a monklike robe. The robe was gathered
at the waist by a braid of rope.

The GC leader identified himself as Loren Hut and

ordered people to stand back. A television camera caught the action as Hut pulled a gun from its holster, scratched himself, and prepared to fire at the man named Micah.

The gun exploded so loudly that the crowd fell back. Expecting to see a lifeless, bloody body, Judd opened his eyes to see Micah alive and well. Loren Hut fired again, only inches away, but again the bullet appeared to miss. Hut fired the gun again and again, but nothing happened.

Someone near Judd laughed and said, "This is a joke! A put-on! He's shooting blanks!"

Loren Hut screamed, "Blanks?" He turned and fired directly into the man's chest. The man fell backward, dead before he hit the ground. Hut turned and fired two more shots at Micah, but neither did any harm. Hut threw his gun away and rubbed his body against a nearby tree, crying in agony.

Minutes later Carpathia arrived by helicopter. He approached the gathering and made sure cameras were trained on his every move. Judd and Mr. Stein stood behind the scene a few yards but could hear every word spoken.

"You are too old to be Tsion Ben-Judah," Carpathia said. "And you call yourself Micah."

Judd saw contempt on Carpathia's face. As Judd studied Micah, he thought it could be Dr. Chaim Rosenzweig, but he wasn't sure.

After one of Carpathia's troops fell to the ground scratching and writhing in pain, Carpathia said, "I concede I have you to thank for the fact that nearly my entire workforce is suffering this morning."

"Probably all of them," Micah said. "If they are not, you might want to check the authenticity of their marks."

"How did you do it?"

"Not I, but God."

"You are looking into the face of god," Carpathia said.

"On the contrary, I fear God. I do not fear you."

"So, Micah, what will it take for you to lift this magic spell that has incapacitated my people?"

"There is no magic here. This is the judgment of almighty God."

Nicolae smiled. "All right. What does *almighty God* want in exchange for lightening up on this *judgment?*"

For the next few minutes Judd watched as God's servant dealt with the evil ruler. Finally, Micah said, "A million of God's chosen people in this area alone have chosen to believe in Messiah. They would die before they would take your mark."

"Then they shall die!"

"You must let them flee this place before you pour out revenge on your enemies."

"Never!"

Judd looked around and realized everyone who had Carpathia's mark was now either on the ground writhing in pain or moving to makeshift medical tents for help.

"Your only hope to avoid the next terrible plague from heaven is to let Israelis who believe in Messiah go," Micah said.

Carpathia's eyes darted back and forth. "And what might that next plague entail?"

"You will know when you know," Micah said. "But I

can tell you this: It will be worse than the one that has brought your people low. I need a drink of water."

Someone brought a bottle of water, and Micah showed Nicolae it had turned to blood.

Nicolae said, "I want my people healthy and my water pure."

"You know the price."

"Specifics."

"Israeli Jews who have chosen to believe Jesus the Christ is their Messiah must be allowed to leave before you punish anyone for not taking your mark. And devout Orthodox Jews must be allowed a place where they can worship after you have defiled their temple."

Judd's mind reeled. He was watching prophecy fulfilled before his very eyes. Carpathia left, and people who had not yet taken the mark volunteered to help set up cameras and equipment. As they followed Micah to the temple, Judd noticed Mr. Stein's lips moving in silent prayer.

"Citizens!" Micah said in a clear voice. "Hear me! You who have not taken the mark of loyalty! There may still be time to choose to obey the one true and living God! While the evil ruler of this world promises peace, there is no peace! While he promises benevolence and prosperity, look at your world! Everyone who has preceded you in taking the mark and worshiping the image of the man of sin now suffers with grievous sores. That is your lot if you follow him.

"By now you must know that the world has been divided. Nicolae Carpathia is the opponent of God and wishes only your destruction, regardless of his lies. The God who created you loves you. His Son who died for your sins will return to set up his earthly kingdom in less than three and a half years, and if you have not already rejected him one time too many, you may receive him now.

"You were born in sin and separated from God, but the Bible says God is not willing that any should perish but that all should come to repentance. Ephesians 2:8-9 says that nothing we can do will earn our salvation but that 'it is the gift of God, not of works, lest anyone should boast.' The only payment for our sins was Jesus Christ's death on the cross. Because besides being fully man, he is fully God and his one death had the power to cleanse all of us of our sin.

"John 1:12 says that to 'as many as received him, to them he gave the right to become children of God' by believing on his name. How do you receive Christ? Merely tell God that you know you are a sinner and that you need him. Accept the gift of salvation, believe that Christ is risen, and say so. For many, it is already too late. I beg of you to receive Christ."

Vicki sat in the backseat as Mark drove through the night. Manny said he could feel the prayers of the people in Wisconsin. Manny tuned in nonstop radio reports from Jerusalem and around the world about the plague of sores that affected everyone who had the mark of Carpathia. Even news reporters were in pain.

He found one station that aired a live broadcast from New Babylon featuring Dr. Consuela Conchita. Her voice was strained as she suggested people bathe often and wear loose clothing.

Mark shook his head. "It's going to take more than soap and baggy pants to stop this plague."

Lionel and Sam drew close to Micah as dozens of unmarked civilians approached the old man and prayed with him. Immediately the mark of God's seal appeared on their foreheads.

Micah rose to speak. "Those of you who are Jews, listen carefully. God has prepared a special place of refuge for you. When Carpathia's plans to retaliate reach their zenith, listen for my announcement and head south out of the city. Volunteers will drive you to Mizpe Ramon in the Negev. My assistant here will tell you how to recognize them by something we can see that our enemy cannot. If you cannot find transportation, get to the Mount of Olives where, just as from Mizpe Ramon, you will be airlifted by helicopter to Petra, the ancient Arabian city in southwestern Jordan. There God has promised to protect us until the Glorious Appearing of Jesus when he sets up his thousand-year reign on earth."

"Praise God," Sam whispered as he looked over the crowd. "I wish Daniel was here to hear this."

"Maybe he is," Lionel said.

As the time of Nicolae's appearance at the temple

neared, Orthodox Jews approached. Micah pleaded with
them to believe the truth about Jesus, but they scowled.

Finally, Carpathia arrived, arguing with Micah and the
holy men and telling them they would know soon that
he was god. He threatened Micah, then turned to the
Orthodox Jews. "You will regret the day Israel turned her
back on me. A covenant of peace is only as good as either
side keeping its word."

"Boo!" an Orthodox man shouted and others joined
in. "You would dare blaspheme our God?"

Carpathia turned toward the temple, then spun back.
"Your God? Where is he? Inside? Shall I go and see? If he
is in there and does not welcome me, should I tremble?
Might he strike me dead?"

"I pray he does!" a rabbi shouted.

Carpathia glared at the men. "You will regret the day
you opposed me. It shall not be long before you either
submit to my mark or succumb to my blade."

Lionel glanced at one of the huge monitors strategi-
cally placed for all to see and noticed the network feed
showed Carpathia going inside the temple. Outside, men
cried out to God.

Now it was Micah's turn. He raised his voice for all to
hear. "If you are God, why can you not heal your own
Most High Reverend Father or the woman closer to you
than a relative? Where are all your military leaders and
the other members of your cabinet?"

Carpathia walked back outside and Micah continued.
"Where are your loyal followers, those who have taken
your cursed mark and worshiped you and your image? A

body covered with boils is the price one pays to worship you, and you claim to be God?"

Nicolae finally went inside again, and Lionel noticed the feed had switched to GCNN in New Babylon. The news anchor explained Carpathia's movements and gave a brief history of the battle over who should be worshiped in the temple. "His Excellency will eventually enter the Holy of Holies," the newscaster said, "but first he is insisting on the removal of the dissidents. Let's go back."

Lionel shuddered as Carpathia appeared in a darkened inner chamber of the temple. "Anyone not here in honor to me may be shot dead," he said. "Are you armed and prepared?"

"No!" someone said.

Another man said, "I am armed."

"You," Nicolae said, pointing to the first man, "take Mr. Moon's weapon and do your duty."

The camera turned and showed the face of the man refusing the gun. Sam gasped and said, "It's Daniel, the man I introduced to you yesterday! He must have volunteered so he could be close to Nicolae."

But Daniel refused the gun. The camera shook and a shot rang out. Someone cried in pain. The camera locked on Carpathia holding the gun. He nodded in the other direction and said, "Show him." The camera panned and Lionel spotted Daniel's body, still and lifeless.

Lionel felt sick to his stomach. Carpathia had killed Daniel without hesitation. Had Daniel refused because he saw who Nicolae really was? Was there a chance he could have become a believer?

Suddenly, the video feed showing the body switched to a close-up of Micah. His voice boomed through the speakers on the monitors overhead.

"Not only does the evil ruler of this world want to rid the priests of their rightful place in their own temple," Micah said, "but it also appears he has personally committed murder at this holy site."

Lionel put an arm around Sam as the boy wept. Lionel knew the world would get violent in the next few years, but how much worse could things get?

25

LIONEL Washington took a deep breath and tried to comfort his friend Sam Goldberg. They had just seen Nicolae Carpathia murder Sam's friend Daniel Yossef inside the temple.

Thousands had gathered to watch Nicolae's every move. Many supported him, flocking outside the temple like it was some sporting event. But Carpathia's words and actions repulsed followers of Jesus Christ and Orthodox Jews. Lionel had heard how cold-blooded Nicolae could be, but he never dreamed the man would kill in front of a live camera. Lionel couldn't understand why anyone would follow this evil man.

Sam looked at one of the huge television monitors and whispered, "Do you think Daniel believed the message about Christ before he was killed?"

"I hope so," Lionel said. "It took guts to refuse Carpathia's order to shoot at those Jewish leaders."

Lionel looked around for Judd. They had become separated earlier, and Lionel yearned for a familiar face. People trembled from the pain of sores breaking out all over their bodies. Many Morale Monitors and GC soldiers had moved to quickly constructed medical tents. Others without Carpathia's mark or the seal of God on their foreheads shook their fists and sprinted up the temple steps.

Through television monitors came the clear voice of God's prophet Dr. Chaim Rosenzweig, who called himself Micah. Somehow the Tribulation Force had broken into a live Global Community Network News feed, and this small, robed man was speaking out against the evil ruler.

"As Carpathia continues," Dr. Rosenzweig said, "you should be able to see the laver where the priests wash their hands before they approach the main altar. The temple was creatively placed over a series of underground waterways where gravity allows constant water pressure for the various cleansings. Of course, he has no business in this place, and even a ceremonial washing of his hands will not exonerate him for defiling it."

For some reason the camera switched back inside the temple, and the scene was so frightening Lionel turned away. Carpathia's eyes seemed to dance with glee as he stood over the dead man's body.

Sam gasped in disgust. "Look at his hands!"

Carpathia stared into the camera and held up two bloody hands. Someone inside the room said something and Carpathia sneered. "My faithful get the message." His voice echoed in the room as he shouted. "Any who dares interrupt my pilgrimage will find his blood on my fingers!"

Judd Thompson Jr. closed his eyes. Was this a bad dream or reality? As Chaim Rosenzweig tried to convince viewers around the world of Carpathia's evil, Mr. Stein drew close and tried to explain why the robed holy men would risk their lives to stop Nicolae. The priests scrambled up the stairs, yelling and shaking their fists. Judd glanced at the video monitor above him just as the camera whirled, the screen filling with priests charging like enraged animals.

"See where this blood comes from!" Carpathia shouted.

The priests stopped at the sight, their faces pale. One at the front glanced at the body on the floor and threw out his arms. "Does your evil know no bounds?"

Nicolae's face reddened. "Are you the god-haters who do not know me as a god, a god acknowledged by all others, but not named by you?"

"It should not surprise you," one man said, "that we showed our loyalty by offering daily sacrifices on your behalf."

"You have made offerings," Carpathia spat, "but to another, even if it was for me. What good is it then, for you have not sacrificed to me? No sacrifice shall ever again be made in this temple except to me. Not *for* me, *to* me. Now leave or face the same fate as this unlucky one who was foolish enough not to believe that I have been allotted the nature of god!"

"God will judge you, evil one!"

"Give me your gun again, Supreme Commander!"

The priests took a step back, but one stood his ground. "We retreat not in fear but rather because you have turned the house of God into a killing field!"

Mr. Stein turned to Judd and whispered, "That is Ethan Ben-Eliezar. We have had many discussions about—"

Carpathia screamed again. "Just go! I shall have my way in my home, and should you be found without proof of loyalty to me by week's end, you shall offer your heads as ransom."

The priests turned, shouting threats and joining their followers outside the temple. When the man Mr. Stein identified as Ethan Ben-Eliezar emerged, other priests cheered. He lifted both hands toward the sky and yelled, "Lovers of God, unite!"

The priests repeated the words until it became a chant. Judd glanced at the monitor again, expecting to see Carpathia mocking them, but Dr. Rosenzweig was back.

"The inner court inside the pillars has stairs that face east and lead to the main altar," Chaim began. "Priests who revere God march around the Court of Priests and the Holy Place with their left hands closest to the altar. This one who would trample holy ground has already begun the opposite way, so his right hand will be closest to the altar. The Scriptures foretold that he would have no regard for the one true God. What plans he has for the beast with which he ridiculed the Via Dolorosa will be revealed only as he invades deeper into God's own territory."

"He's going to do something with the pig he rode?" Judd said.

Mr. Stein pursed his lips.

Chaim continued, contrasting Carpathia's rantings with the way God had displayed his glory. "God appeared to Moses on Mount Sinai when the Ten Commandments were handed down. He appeared again when Moses dedicated the Tent of God. And finally he showed himself at the dedication of Solomon's Temple on this very site. Should God choose, he could reveal himself even today and crush under his foot this evil enemy. But he has an eternal plan, and Antichrist is merely a bit player. Though Antichrist has been granted power to work his horror throughout the world for a time, he shall come to a bitter end that has already been decided."

Vicki Byrne was riveted to the radio coverage from Israel. The news anchor explained that the audio was being taken from the video feed and broke in to talk over the man named Micah.

As Mark drove south, Manny Aguilara, the new believer who had escaped the Global Community, studied a map. Their plan was to rescue Morale Monitor Claudia Zander with the help of one of Manny's gang friends.

Between Carpathia's pig ride down the Via Dolorosa

and his assault on the temple, Manny told his story. Vicki was astounded when she heard how Manny had been placed in a cell next to Zeke Sr.

"Sure, I went to church with my mother when I was little. But when it came time to choose between the gang and God, the decision was simple. The gang gave me money, protection, and friends. It made sense to me back then."

"Did you ever try to get out?" Vicki said.

Manny shook his head. "I thought about it once or twice when things heated up. The police would get close or somebody would get shot and I'd wonder if it was worth it, but getting out is more dangerous than staying in."

"What do you mean?" Vicki said.

Manny pointed to a tattoo on his face, a small x. "I got this when I joined. Everyone knows you're part of the gang by this. They fear it. But try to leave, and your own gang wants you dead. Then other gangs come looking for you. It's easier and safer to stay in."

"Did anybody ever try to kill you?" Mark said.

Manny looked at the floor. "Our gang was into drugs. We had our territory and no one was supposed to cross the line. Our rivals violated the boundary, so our leader said I should go along to help end the problem."

"What do you mean, end the problem?" Vicki said.

"Usually you take a couple of guys and talk with the people, to scare them. But things had gone way past scaring. The disappearances changed everything. I don't know how to explain it, but we had lots more business and the violence was getting worse.

"The meeting with this rival turned ugly. Hector pulled his gun first, so it forced me to as well. Four people died that day."

There was silence in the car. Finally, Vicki said, "Four died because of a territory dispute?"

Manny nodded. "Sounds stupid now, but back then I dreamed about killing or being killed. Dying was just part of life."

"And you think one of these gang guys will help us?" Mark said.

Manny hesitated, then nodded. "The leader, Hector."

As they drove on, Vicki thanked God that Manny's life had changed. She knew they would be in great danger and was glad people were praying for them back in Wisconsin. The kids had set up a room where at least one person would be praying at all hours.

Now, listening to Carpathia on the radio and the voice of his right-hand man, Leon Fortunato, Vicki snapped back to reality. Leon had joined Carpathia in the temple and weakly said, "You, my lord, are the good spirit of the world and source of all good things."

Judd stayed close to Mr. Stein, asking questions when there was a lull in the action. He knew Carpathia wasn't finished defiling the temple, but he couldn't believe it could get worse.

"I don't understand how these people are going to get away from here," Judd whispered. "When is Operation Eagle going to begin?"

Mr. Stein looked concerned. "That is my question as well. We must take advantage of this window and put out a call to everyone to flee before Carpathia attacks."

Jewish priests filed by them, and Mr. Stein called out for Rabbi Ben-Eliezar. They were making such a commotion, still chanting, that the man didn't hear. Mr. Stein turned to Judd. "Stay here. I will talk with the rabbi and return."

Judd nodded, leaned against a stone, and surveyed the crowd. At times the noise was deafening, with Carpathia supporters trying to shout down the Orthodox Jews. Others who had taken the mark, Morale Monitors and soldiers, could barely stand. That seemed to give energy to the anti-Carpathia group, and they grew louder and more menacing as each minute passed.

Judd took a breath and prayed silently. "God, you know how much these people need to know you. You know how powerful the evil one is. I pray you would remove the blinders from those who haven't taken the mark yet. Help them see the truth about Jesus. And help us get out of here alive."

Lionel stayed with Sam as the crowd turned into a mob. There was so much noise around them—shouting, arguing, and people throwing dirt and stones—that the two had to huddle in a corner.

Sam finally stood, his face streaked with tears. "We'll never know if Daniel truly believed in God or not. Carpathia took his life in front of all these people and we're not doing anything."

Lionel put a hand on Sam's shoulder. "Calm down. We're going to get out of here."

"Is that what you want to do?" Sam said, pulling away. "You want to be safe?"

Sam suddenly glanced up. He whispered something under his breath as Lionel came out from behind their shelter and looked at the huge monitor nearby. Nicolae Carpathia approached a curtain that stretched out of the camera's view. Lionel noticed the crowd had quieted, mesmerized by what was on the screen.

"He's in the Holy of Holies," Sam whispered. "He's ready for the final defilement."

Carpathia grabbed the handle of a long knife he had tucked in his belt and dramatically raised it over his head. He reached as high as he could and plunged the gleaming steel through the veil. The fabric ripped as he pulled the blade all the way to the floor. Nicolae pushed each side of the curtain back, revealing the altar and the massive pig from the day before. There was no saddle this time. The pig struggled and tugged at ropes held by two men. Lionel wondered if this animal sensed evil.

Sam clenched his teeth. "I can watch this no longer. I have to do something!"

"Sam, wait!" Lionel said, trying to grab the boy's arm, but it was too late. Sam disappeared into the crowd of priests and Carpathia loyalists.

Vicki listened as the reporter in Jerusalem tried to describe the scene. Before he mentioned the pig, she heard it squeal in the background and guessed what was about to happen.

"Pull over right here," Manny said suddenly. He wiped his forehead with the back of his hand and squirmed in his seat.

"We're not that close, are we?" Mark said.

"Just pull over."

Mark parked on the darkened street and turned off his lights. Manny switched the radio off and sat back.

"What's the matter?" Vicki said.

"I didn't tell you the whole truth," Manny said. "In fact, I lied."

26

LIONEL raced into the crowd and caught up with Sam as the boy fell to the ground and buried his face in his hands. Lionel knelt beside him and put a hand on his shoulder.

"Look!" a man behind them shouted. "He's preparing the sacrifice!"

The holy men cried out, tearing their robes as Nicolae approached the huge pig. In the street, the animal had been slow and seemed drugged. Now it was thrashing around, squealing, and straining at the ropes. Two men struggled to hold it as Nicolae laughed. He jumped at the animal and slipped, the pig dodging him.

"Want to play?" Nicolae howled. Then he leapt onto the pig's back, sending the animal to its knees. For the next few seconds the pig tried to knock Nicolae off, but it was no use. Finally, Carpathia plunged his knife into the animal's throat.

Nicolae fell to the ground, a flood of blood soaking his clothes. The pig went wild, thrashing and pulling its handlers. As the blood flow slowed, the pig fell and Nicolae cupped his hands under its neck. Lionel had to look away.

The crying and wailing of the holy men reached a crescendo and one priest screamed, "He has thrown the animal's blood on the altar!"

Lionel couldn't watch the gory scene that followed, but he could hear Nicolae trying to butcher the animal. Lionel turned to Sam. "Come with us. We're leaving soon."

"I must stay with my people," Sam whispered. "These men need to know that Jesus is the perfect sacrifice. How will they know if someone doesn't tell them?"

"I understand, but—"

More shouts from the crowd stopped Lionel. He stood for a better view of the screen. Nicolae had given the order to take the pig away and bring in his image. The holy men went berserk.

Carpathia washed off the blood and dried himself. Someone off camera handed him the shimmering white robe, silver sash, and gold sandals he had worn the day before. He put them on and looked at the camera. "Now, once my image is in place, we are out to Solomon's scaffold."

Suddenly the camera switched to a brown-robed man, shaking his head. The holy men around Lionel seemed hopeful again. Lionel studied the camera shot to try and figure out where Chaim Rosenzweig was, but the man's face filled the screen.

"Is this not the most vile man who ever lived?" Rosenzweig said. "Is he not the opposite of whom he claims to be? I call on all who have resisted or delayed in accepting his mark and plead with you to refuse it. Avoid the sentence of grievous sores and certain death."

"What do you mean, you lied?" Vicki said.

Mark clenched his teeth. "This group is built on the trust of its members, and if you've—"

Manny held up a hand. "Let me explain."

"You've got thirty seconds," Mark said.

"What are you going to do, shove me out on the street?" Manny said. "Is that how you treat a fellow believer?"

"People who lie to us can't be part of the group," Mark said. "It's as simple as that."

"Just let him talk," Vicki said.

Manny sat back and took a deep breath. "When I spoke with Hector on the phone . . . I wasn't honest about what he said."

"You told us he would help us see if Claudia was legit," Mark said.

"You have to understand. My life has changed so much. When you helped me escape, I thought about all my friends who don't know God. That's everyone I know."

"What did you lie about?" Mark said.

"Hear me out," Manny said. "I was in jail because the Global Community knew I was involved with the shooting of those four people. They promised if I testified against Hector and a few others that I wouldn't see jail time."

"So you told them what they wanted to hear?" Vicki said.

"No. I didn't tell them anything. Maybe I should have. I don't know. I was more scared of Hector and the others than the GC. The point is, after I prayed and asked God into my life, I haven't been able to get Hector and the others out of my mind. Once we made it to Wisconsin, I figured I'd never have a chance to see the gang again."

"So you used this situation with Claudia to make contact," Mark said. "You've put us in danger."

"When you explained about this girl, I thought it would be the perfect way to help you and reach out to my friends."

"What did Hector say when you called him?" Vicki said.

Manny frowned. "He didn't believe me. I told him I was free and he said it was a GC trick, that they were using me."

"Did you explain about Claudia?" Mark said.

"Hector blew up and said he would see me dead if I came back."

Mark rolled his eyes. "Great. Then why are we going there?"

"I know it sounds weird, but if I can see them one more time, I know I can get them to understand."

Vicki put a hand on Manny's shoulder. "We both

understand how much you want to reach out to your old friends. All of us have felt that way."

"Yeah, but putting us in this situation isn't right," Mark said. "You could have the best intentions and go in there and—"

"I've been praying and asking God to get them ready," Manny interrupted. "I heard Dr. Ben-Judah or someone say that people's hearts will be hardened. I'm hoping I can get to the gang before any of them take Carpathia's mark."

"This throws everything off," Mark said. "How are we going to get to Claudia?"

"Please," Manny said, "take me to the gang. I'll go in alone. And I promise you, someone will help us."

Judd watched in horror as the angry mob reacted to Nicolae. The Temple Mount was near a riot with loyalists yelling support for the potentate and crying out in pain because of their sores. Christ followers and Orthodox Jews protested, while many undecided were caught up in the turmoil.

Judd wondered what it would take to convince the undecided about the potentate's identity. He had committed murder in front of the world and was acting like a wild man, calling for people to sacrifice offerings to him and saying the temple was his house.

Judd looked for Mr. Stein amid the group of priests but couldn't find him. Men with long beards fell to their knees, crying. "He would sacrifice a *pig* in the Holy of Holies and cavort in its blood?"

Another priest climbed to the top of the steps. "Those who live by the sword shall die by the sword! He has killed an innocent man in cold blood, and we demand his blood!"

A few men without Carpathia's mark came outside to move the golden statue. The holy men called for quiet as Nicolae's face appeared on-screen.

"Why worship at an altar of brass?" Nicolae sneered. "If this is indeed the holiest of holy places, every worshiper should enjoy the privilege of bowing to my image, which our Most High Reverend Father has imbued with the power to speak when I am not present!"

A murmur ran through the crowd, and Judd saw scores of priests running for the stairs. When the workers were ready to carry the golden Carpathia statue inside, a crowd surrounded them.

Mr. Stein rushed back to Judd's side. "I talked with Ethan briefly, and he said he would meet with me later if possible."

"Did you expect this?" Judd said, nodding to the ugly scene on the stairs.

Suddenly gunfire rang out and Judd hit the ground. Protesters surrounding the statue pulled back, cursing and waving their fists. The statue was moved inside to the Holy of Holies.

The human storm finally erupted. Morale Monitors and Peacekeepers, many too weak to lift a weapon, were attacked by the mob and trampled. A few managed to get off a shot or two, killing several protesters. Judd stayed down as a bullet struck a rock nearby. The shots sent the people into a frenzy. Medical tents fell, the guillotine was smashed to pieces, and GC vehicles turned on their sides. Several TV monitors crashed to the ground, scattering shards of glass.

"Kill Carpathia!" someone screamed.

"Death to the monster!" another said. "I hope he dies and stays dead!"

Judd noticed one TV monitor that hadn't toppled. Carpathia stepped back, his eyes wide. He said something Judd couldn't hear into the camera. Seconds later Mr. Stein pointed to the temple entrance where cabinet members, including Leon Fortunato, joined Carpathia. Rioters yelled.

Nicolae tried to speak, but the noise was too great. Finally, someone found a microphone that weakly amplified his voice through the remaining speakers in the outer court. Judd thought the man would try to soothe the people, but Nicolae raised a hand and said, "You have breached the covenant! My pledge of seven years of peace for Israel is rescinded! Now you must allow me and my—"

Thousands hollered, overwhelming the potentate's voice. Holy men pressed close to the temple entrance, keeping Carpathia and anyone else from exiting.

"You think Fortunato will call down fire like he did yesterday?" Judd said.

Mr. Stein pursed his lips. "I pray no more will die before they have a chance to hear God's man again."

Carpathia tried to capture his followers' attention. "My brothers and sisters of the Global Community! I will see that you are healed of your sores, and you will again see that it is I who love you and bring you peace!"

A young voice shouted, "You'll not leave here alive, pretender!" It was Sam, halfway up the steps of the temple.

The mob shook their fists and cheered, repeating Sam's words, laughing, screaming more death threats at Global Community leaders.

Leon Fortunato braced himself against a wall and said something to another GC cabinet member. Everyone behind Nicolae looked like they were at a funeral, and Judd wondered it if might be their own.

Piercing the din of the crowd came the voice of the man in the brown robe. Everyone hushed and remained riveted on him. "Yes," Mr. Stein said softly as Chaim began.

"It is not the due time for the man of sin to face judgment, though it is clear he has been revealed!" Dr. Rosenzweig said to the crowd. People murmured as Chaim walked through the main group of protesters. Out of respect, people took a step back as he ascended the temple steps. Judd thought it amazing that Nicolae had used a microphone and he could barely be heard, while Chaim spoke in a normal tone and everyone understood him.

"As was foretold centuries ago, God has chosen to allow this evil for a time, and impotent as this enemy of your souls may be today, much more evil will be perpetrated upon you under his hand. When he once again gains advantage, he will retaliate against this presumption on his authority, and you would do well to not be here when his anger is poured out."

Carpathia swung the microphone to his lips. "That is right! You will rue the day when you dared—"

"You!" Chaim roared and pointed at Nicolae. "You shall let God's chosen ones depart before his curse is lifted, lest you face a worse plague in its place."

"I have always been willing to listen to reasonable men," Carpathia said. "I will be at the Knesset,* available to negotiate or to answer honest inquiries from my subjects."

Judd stood, amazed, as the crowd parted for Nicolae and his people. As they left, Chaim raised his arms and spoke. "Let those who are in Judea flee to the mountains. Let him who is on the housetop not go down to take anything out of his house. And let him who is in the field not go back to get his clothes."

"Why should we flee?" a man yelled. "We have exposed the potentate as an impotent pretender!"

"Because God has spoken!" Dr. Rosenzweig said.

"Now we're to believe *you* are God?" the man said.

"The great I Am has told me. Whatsoever he even thinks comes to pass, and as he purposes, so shall it stand."

"Praise God," Mr. Stein whispered. "Listen to the people. They are calm."

"Where shall we go?" someone asked.

"If you are a believer in Jesus Christ as Messiah," Chaim said, "leave now for Petra by way of Mizpe Ramon. If you have transportation, take as many with you as you can. Volunteers from around the globe are also here to transport you, and from Mizpe Ramon you will be helicoptered in to Petra. The weak, the elderly, the infirm, find your way to the Mount of Olives, and you will be flown in from there."

*Israel's Parliament

"And if we do not believe?"

Chaim paused. "If you have an ear to hear, make your way to Masada, where you will be free to worship God as you once did here at his temple. There I will present the case for Jesus as Messiah. Do not wait! Do not hesitate! Go now, everyone!"

27

WHILE Mark phoned their hideout in Wisconsin, Vicki talked with Manny. He apologized for his mistake and said he wouldn't blame them if they turned around and headed for safety.

"We decided a long time ago that we would do whatever we could to help people understand the message," Vicki said. "We want to stay away from Peacekeepers and Morale Monitors, but our first priority is reaching people with the truth."

Manny looked out the window. "I've been practicing what I'll say to Hector and the others. I'm not sure I can speak as well as you."

"You want me to go with you?"

"I couldn't ask that."

Mark hung up the cell phone. "Colin is ticked. He wants us to turn around."

Manny scratched his head. "Which one is Colin?"

"Colin Dial, the guy who owns the house where we're staying. He said we should get out of here and they'd figure out another way to help Claudia."

Manny sighed and reached for the door handle. "I guess this is where I get out."

"Stay where you are," Mark barked. "Some of the others were up and I talked to them on the speaker-phone. They all thought after Claudia's latest e-mail that we should—"

"She wrote again?" Vicki said.

Mark nodded. "She said she's leaving her hotel by noon today and wants to know where she should go."

"Did they write back?"

"Yeah. They said they would send her instructions before noon."

"Good," Vicki said. "That makes it sound like we're going to send a message rather than show up."

"The kids voted to make Claudia our priority," Mark continued. "If we can help Manny meet with his friends and do it safely, they gave us the thumbs-up."

Manny smiled and glanced at Vicki. Suddenly his face contorted and he gasped.

"What is it?" Vicki said.

"GC squad car!"

Lionel moved along with Sam and the crowd making its way from the Temple Mount. He kept looking for Judd but couldn't find him. Many who had Carpathia's mark were trying to leave for Masada, and Lionel felt sorry for them. Though they didn't realize it, these people had decided their eternal fate when they had taken Nicolae's mark.

As they followed the crowd, Lionel turned to Sam. "You told me about Petra, but what's Masada?"

"It is an ancient site revered by the Jews," Sam said. "It looks like a huge boat in the middle of the desert."

"And it's made out of rock?"

"Exactly. In the first century, a Jewish uprising threw out the Romans who occupied the fort. Later, the Romans came back and attacked. After a long battle, the Jews realized they would be defeated, so they killed themselves rather than be captured by the Romans."

"Now I remember," Lionel said, still scanning the crowd for any sign of Judd. "What are you going to do?"

"I will eventually go to Petra, I think," Sam said, "but I have to go to Masada and see if I can help my fellow countrymen become followers of Messiah."

Lionel walked close to Sam, wishing he had stayed with Judd. Now there was no turning back.

Judd remained with Mr. Stein as the Temple Mount quickly emptied, leaving bodies, splintered wood, and trash. Judd even spotted a few Global Community issued handguns thrown on the ground.

Judd's cell phone rang.

"Where are you?" Chang Wong said.

Judd told him.

"I have just communicated to the rest of the Tribulation Force that I'll be able to let everyone hear exactly what happens between Carpathia and Dr. Rosenzweig at the Knesset."

"How did you manage that?" Judd said.

"Buck Williams is with Chaim and he's going to keep his cell phone on during the meeting. The sound won't be perfect, but we'll be able to hear most of what happens. Would you like to be included?"

"Yeah, but I don't have a computer right now—"

"That's okay. I'll patch your phone into the system. I'll call when they arrive. Would you like to hear my good news?"

Mr. Stein motioned to Judd that he was going to speak with one of the rabbis and Judd nodded. "Sure."

"You know how concerned I was over my dual marks," Chang said. "When I heard there was a plague of boils, I even felt an itch on my leg and was afraid I was being affected. Now I know for sure what happened to me the morning I received Carpathia's mark."

Vicki whirled and noticed a GC squad car moving slowly toward them, less than a block away. Using its side-mounted searchlight, it illuminated parked cars and checked license plates.

"Quick decision," Mark said. "Do we stay or risk pulling out?"

"It looks like a routine canvas," Manny said.

"But if we stay, they'll see us," Vicki said.

"Keep your lights off and ease out," Manny said. "Don't touch your brake or the lights will tip them off."

Mark started the car and slowly pulled forward, angling toward the street. Vicki rolled down her window slightly and studied the squad car behind them. "I don't think he's seen us yet," she said. Mark leaned over the steering wheel and peered into the dark.

"Another few blocks and I'll show you a place you can hide," Manny said.

Vicki heard a metal clinking and something darted across the road. "Mark, watch out!"

Mark slammed on the brakes, narrowly missing a small white dog that rushed in front of them. The dog scampered safely into the night, its tags tinkling as it ran.

"Move fast," Manny said. "They saw your brake lights."

The squad car turned its searchlight forward. Mark hit the accelerator and sped into the darkness, swerving wildly to miss a giant pothole. Flashing lights swirled and the car raced toward them, its siren blaring.

"Turn here!" Manny yelled.

Mark turned sharply and sped down a dark alley. "I have to turn on my lights!"

"Keep them off. I'll tell you where to go."

They passed a fenced-in area and several crumpled buildings. Vicki's heart raced as the squad car shot past the entrance to the alley. "They didn't see us turn!"

"Keep your lights off. They might be—"

The swirling lights returned as the squad car backed up and entered the alley.

"Turn left here," Manny said. "No brakes!"

Mark careened around the corner, barely missing a

telephone pole and smashing into several trash cans. They were on gravel now, and the tires crunched bits of rock as they flew along the darkened side street. Manny leaned forward, struggling to see the next turn.

"They passed us again," Vicki said. "Wait, they're backing up!"

"Okay, a right turn coming up after an apartment building," Manny said. "Almost there, but we have to put some distance between us and them."

Mark pushed the car faster until Manny screamed. Mark had to hit the brakes and slid within a few inches of a concrete wall. A few yards more and they were back on a paved road. "Where are you taking us?"

"Just keep going," Manny said, looking behind them. "If they catch us, we'll lose our heads."

Mark strangled the steering wheel. "You two get out and hide, and I'll—"

"No, we're close," Manny said. "Keep going."

There were no working streetlights, and Vicki couldn't imagine how Mark drove without hitting something. The road was bumpy and at these speeds there was a chance of blowing a tire. Vicki closed her eyes and prayed. "God, help us get out of this without getting caught."

When she opened her eyes, the lights of the squad car seemed closer.

Lionel followed Sam through the streets of Jerusalem. The uproar of the crowd at the Temple Mount continued as looters smashed windows and knocked over tables outside businesses. Outside bars, drunken men and women celebrated—though Lionel couldn't figure out why—by dancing and singing. Those who had Carpathia's mark soon fell behind, wailing in agony at sores that appeared on their feet.

Lionel saw one man shriek as he tried to wrestle a gun from an equally sick GC Morale Monitor.

"I can't go on like this!" the man screamed.

The Morale Monitor gained control of the weapon, took a step back, and aimed. "Stay where you are or I'll shoot!"

The man howled like a hurt animal and lunged wildly. The Morale Monitor fired, and the man crumpled to the ground. Lionel and Sam rushed over with several others. Someone rolled the man on his back, and blood poured from a wound in his chest. He gasped for air as his head lolled to one side. When he saw the Morale Monitor, he smiled slightly. "Thank you . . ."

One of the rabbis felt the man's neck and said he was dead. The Morale Monitor, who looked only slightly older than Lionel, seemed near hysterics. "I didn't have a choice! I told him to stop!"

Lionel and Sam left the group huddled around the man's body and kept following the crowd.

Judd thought Chang sounded more excited than he had ever heard him. The young man had pieced together video and audio clips from secret recording devices planted throughout buildings in New Babylon.

"My father and Walter Moon gave me a tranquilizer," Chang said. "The drug made me forget the whole thing, including a conversation I had with my mother about being a believer."

"She's a believer?"

"Not yet, but she knows my sister, Ming Toy, and I are followers of Christ."

"That sounds like trouble. What if she tells your dad?"

"I'm praying both of them will see the truth before it's too late."

"What did you find out from the recordings?" Judd said.

Chang laughed with delight. "You don't know how relieved I was when I found video from a surveillance camera in one of the hallways. As my father and Walter Moon helped me walk—they pretty much carried me—I made the sign of the cross on my chest!"

"Incredible," Judd said.

"I don't even know where I got that! And then I pointed toward heaven and tried to say something."

"So it's clear you were resisting."

"Yes," Chang said. "God knew my heart and that they made me take the mark. Now I'm ready to do whatever I can to help the Tribulation Force."

Judd described the mayhem at the Temple Mount and asked Chang to call back when he had news from Carpathia's meeting at the Knesset.

"Watch for members of Operation Eagle," Chang said.

"How will I recognize them?"

"You'll know them when you see them."

Lionel became more concerned the farther he and Sam walked away from the Temple Mount. *Where are we going? How will we reach Judd?*

In the street ahead he noticed several parked vehicles. Men and women stood on top, waving and calling. These weren't Morale Monitors or Peacekeepers. They didn't wear uniforms and seemed too energetic.

As they drew closer, Lionel realized that all the people calling from the tops of their vehicles had the mark of the believer! Some yelled, "He is risen!"

Believers in the crowd answered, "Christ is risen indeed!"

Operation Eagle.

Vicki held on to the backseat as they drove across a deserted parking lot and into a run-down area. The GC squad car continued pursuit but seemed farther behind.

Manny grabbed the cell phone and punched a few numbers. He screamed something in Spanish and hung up.

"What was that about?" Mark said.

Manny ignored him and pointed Mark to a battered brick building in the middle of the block. Mark pulled up to a garage door marked with graffiti, and Manny leaned over and gave the horn two short honks. The door opened and Mark drove inside. As soon as they stopped, the door banged shut behind them.

Seconds later Vicki heard the squad car siren approach.

28

VICKI held her breath. The only light in the garage came from the reflection of the red taillights, which cast an eerie glow about the room. Manny held up a hand for quiet and Mark turned. Vicki had been through many scrapes with Mark, but she had never seen him this frightened.

The siren grew louder, wailing and warbling, until it screamed outside the building. It surged, then quickly subsided as the car flew past the building.

"Stay where you are," Manny whispered. "We have to make sure they're not coming back."

The phone rang and Mark handed it to Manny. "It's for you."

Manny answered and listened. After a few moments he said something in Spanish, hung up, and turned to Mark and Vicki. "The squad car is gone, but I'm afraid we have another problem."

"Who were you talking to?" Vicki said.

"Hector. There's an observation room in the top floor—"

Before Manny could finish, a door opened and a shaft of light pierced the darkness. Vicki noticed a rickety staircase in front of them. A man stepped onto the landing above and pointed a gun. "Get out slowly," he said.

Lionel rushed to the waiting cars behind a wave of Orthodox Jews, who had neither the mark of Carpathia nor the mark of God. Operation Eagle members waved people farther back, filling up vans, cars, and trucks. One man had brought several ancient school buses, and people filled them in minutes.

"Lionel!" someone yelled from atop a Humvee ahead. At first, Lionel thought it might be Judd, but as he moved closer he saw Westin Jakes.

Westin jumped down and Lionel introduced Sam. Lionel explained that Westin was a pilot for the famous singer Z-Van and that he had flown Judd and Lionel to Israel.

Westin smiled. "Lionel is the one who explained the truth to me after old Nicolae sat up in his glass coffin."

"What are you doing here?" Lionel said.

"Couldn't miss out on the excitement. I was at the airport, waiting for instructions from the boss, when I saw a lot of small plane activity. There were charters going out and some choppers, so I walked up to one of the guys doing his preflight and noticed he had the mark of the believer. He said he was with Operation Eagle.

After he described it, I didn't have to think long. I knew I had to be part of it."

"What about Z-Van?" Lionel said.

Westin rolled his eyes. "I told you there would come a time when I'd have to stop working for him. I left a message at his hotel, but I haven't heard anything. I think he's brooding over the fact that he hasn't been able to perform his new material."

Lionel ran a hand along the Humvee. "Where'd you get this?"

"Airport rental." Westin winked. "I'm supposed to have it back the day after tomorrow, but I'm not sure where I'll be the day after tomorrow."

Lionel and Sam got in, and Westin fired up the big vehicle. "You guys can help. I'm supposed to find people who can't get around very well and take them to the Mount of Olives. Then it's off to Masada."

Sam spotted someone in a wheelchair and Westin stopped. For the next few minutes they picked up as many feeble or ailing people as they could cram into the Humvee.

"Are you flying today?" Lionel asked.

Westin shook his head. "I'm only doing ground transportation for now. This is one big escape plan. The goal is to get as many people out as we can before Carpathia attacks."

"Which way to Masada?" Lionel said.

"It's south toward En Gedi," Sam said, "just a couple of miles off the western shore of the Dead Sea."

"Where's Judd?" Westin said.

"Good question," Lionel said.

Judd watched the evacuation with a mixture of delight and horror. From the frenzy Carpathia had put the people in, Judd hadn't expected anyone to leave. After all, the crowd had Nicolae trapped. But something Dr. Rosenzweig said—or maybe it was the way he had said it—convinced people there was real danger.

Judd and Mr. Stein followed one of the Jewish leaders, Ethan Ben-Eliezar, to his home. The rabbi tried to convince his wife to join the exodus.

"Why do we need to leave?" the woman said.

"We have been warned by a man who speaks with great authority. He may be a prophet of God."

"He's not a follower of Tsion Ben-Judah, is he?"

The rabbi glanced at Mr. Stein and Judd and took his wife by the arm. "We are only going to listen to what he has to say. It can't be any worse than what I just witnessed at the Temple Mount."

Judd wanted to find Lionel and Sam, but Mr. Stein insisted they keep moving. "I hope they have gone ahead to Petra. We will find them after we leave Masada."

Vicki shook as she slowly got out of the car with Mark and Manny. The three held up their hands and walked toward the stairs.

"Boss said he told you not to come here," the man with the gun said. "You must want to die."

"You didn't have to open the garage," Manny said.

The man squinted and stepped back, making way. Manny led Mark and Vicki through a series of steel doors to a loft area. An old couch and several chairs had been thrown about the room. The wooden floor creaked when the three walked across it.

The man with the gun told them to sit. He glared at Manny. "Boss'll be down soon."

While they waited, Manny told them more about how he had gotten involved with the gang, the regular payoffs to GC authorities, friends who had died, and how his mother had reacted to his gang involvement.

"I kept it a secret from her for a long time, but she finally found out. She had talked about me going to live with relatives, and I found a letter from an uncle in Georgia saying he would take me in, no questions."

"Why didn't he?" Vicki said.

"That's when everybody disappeared. My mom was gone, and for all I know, my uncle too. I decided to move in here."

"How did you know they'd open the garage when you called?" Mark said.

"I gave them the signal and hoped. There's somebody up all the time, waiting for anybody in trouble." Manny rubbed his hands and looked at the floor. "I know you wanted to focus on getting Claudia out, but I figured this was our only shot to get away from the GC."

"Do they let people come in here who aren't part of the gang?" Vicki said.

"I've only seen it happen a couple of times, and the people they brought here didn't make it out alive."

Judd squeezed into the backseat of Rabbi Ben-Eliezar's car with Mr. Stein. As the rabbi drove, he described to his wife what had happened at the Temple Mount and the awful display of Nicolae Carpathia.

Mrs. Ben-Eliezar put a hand to her head and gasped.

Judd's phone rang and Chang talked quickly. "You'll just get the raw feed from the Knesset. I won't be able to explain who's talking or what's going on, okay?"

"Got it."

The phone line crackled, and Judd heard groaning in the background. He had always had a good ear for voices, being able to identify people after only a few words on the phone.

Nicolae Carpathia said, "Forgive me for not standing."

"I represent the one true God and his Son, Jesus, the Christ," Dr. Rosenzweig said. "I prefer to stand."

After a moment, Nicolae said, "All right." The man seemed furious. "I am letting these people run off to the hills. When do the sores go away? I upheld my end of the bargain."

"We had a bargain?" Dr. Rosenzweig said. Judd pictured him in his brown robe, standing up to the most powerful ruler in the world.

"Come, come! We are wasting time!" Carpathia sneered. "You said you would lift this spell if I—"

"That is not my recollection. I said that if you did *not* let them go, you would suffer yet a worse plague."

"So I let them go. Now you—"

"It is not as if you had a choice."

Something banged on the table and Carpathia screamed, "Are we here to play word games? I want the sores on my people healed! What do I have to do?"

"Make no attempt to stop Israeli Messianic believers from getting to Petra."

Carpathia paused. Judd wondered how many of his top cabinet members were in the room, suffering from sores. "Have you not noticed? I am the only full-time employee of the Global Community not suffering from the plague!"

"And that only because you have not taken your own mark, though I daresay you worship yourself."

Footsteps. Nicolae came close to the phone. "Our medical experts have determined there is no connection between the application of the mark of loyalty and—"

"Why does your bad breath not surprise me?"

Judd laughed.

"You do not dare to lift the curse for fear your fate will be the same as that of your two associates at the Wall."

"If your medical experts know so much, how is it that they have been able to offer no relief?"

"What is going on?" Mr. Stein said.

Judd put a finger to his lips. "I'll tell you as soon as the meeting's over."

Carpathia had just finished asking a question when Judd put the phone to his ear again. Dr. Rosenzweig said, "I am here to remind you that this script has already been written. I have read it. You lose."

"If I am not god," Carpathia said, "I challenge yours

to slay me now. I spit in his face and call him a weakling. If I remain alive for ten more seconds, he, and you, are frauds."

Judd shook his head. He wished God would take Nicolae up on his challenge.

"What kind of a God would he be if he felt compelled to act on your timetable?" Dr. Rosenzweig said, a smile in his voice.

Something happened in the background. Carpathia was talking with others in the room. Finally, Nicolae said, "My people are pleading for respite. I recognize that I am forced to concede something."

"And that would be?"

"That . . . I . . . must . . . submit to you in this. I am prepared to do what I have to do to enable a lifting of the plague."

Dr. Rosenzweig spoke slowly and firmly. "You are under the authority of the God of Abraham, Isaac, and Jacob, maker of heaven and earth. You will allow this exodus, and when I am satisfied that the people under my charge are safe, I will pray God will lift the affliction."

"How long?" Nicolae said.

"This is a huge undertaking. Six hours should be telling. But should you attempt to lay a hand on one of the chosen, the second judgment will rain down."

"Understood," Carpathia said quickly.

There was movement in the room, and Judd assumed Buck and Dr. Rosenzweig were leaving. Before Judd turned off the phone, Carpathia growled, "Your days are numbered."

Judd put the phone down, his hands shaking. He had seen Carpathia's evil display, but he had never heard his voice so close.

Judd told the others what he had heard and Rabbi Ben-Eliezar asked how he had access to such a meeting. Without giving away anyone's identity, Judd explained that the Tribulation Force had contacts throughout the Global Community.

"It is our desire to convince as many people as possible of the true identity of Nicolae Carpathia," Mr. Stein said, "and the identity of Carpathia's heavenly foe."

"Who is that?" Mrs. Ben-Eliezar said.

Vicki watched the seconds tick by on a digital clock. Finally, a door opened and a heavyset man with a mustache walked into the loft.

Manny stood and the man waved at him to remain seated. "Hector, I'm sorry—"

"You must not have understood me on the phone. Did you bring the GC or just these two?"

"Please let me explain."

Hector looked out a window behind Vicki. A pink strip of light shone on the horizon. "I'll give you until I can see the sun peek over those buildings, which won't be long."

Vicki glanced at Mark, who had his eyes closed. She hoped the kids in Wisconsin were still praying.

29

JUDD listened as Mr. Stein explained from both the Old and New Testaments what he believed about Nicolae Carpathia. Mrs. Ben-Eliezar listened with interest as the rabbi drove silently. When he had talked for many miles, Mr. Stein switched the conversation to Mrs. Ben-Eliezar and asked about her family.

"We have two grown boys. One is in Haifa, the other in Tel Aviv. Things have been very hard, but they come to see us as often as they can. We had a girl. . . ." The woman glanced at her husband.

Mr. Stein sat forward. "What happened to her?"

Mrs. Ben-Eliezar clutched a tissue, as if she knew she was going to need it. "She went to America a few years ago to study. Anyway, she passed away."

"Was she part of the disappearances?"

"We should not talk of this," the rabbi said.

Mrs. Ben-Eliezar turned, tears in her eyes, and nodded.

"Let me guess," Mr. Stein said. "At the university, she met some religious fanatics. Maybe had one for a roommate. And they convinced her to turn her back on her beliefs. It broke your heart."

The woman hung on every word, wiping away tears. She looked at her husband. "Did you tell him?"

"I've heard this story before," Mr. Stein said. "My own daughter, Chaya, was also taken in by the message your daughter—"

"Meira was my daughter's name," Mrs. Ben-Eliezar interrupted.

"—yes, Meira. She no doubt tried to convince you that the Messiah had already come."

"She wrote letters, called, even made a special trip home from school. We were all heartbroken."

"When Chaya talked to my wife and me, I was so upset that I turned my back on her." Mr. Stein's lip quivered. "I considered her already dead, told my wife that she was to no longer speak Chaya's name in our home."

Judd noticed the rabbi had gripped the steering wheel tighter.

"Did your daughter disappear?" Mrs. Ben-Eliezar said.

Mr. Stein told Chaya's story, how she had heard of Messiah after the vanishings and had convinced her mother that Jesus had come back for his own. "Chaya died during the great earthquake."

"I'm sorry," Mrs. Ben-Eliezar said. "Meira went back to the States and only a short while later came the worldwide disappearances. We received word from the school that her things were found in her dorm room, but she was gone." The woman put her head in her hands and her shoulders shook. "I have heard all the theories. Do you have an explanation?"

Mr. Stein put a hand on her shoulder. "Yes, I know exactly what happened to your daughter, and I have good news."

"You do?"

"I believe you and your husband can see her again."

Vicki sat perfectly still, silently praying for her new friend. Manny told Hector about his interrogation by the Global Community and what they had promised if he testified.

Hector sipped coffee and listened. When Manny described his escape from the GC jail, Hector looked at Vicki. "Why would you risk going to jail for someone like him? Do you know what he would do to you if he had the chance?"

"Manny is our brother now," Vicki said. "We couldn't leave him behind."

Hector gently placed his mug on a wooden table. "What if your brother is a murderer?"

"He's told us about the things he's done. He's changed."

Hector sat back and folded his arms. "And what brought about this *change?*"

"Did you hear about the man who chose to take the blade instead of Carpathia's mark?" Manny said.

Hector nodded. "The fool. It's just a little tattoo, nothing to worry about."

"Whatever you do, don't take that mark," Manny said. "It will seal your destiny forever."

The man holding the gun in the corner laughed and Hector joined in. "Did you get religion in that jailhouse?" Hector said. "Is that why you want me to trust you and help you with some Morale Monitor whose soul you're also trying to save?"

"What I heard in prison made me want to risk my life and come here to tell you the truth."

Vicki glanced over her shoulder. The sun was an orange ball peeking over the horizon. Hector seemed intrigued. "So if I search you three, I won't find a recording device or a locator. The GC aren't going to be bursting in with guns blazing?"

Manny stood and pulled up his shirt. "Search all of us. I swear to you, we're not working with the GC."

Hector rose and turned to the man with the gun. "Make sure they're clean and get them something to eat."

"Don't you want to hear what I have to say?" Manny said.

"Get something to eat. I'll be back."

Lionel watched eagerly as Westin took a small road through the Dung Gate and headed for the Mount of Olives. Two of their passengers were believers going to Petra, the rest to Masada. People streamed past, heading for the Mount, passing ancient trees and historical sites along the winding road. Westin drove around the Kidron Valley and pulled as far up on the Mount as he could.

Lionel and Sam got out to help two elderly believers climb the rest of the way to the shuttle area. The view took Lionel's breath away. From here, he could see a panorama of the Old City of Jerusalem, the walls, the new temple, and a line of thousands moving into place on the Mount.

Operation Eagle volunteers greeted people and gave them instructions. "Helicopters will move into position here within a few minutes," one man said through a bullhorn. "Be patient with us as we try to go as quickly as we can."

"How long do you think it will take to move this many people?" Sam said.

"Depends on how many choppers they have lined up," Westin said. "Let's go."

They hopped back in the Hummer, headed toward Masada, and picked up three more passengers who had mistakenly come to the Mount of Olives.

Westin's phone rang and he looked at the readout. "Brace yourself—it's him." He turned the speaker on and answered.

Z-Van yelled a string of profanities at Westin. When the man took a breath, Westin interrupted. "I take it you're not happy with me."

Z-Van groaned, clearly in pain. "Get back here right now! We're playing tomorrow for the potentate's celebration. I want you ready to leave when we're done."

"I don't think you should plan anything with the potentate right now," Westin said. "From the amount of people I see leaving Jerusalem, he's going to have his hands full the next few days."

"When I want your opinion, I'll ask. I want you to make sure the plane's ready."

"With all due respect, you sound awful," Westin said. "How are you going to perform with sores all over your body?"

"How did you know I had sores?"

"Lucky guess."

"It doesn't matter. The potentate assured me personally that the problem would be gone within a few hours."

"How can he do that?" Sam whispered.

Lionel shrugged as Z-Van ordered Westin to return to the airport.

"No can do, sir. I'm driving some people to Masada. You can probably hire a pilot for a lot less than you pay me."

Z-Van cursed again. "I've paid you to do a job. You're under contract! I can sue you for everything you're worth."

"Which is not much, sir. I think it's time we go our separate ways."

"I'll decide when that is," Z-Van screamed. "Just finish whatever you're doing and get back here, understand?"

"I'll check back after my trip."

Click.

"You could have just told him you were a believer now," Sam said.

Westin smiled. "Want to hear my wild dream?"

"What?" Lionel said.

"We wind up using Z-Van's plane for believers."

As they drove south, Judd listened to Mr. Stein explain the truth about the disappearances to Rabbi Ben-Eliezar and his wife.

After a few minutes of conversation, the rabbi asked him to stop. "You're asking me to do the same thing my daughter wanted me to do."

"If you put your hope and trust in Christ, you will see your daughter again."

"We may not survive the night," the rabbi said. "You expect me to believe that Carpathia will live up to another agreement?"

"Carpathia is a liar at heart," Mr. Stein said. "You cannot trust anything he says. Besides, I already know he is going to break his agreement."

Mrs. Ben-Eliezar turned. "How could you know that?"

"This is from careful reading of Revelation, chapter 12. Tsion Ben-Judah agrees. In that chapter we are told that Israel will be given two wings like those of a great eagle. Israel flies to a place prepared for her in the wilderness. She will be cared for and protected there."

"But what makes you think Carpathia will attack?" the rabbi said.

"It says the dragon will try to drown Israel with a flood that comes from the dragon's mouth. Dr. Ben-Judah believes this flood refers to the Antichrist's army."

"Oh dear," Mrs. Ben-Eliezar said.

"But the Scripture goes on to say that the earth will help Israel by opening its mouth and swallowing the river that gushes from the dragon's mouth."

"What could that mean?" the rabbi said.

"I don't know exactly, but as the Lord has shown himself faithful in the past, I believe it means he will somehow overcome this military operation."

Judd checked his watch. If he was right, the plague of boils would end at about nine that evening. Would Carpathia test God again? He phoned Chang and thought he heard Nicolae's voice in the background.

"Hang on," Chang said, putting down the phone. When he came back on the line, he said, "I've just heard a conversation between Sick Nic and his top people."

"Sick Nic?"

"If I had time to play this back, you'd understand. It gave me major goose bumps. Where are you?"

"Headed toward Masada. Lionel and I got separated, so—"

"You may want to rethink that."

"Why? What did Carpathia say?"

"It's not only what he said, but what he did. You were at the Temple Mount when the head of the Morale Monitors tried to kill Dr. Rosenzweig, right?"

"Yeah, Loren Hut."

"Right. He's dead."

Judd gasped. "What happened?"

"Hut talked back to Carpathia, was sarcastic, and Nicolae shot him."

Judd shook his head. "Carpathia's out of control."

"He sure is. And he says once the curse is lifted, his enemies will be bunched up in four places or in the air."

"Mount of Olives, Masada, Mizpe Ramon, or Petra."

"Exactly, and he's declared all of Israel a no-fly zone at 9:15."

"There could still be planes and helicopters in flight."

"And my guess is, the GC will try to shoot them down. They're also planning an attack on Masada at 9:30."

"What?" Judd said.

"Carpathia wants to wipe out the Orthodox Jews and the Judah-ites wherever they are."

"Then everybody needs to head to Petra," Judd said.

Mr. Stein asked what was happening and Judd held up a hand.

"Carpathia says Petra is just as defenseless against their weapons as Masada," Chang said. "Judd, if God doesn't do something miraculous, you guys could all die out there tonight."

30

VICKI ate some fruit and toast and tried to fight fatigue. She didn't know how long she had been up or how long she had been running on adrenaline. It had to catch up soon, but she reminded herself of their mission. Claudia Zander was out there, running from the GC, and needed help. At least, that's what she said.

Vicki drank coffee and winced. It perked her up a little but left a bad taste. Another gang member walked into the garage and came out a few minutes later and spoke to the man with the gun.

"What do we do about Claudia?" Vicki said.

"If they let us go," Mark said, "I say we go get her."

Vicki put the cell phone in her lap and redialed the Wisconsin hideout. Darrion answered and sounded like she had been asleep. Vicki spoke softly and told Darrion what had happened. "Have we gotten any more messages from Claudia?"

"I'll check," Darrion said. The girl asked someone to wake up. *Probably Janie,* Vicki thought.

"Okay, it looks like a message came in from her a few minutes ago."

"Read it."

" 'Dear Young Trib Force, it looks like time is running out. I don't think I can wait much longer. Please tell me if you're coming or not. Claudia.' "

The man with the gun stirred, walking closer.

"Write her back and tell her—"

"Hey, no phone calls!" the man yelled.

"—to stay where she is. We'll be at her place as soon as we can get there."

"I said, no phone calls!" the man said, grabbing the phone and turning it off.

"She's not calling the GC," Manny said.

"Shut up, traitor!"

Manny stood, eyes flashing. "I'm a traitor? I'd like to see how long you would last in a GC jail cell, Carlos. How long would you hold out until you squealed on your friends and turned them in?"

"I know one thing," Carlos answered. "I wouldn't use religion as a crutch."

Manny shook his head. He was about to say something when a door opened and a young woman walked in.

Carlos smiled. "Now let's see what a tough guy you are."

The girl was dressed in a jogging suit and wore a scarf over her brown hair. Her brown eyes locked on Manny as she marched across the room. She stopped inches from his face and stared.

Before Manny could speak, the girl slapped him hard. The blow left a handprint on his face. He turned his head slightly, then looked into her eyes.

The girl clenched her teeth. "That was for getting caught!" She swung again. "And this is for leaving me alone!"

Manny caught her right hand in midair. She swung the other and he blocked it. They stood facing each other until the girl's shoulders shook. Manny let go of her arms, and the girl hugged him tightly and wept. "I thought you were dead."

Mark whispered to Vicki, "Looks like he had more people to talk with than Hector."

"Anita," Manny said, "I told you to leave and go to—"

The girl put a hand over his mouth and shook her head. "I couldn't leave. I knew you'd find a way to get back."

"I'm sorry you got involved in this. Have they taken care of you?"

The girl nodded. "Hector brought me here soon after you were arrested." Manny grabbed her shoulders and Anita smiled. "They haven't hurt me."

A wave of relief showed on Manny's face. He turned to Vicki and Mark. "I want you to meet my new friends." He put his arm around the girl and kissed her cheek. "This is my sister, Anita."

Lionel marveled at the Hummer's electronic navigation system. He had used global positioning devices before— his mom and dad had both had one—but this one included a computer screen with 3-D images of what was ahead and behind them on the road, their speed, distance to their destination, and a projected arrival time.

"Will that thing tell us if the GC are going to attack?" Lionel smirked.

Westin touched a button on the screen. "Watch this."

A number flashed at the top indicating the current temperature. The readout also included wind velocity, barometric pressure, and humidity. As the statistics flashed on the screen, the 3-D image tilted skyward, revealing a gridded outline of the sky. "I've got it on ten miles right now, but you can set it for twenty, fifty, a hundred, or more."

"What's it do?" Sam said.

"Lets you know about aircraft activity," Westin said. "Some use it to avoid radar detection from choppers. It could also be used in a military situation. These rigs are usually decked out with lots of gizmos people never use."

"Can you set it to look back at the Mount of Olives?" Lionel said.

Westin touched the screen a few more times and the grid enlarged. He pointed to the left side of the screen. "I could put in the coordinates, but this is basically the location of Jerusalem—here. The Mount of Olives is about here."

"What are all those dots to the right?" Sam said.

Lionel leaned closer and smiled. "Operation Eagle!"

Judd told Mr. Stein what Chang had said about Carpathia's plans. As he described the situation, Judd saw fear on the faces of Rabbi Ben-Eliezar and his wife.

"I think we should continue to Masada," Mr. Stein said. "The prophet God has sent told us to—"

"Your prophet told you to go toward Petra," Rabbi Ben-Eliezar said. "Only people like us should go to Masada, right?"

Mr. Stein rubbed his forehead. "True. But I feel called to Masada to help unbelievers in any way I can."

"Is that what we are to you?" Mrs. Ben-Eliezar said.

Mr. Stein leaned close. "I don't mean to offend you with my words about the Messiah. You have a knowledge of God and a zeal for him." He looked at Rabbi Ben-Eliezar. "You risked your life because you love God's house and didn't want to see it defiled. But God is asking you not just to be zealous for him, but to know his Son. He sent Jesus as the perfect sacrifice for sins so that—"

"Enough," the rabbi said. "I know your position."

"Please do not harden your heart," Mr. Stein said. "God has given you an opportunity to know him fully, through Jesus."

The line of vehicles stretched for miles toward Masada. Judd phoned Chang again but his line was busy. He wondered what new plans Chang might uncover that could help believers in the coming days.

Judd sat back and prayed that Lionel and Sam would find a way to the safety of Petra—if Petra truly was safe. Would God's protection extend to all believers, or was it only for those who were Jewish?

Judd watched the terrain change as they drove closer to Masada. He thought of others in the Young Trib Force and prayed for their safety. When he thought of Vicki, he felt a strange ache. He believed his time spent in Israel and the Middle East was something only God could orchestrate, but he longed for home, to see his friends, and especially Vicki. So much had happened since he had last seen her. Maybe he wouldn't make it back to the States at all. Perhaps the next few days would decide that.

Still, Judd held out hope that he would return one day soon and put his troubles with Vicki behind him. Judd laid his head against the door and closed his eyes. Though there was much to fear, he knew the best and safest place to be was where God wanted him.

"I'm yours, God," Judd prayed. "I'll do whatever you want."

Vicki listened as Manny told Anita how the Global Community had caught him and what had happened in jail. When he described his conversation with Zeke, Anita looked away.

"I've heard of jailhouse conversions, but I never thought you'd be one of them," Anita said.

"Me either. But I've wanted to find you and tell you since it happened. You have to listen."

Vicki turned as Hector approached Manny. "No bugs in the car. Your story checks out. Our guy close to the GC says they're still looking for you. Go."

Vicki and Mark stood. Manny looked at them, then at Hector. "I'd like your permission to stay."

"Why?"

Manny took a breath. "I could leave here right now

and do lots of good things with my life. I could tell other people I meet what has happened to me and what a change I've experienced, and maybe it would help them. But I've been thinking that I was given this gift so I could give it to the people I care about most."

Hector smiled. "You want to be a preacher to the gangs? You think you'll get brownie points in heaven?"

Manny looked at Vicki and Mark again. "I know how much these people did for me, and they didn't even know me. How much more should I care about the only family I have left? How could I live with myself if I kept life from you? The stinging locusts, the earthquake, everything we've seen the last few years has a purpose, and it's to get our attention. Let me stay and tell you."

"Keep your religion," Hector said. "It would spoil our business."

Manny walked closer. "If you harden your heart against God, you will never know true freedom."

Hector shook his head. "Freedom? The only freedom I need is from nuts like you. Stay if you want, but you'll obey orders like before." He walked out of the room.

Mark put a hand on Manny's shoulder. "This is suicide. If you don't get out—"

"I know," Manny interrupted. "I think this is where I'm supposed to be."

Vicki looked at Mark. She knew Manny had made up his mind. "If you need help, you know how to reach us. We'll do all we can. Take this." She handed her watch to Manny and showed him how to work The Cube, a high-tech, 3-D demonstration of the gospel.

Manny looked at Vicki and Mark through tears. "What would I have done? Where would I be today, if you had not helped me?"

"Be faithful with the message," Vicki said. "God put you here for a reason."

"But what about Claudia?" Manny said.

Vicki shook her head. "Stay. We'll sort that out."

"Vicki's right," Mark said. "This may be your only chance to talk with your sister and the others."

Manny gave specific directions to Claudia's hotel and retrieved their cell phone. Manny led them to the garage and Vicki waved as they pulled away.

Vicki sighed. "What now?"

"We have two options," Mark said. "Head back to Wisconsin or go after her."

"We haven't come this far to turn back," Vicki said.

Colin Dial answered when Vicki called the Wisconsin safe house. "Darrion sent your message, and Claudia said she was still at the hotel. Room 223. What's going on down there?"

Vicki quickly explained how they had eluded the GC and that Manny had chosen to stay with the gang. As she talked, Vicki kept an eye out for any GC squad cars. Mark spotted one coming the other way and calmly kept driving. The officers seemed not to notice them.

A few minutes later, Mark pulled into a parking lot a block from the hotel. He got the phone number from a sign on the side of the building advertising weekly rates and told the desk worker he was looking for a safe place to have a family reunion.

After a few minutes he hung up. "She said there hasn't been any GC activity there that she knows of, so our reunion looks like a go."

Vicki shook her head. "You know I don't like it when you lie to people."

"Sorry. I thought it would help to know if—"

Vicki held up a hand and looked at her watch. They had plenty of time to find Claudia and leave.

Mark unbuckled and opened the door.

"You're not going without me," Vicki said.

"They'll recognize your face."

Vicki pulled out a hat Manny had given her and pushed her hair underneath. She put on bright red lipstick and a pair of sunglasses. "Let's go."

Mark shook his head. "Okay, but follow my lead."

Mark and Vicki stole through an alley and around a concrete barrier to the street. They crossed a half block from the hotel and worked their way back, keeping a close watch for any GC vehicles. The hotel rose six stories and Vicki kept an eye on the windows for anyone watching.

Several people sat in the lobby eating breakfast when Vicki and Mark walked inside. Vicki's heart beat faster as they approached the front desk. She saw a surveillance camera in the corner so she picked up a newspaper and pretended to read while Mark approached a woman clicking at a computer screen.

"I called a few minutes ago about a family reunion," Mark said.

"Yes?" the woman said, not looking up.

"Would it be possible for my sister and me to look at one of your rooms?"

"How many in your party?"

"We'd probably be renting a whole floor."

The woman looked up. "Most rooms have two double beds. A few have king-size with whirlpool baths."

"And meeting rooms?" Mark said. "How many will those hold?"

"Up to two hundred," the woman said. "You'll have to make food arrangements outside. We don't provide that."

"Of course," Mark said. He studied a layout of the building as the woman grabbed a key. "Could we see something close to the pool? I think that's on the second floor, isn't it?"

The woman nodded. "Yes, if you'll let me see some identification, you can go right up."

Mark dug out the fake ID Colin Dial had helped him create and handed it to her.

She wrote down the information and gave him a card. "Room 264 is down the hall and around the corner from the pool, but that's the closest I could find that's clean. Take the elevator across the hall or the stairs down there."

"Great," Mark said. "We'll be right back."

Vicki followed Mark to the stairs. He paused and held the door slightly open.

"What?" Vicki said.

"I want to make sure that woman's not calling anybody."

He finally closed the door and they ran to the second floor and opened the door quietly. A soda machine hummed around the corner. Room 201 was directly across the hall.

"You ready?" Mark said.

"Yeah, let's go."

31

VICKI followed Mark into the hallway, and a wave of chlorine assaulted her senses. Before her sister, Jeanni, had been born, Vicki's family spent a couple of weekends every year at what her dad called "a fancy hotel." Vicki spent hours at the pool with her older brother, Eddie, ate at nearby restaurants, and once she remembered getting room service.

The door to the pool opened and Vicki heard splashing. She missed the laughs and giggles of kids around a pool, of kids in general. An older woman carried a bucket of ice inside and closed the door.

"Her room is right up there," Mark whispered. "Play it cool when we go by. Don't stare."

They walked confidently down the hall. 215. 217. 219. Vicki slowed a little and listened for a television, someone talking, perhaps a GC radio. They passed 221. Mark squeezed by a laundry cart ahead, and Vicki paused as she passed 223. A maid across the hall loaded wet towels into a basket. Covers and sheets lay strewn on the floor.

A door opened suddenly behind her and Vicki nearly screamed.

"Excuse me," a man said loudly.

Vicki stopped, took a breath, and turned. She expected a Peacekeeper or Morale Monitor, but instead saw a man in his undershirt, his hair neatly combed back and parted in the middle, hands on hips. "I called down to the front desk twenty minutes ago and asked about an ironing board!"

The maid walked into the hallway. "Very sorry, sir," she said in broken English. "I . . . get now." The woman hurried to the elevator as Vicki followed Mark to 264. He had the door open when she got there.

"It's going to take that cleaning woman a few minutes to get back," Vicki whispered. "Let's go into the room that's being cleaned."

Vicki led the way back down the hall and slipped into room 224. Mark closed the door behind him and watched the hallway through the tiny hole in the door. "Call her."

Vicki scanned the directions and figured out how to dial the room directly. As she was about to punch in the final number Mark put up a hand. "Hang on, somebody's coming."

"Is it Claudia?"

"Only if she's six feet tall and has a mustache. Okay, he's going into that guy's room. Go ahead."

Vicki dialed 2-2-3 and heard a faint ringing through the door. Someone answered on the second ring.

"Claudia?" Vicki said.

"Who is this?" a girl said.

"Claudia, if this is you, please—"

"Vicki? I hope you're not anywhere near here."

"Why? What's wrong?"

"A GC cruiser just pulled up in front of the hotel. I think somebody saw my picture and identified me. Are you outside?"

"We're close," Vicki said.

"We? You shouldn't have risked bringing anybody else. But I'm glad you're here."

"We need to get you out," Vicki said. "What's the best way?"

"The back of the hotel! I'll take the stairs and meet you there."

A knock outside. "Housekeeping!"

"Cleaning woman's back with the ironing board," Mark whispered.

"Wait a minute," Claudia said. "Are you guys in the hotel?"

The door slammed across the hall. "Go toward the back and we'll meet you," Vicki said. She hung up as the maid put her key card in the door.

Mark opened it and the woman jumped back. "Sorry," he said, holding up both hands.

Vicki and Mark scooted past her as the door to room 223 opened. Vicki glanced at a tall, blonde girl and recognized Claudia from her picture on TV. Vicki stared at the girl's forehead where she expected to see the mark of the believer.

Nothing.

"I told you they'd come!" Claudia yelled into a radio. "Where are you guys? There's two of them! One male, one female!"

"Run!" Mark yelled, shoving the heavy laundry cart to block the hallway.

"You'll wind up just like Bishop, with your head in a basket!" Claudia shouted. She tried to get around the cart as Mark and Vicki sped down the hall. "They're heading away from the pool on the second floor. Somebody watch the exits!"

Vicki turned the corner with Mark not far behind. Claudia cursed and screamed at the maid. "Get this out of my way!"

Footsteps pounded up the back staircase as Vicki put the key card into the door of room 264. Mark ducked in behind her and closed it quickly. The two struggled for breath and listened as someone ran past, wheezing and groaning.

"Where are they?" Claudia demanded. "You're moving so slow!"

"They didn't come out the southeast stairs!" a young man said. "And take it easy, you don't have sores all over—"

"Quit making excuses!" Claudia sighed and moved down the hall. "I told those guys to give me another hour!" She clicked her radio and gave the name of the hotel. "We have two Judah-ites cornered and need some help!"

Vicki closed her eyes and whispered, "The whole thing was a setup. That commander guy on TV set the trap and Claudia lured us here."

"We have to find a way out," Mark said. He rushed to the window and peeked through the curtains. "No GC cars out front. Sounds like they thought we weren't coming, so we might have a chance if we hurry."

Vicki slipped out of the room behind Mark, whispering a prayer. "Please, God, protect us."

A room at the end of the hall was open and Mark ran for it. Vicki ducked inside and realized it was the second floor maid's station. Mark closed the door quietly and Vicki looked around. Cleaning supplies, sheets, blankets, and towels were stored neatly on shelves. In the corner, two carts, fully stocked.

"Maybe they have a laundry chute," Vicki said.

They searched but couldn't find one. "Must be someplace else in the building."

"What about a fire escape?" Vicki said. "A building this size has to have one."

Mark checked on the back of the door for directions in case of a fire. "It only shows stairs."

Vicki opened a locker and found a maid's dress. She held it up and looked at Mark. "You think you could fit on the bottom of one of those carts?"

Mark pulled away towels and supplies from the bottom and tried to squeeze onto it, but his legs stuck out.

"We'd better just make a run for it," Vicki said. "The longer we wait—"

Footsteps in the hall. Wheels squeaking. Vicki looked

for a place to hide but it was too late. The door opened and a black woman backed in, pulling her cart. She hummed a familiar tune.

Before they could run, the woman turned and was so startled that she fell back, a hand on her chest.

The woman had the mark of the true believer!

"Land sakes, you two just about scared me to death," she said with a thick Southern accent. She looked them over and smiled when she saw their marks. "So you're what all the commotion is about."

Mark started to explain, but the woman put her hand in the air as someone ran down the hall. "GC officers are checking each room," she whispered. "What did you two do?"

A radio squawked. "Check 264! Front desk says they have a key to that room."

Vicki trembled as she whispered, "We thought we were helping another believer but the GC tricked us."

"Mm mm mm," the black woman said. "Looks like it's time for me to take out the trash." She pointed to two huge garbage cans with rollers on the bottom.

Mark nodded and helped Vicki inside one. He climbed in the other, and the woman piled wet towels and trash on top of them. "Can you still breathe?" she said.

"We're fine," Mark whispered.

The woman hummed the tune again, stopping long enough to say, "My job's the same as the Lord's in a way. I take the trash out and make sure it gets put in the right place. He takes our trash and puts it on the cross where Jesus can take care of it. Simple as that. Hmm hmm hmm hmm . . ."

The woman wheeled the two trash cans down the corridor. Vicki heard the splash of the pool and the hum of the soda machine as they rolled along.

Someone yelled, "Florence! There are two teenagers running around here. If you see them, holler."

"All right, then," Florence said at the top of her lungs, "I will!"

The wheels squeaked as Florence pushed and pulled the trash cans. "I sure hope those kids haven't done anything to get the Global Community upset. That would be just awful."

Vicki smiled. Moments before she had felt there was no way out of the hotel. Now she felt cared for and safe.

A service elevator opened and Florence pushed them inside. "Look at that itty-bitty little camera up there in the corner, watching everything I do. I tell you, if I was trying to get away, I'd stay right where I was in case somebody's watching."

Vicki noticed a strong smell when they made it outside. She peeked over the edge and saw a huge, green garbage container at the edge of the building. Florence wheeled the two containers close, turned them on their sides, out of sight, and sighed. "Now I hope you two won't come round here very often, 'cause you nearly gave old Florence a heart attack."

"How will we ever repay you?" Vicki said, her voice muffled by the trash and wet towels.

"Honey, you can repay me by getting out of here in one piece and staying away from all these people who want to chop your head off. I'll go back inside while you two climb out of there and get over the fence. Directly I'll come back for my trash cans and hopefully nobody'll know the difference."

"Wait," Vicki said. "That song you were humming. What's it called?"

Florence laughed. "Everybody knows 'Amazing Grace, how sweet the sound.' Learned it from Momma when I was little. Wish I'd have listened to her when she tried to tell me about God, but I expect I'll be seeing her again one of these days." Florence hummed the old hymn as she walked back into the hotel.

Vicki and Mark crawled out, climbed to the top of the bin above, and hopped over the fence. They crouched low, walking between newly planted pine trees that shielded them from view of the building and the street. Two blocks away from the hotel, they cut across the street and made their way back to the car.

Vicki's heart pounded as they neared the parking lot. Mark held up a hand and told Vicki to wait in the alley. When they were sure no GC squad cars were nearby, Mark casually walked to the car, started it, and returned.

Mark drove away from the hotel, using side streets until they found their bearings and headed north. Vicki called the safe house in Wisconsin and Shelly answered.

"It was all a hoax, Shel. You should have seen Claudia's face when we came out of that room. She hated us."

"You tried," Shelly said. "And you're safe. That's what's important."

Vicki asked Shelly and the kids to pray that Anita and other gang members would believe the truth.

"We've been praying for you guys nonstop," Shelly said. "Charlie even prayed that God would send an angel to show you the way back."

Vicki smiled. "Tell Charlie God answered his prayer with a woman named Florence."

After she hung up, Vicki thought of Claudia. When the girl had first written, Vicki sensed something was wrong. Claudia's bosses had probably written her notes.

Vicki remembered the questions she had asked herself after the first e-mail. *How do I know the right thing to do when the choices aren't clear? How do I follow my heart when my heart doesn't know what to do?*

"Why do you think Claudia didn't have the mark of Carpathia?" Vicki said to Mark.

"They probably thought it would give her away if we had a face to face with her. That also explains why she didn't have sores."

Vicki sighed and vowed never again to dismiss her feelings about such things. As Mark drove north, Vicki quietly hummed and thought of Florence.

32

DARRION Stahley breathed a sigh of relief when she heard Vicki was okay. The kids focused their prayer effort on Manny, his sister, and the gang members.

In addition to her work on the kids' Web site, Darrion kept an eye on what was going on in Israel. She hadn't heard anything from Judd and Lionel and hoped they would call. Global Community Network News reported the strange sickness affecting people all over the world, but they didn't connect the sores with the mark of Carpathia.

One commentator speaking about the scene at the temple said the actions of the potentate showed his true leadership abilities. "You saw in the Holy of Holies the perfect use of force when it was needed. Anyone who disregards a direct order from this man deserves death."

A woman nodded in agreement. "But the skill and

diplomacy of Potentate Carpathia is also evident. You saw his humility. Even though the temple is now his 'house,' as he called it, he stooped to negotiate with this Micah, the monklike character in the robe."

"And we receive word now that His Excellency the potentate guarantees healing from the affliction of sores by 2100 hours Carpathian Time."

Darrion tuned out the news and studied the kids' Web site. More people were writing than ever before, and Darrion felt privileged to attach information to each e-mail about how to become a believer. Some people wrote heart-wrenching notes asking how to get rid of the sores that had broken out all over their bodies. Darrion knew these people had taken the mark of Carpathia.

The phone rang and Darrion picked up.

It was Judd. "We're headed to Masada, but I have a situation here," he said. "I lost contact with Lionel. If you hear from him, tell him where I'm going and have him call me."

Darrion made sure she had the right phone number for Judd. "Anything else?"

"Yeah, I just got a call from Chang in New Babylon. They're having trouble reaching the guy who's setting up all the computer stuff in Petra, David Hassid."

"What could have happened?" Darrion said.

"Chang says Mr. Hassid was alone and there may have been some GC Peacekeepers left in the area. Have everyone pray he'll be okay and that the equipment won't fall into the wrong hands."

As Darrion wrote down the information, Judd asked

about Vicki. Darrion told him what had happened in Des Plaines.

"When she gets back, have her call me too," Judd said.

Lionel noticed a line of helicopters to their left and assumed they were heading for Masada. In a short time, thousands of curious Israelis had converged on the fabled fortress.

Westin parked as close as he could, and everyone got out and began the long climb up the stone steps. As they walked, people talked about Carpathia's actions in the temple and what he might do next. Someone near Lionel questioned whether the whole crowd could be transported to Petra. Others walked in silence, seemingly drawn to the ancient site.

Lionel knew that God was calling these people to follow him, but would they be convinced?

Judd let Mr. Stein and the others walk ahead to Masada while he stayed in the car. Huge crowds moved on foot and helicopters landed nearby, filled with anxious participants. Judd was sure it would be after dark before Chaim would speak. He looked at his watch and counted the hours before Carpathia's attack.

Judd felt angry at Lionel for getting separated. He had made it clear many times that they had to stick together, and Lionel had wandered off with Sam. Judd lay down in the back of the rabbi's car and put an arm over his forehead.

Judd had no trouble thinking the worst about people. When a problem arose, he found someone to blame. *Maybe it's not Lionel's fault,* he thought. *Lionel wasn't trying to get separated. It just happened.*

Judd thought about the people he had hurt with his quick anger. He had been insensitive to Ryan Daley several times, and Judd regretted that he would never get to apologize and make things right.

As Judd listened to the noise outside, he smiled. Ryan would have loved to see God reaching more and more people around the world.

What about the others I've hurt? Judd thought. Mark and Shelly . . . and Vicki.

Judd cringed when he thought of what he had said about Vicki in his last conversation with Shelly. Vicki had been out late with some guy in Iowa, and Judd had assumed the worst. Judd shook his head and rubbed his eyes. He had to stop saying the first thing that came into his mind.

The phone startled Judd and he sat up, disoriented. He had no idea how long he had been there, but the sun was going down and people were still coming into Masada.

"Judd, it's Lionel. Where are you, man?"

"I'm in a car about a mile away from the fortress. How about you?"

"I'm inside with Sam and Mr. Stein. He told me about your ride with Rabbi Ben-Eliezar."

"Did you fly down in a chopper?" Judd said.

"Westin brought us," Lionel said, and he explained

what had happened to them. "They're setting up a small medical tent outside the fortress. Why don't you meet me there in an hour?"

Judd agreed and sat back. He didn't want to frighten Lionel with the information about the impending attack, so he decided to tell him when they met at the tent.

Vicki slept while Mark drove toward Wisconsin. She awoke several times to find Mark pulled over on a side street or a crowded parking lot making sure they didn't cross paths with any GC vehicles.

While she was awake, Vicki found herself praying for Manny and wondering how the other gang members had reacted to his message. She thought about Anita and her difficult life. The girl wasn't a believer, but she had still resisted the mark of the beast.

Vicki dialed the safe house and Shelly answered. There was noise in the background, and Shelly said the hideout seemed crowded. "The Fogartys and Cheryl have been praying for you a lot."

"Tell them I appreciate it. We'll talk about the over-crowding issue when we get back."

"Colin already has a plan," Shelly said. "One of his friends has started an underground group in the western part of the state. Charlie's excited and wants to take Phoenix, and some of the others think it's a good idea."

"Okay, but don't decide anything until we get there."

"Oh, and Darrion said to tell you she talked with Judd."

"Where is he?"

"Still in Israel, at Masada. And get this, he told Darrion to have you call him as soon as you get back."

"Did she say what he wanted to talk about?"

"Nope. You should call him."

Judd walked with a crowd of excited Israelis approaching Masada. Men spoke with disgust about Carpathia. "Yes, but I am equally distrustful of this Micah," one man said. "You know he will talk to us about Jesus being the Messiah."

"I'll listen to anyone if they can scare Carpathia away," the man said. "Did you see the way Micah spoke to Nicolae?"

Thousands milled around inside the fortress, while others stayed outside. Many carried a simple meal of bread and cheese and shared with those who had nothing. As Judd came close to the medical tent being set up, his phone rang.

"Judd, it's Vicki. I heard you wanted to talk."

Judd smiled. "Are you back in Wisconsin already?"

"Almost. Mark just fueled up and is getting something to eat. We're both pretty tired."

"Darrion told me about your brush with the GC. Sounded pretty hairy."

"You're saying that from Israel where Carpathia could bomb you any minute. That's the hairiest place on earth right now."

Judd hesitated and the silence unnerved him. Vicki

asked what Masada was like and he tried to describe it. "I wish you could be here. I have a feeling a lot of Israelis are going to believe once Micah—Dr. Rosenzweig—talks."

"Is that who Micah is?" Vicki said. "I didn't recognize his voice." She paused. "I was thinking how long you and Lionel have been over there. Do you realize when we last saw you two?"

"When you're in the middle of everything, time goes pretty fast. Then when I stop to think about it . . . well, it feels like decades since we've seen each other."

Vicki gave a nervous laugh. "So, are you headed home?"

"I can't say for sure, but I've been having these feelings like our time here is about over." Judd took a deep breath and turned from the crowd, finding a place behind the tent where no one could hear him. "Vicki, I know we've talked about this, and maybe now's not the time . . ."

"No, go ahead."

"We've had our problems, butting heads and lots of angry words. I want you to know I'm really sorry for the stupid stuff I've done. I think maybe God brought me over here to knock some of the rough edges off. Lionel's been a big help with that."

Vicki chuckled. "He's been a good friend to both of us."

"I was thinking about Ryan earlier and how hard I was on him. You always stuck up for him."

"You mean about Phoenix?" Vicki said.

"I was on him a lot for different things. I wish I could take all that back."

"Ryan knew how much you cared. I'm sure of it. And while you're apologizing, I have to admit I haven't been the best friend. I was always thinking you were looking down on me because my family wasn't as rich as your family."

"You know that stuff doesn't mean anything now," Judd said. "When the disappearances happened, we were all in the same condition. We needed God. That was the only thing that mattered."

"Soooo," Vicki said. "What does this mean?"

Judd glanced at the front of the tent and saw Lionel. He waved and Lionel started over. "I think it means when I get back, we should take some time and talk."

"Good," Vicki said. "I hope you get back sooner rather than later."

Judd said good-bye and handed the phone to Lionel. He talked with Vicki a few moments and hung up. "So you two are back on speaking terms?"

Judd smiled and put an arm around Lionel. He told him what Chang had said about Carpathia's plans. "I've been thinking we ought to go home."

"You and me both," Lionel said. "Westin talked with Z-Van again a few minutes ago and tried to convince him to head back to the States before things blow up here."

"What did he say?"

"No luck. Z-Van's committed to a concert that'll be beamed by satellite all around the world. The GC is hoping it will encourage people in the less populated areas to come out and get their Nicolae tattoo."

Judd looked at the massive crowd now pushing its

way up the steps of the fortress. "It'll take more than a couple songs from The Four Horsemen—"

Lionel held up a hand. "Is that who I think it is?"

Judd turned and saw two women helping a man with medical supplies. Judd recognized Mac McCullum, their friend from the Tribulation Force.

Judd and Lionel yelled and rushed to the edge of the tent.

Mac smiled and shook hands with the two. He was surprised but glad they were reaching out to unbelievers. "Sorry I'm not more excited right now. We just got some bad news."

"What's that?" Judd said.

"One of our members, David Hassid, was killed earlier today." Mac explained that David was alone at Petra setting up their computer equipment when two GC Peacekeepers stumbled upon him. "They didn't find the equipment, but needless to say, we're all pretty upset."

Judd's mind reeled. He had hoped the protection of God would cover all believers involved in the operation. If David Hassid was dead, that meant other believers might die.

Will God protect Lionel, Sam, and Mr. Stein? Judd thought. *Will he protect me?*

33

JUDD and Lionel talked briefly with two women helping Mac, Hannah Palemoon and Leah Rose. Leah had come from the States to help in Operation Eagle, while Hannah had worked in New Babylon. Leah gave Judd and Lionel food, and they thanked her.

Lionel led Judd up the crowded stairway to rejoin Mr. Stein and Sam. As they slowly inched through the masses, Judd asked Lionel how they should get home.

"Westin's a man of his word. He told us he'd take us back. If anybody can get us there, he can."

Judd's phone rang and it was Chang. While Judd talked, Lionel went ahead, taking some food to his friends who were seated on a ledge above them. The phone beeped a low-battery message, so Judd quickly told Chang what was happening at Masada. Chang informed him that Dr. Rosenzweig was there waiting for the chance to speak.

"There are no speakers or microphones," Judd said. "How are all these people going to hear him?"

"There wasn't time to set any of that up," Chang said. "I'm praying God will enable everyone to hear."

"Any problems with the airlift out of Jerusalem?"

"The return runs from Petra to the Mount of Olives have been delayed slightly, but things have gone smoothly. It seems a miracle that such a massive relocation has not had one mechanical failure." Chang paused. "I didn't expect one thing—my mother e-mailed a message."

Judd had met Mrs. Wong in New Babylon and knew she wasn't a believer. "Has she taken the mark of Carpathia?"

"I don't think so. She said my father was upset about what Carpathia did in Jerusalem and he wondered what I would think about it."

"Good," Judd said. "They both sound more open to the truth."

"Perhaps. My mother is the one who has visited Tsion Ben-Judah's Web site. She wanted to know how he could predict things so accurately."

"I'll tell the others here and we'll pray for them," Judd said. "Did you write back?"

"Yes. I pleaded with her to give her life to God before it is too late."

"I hope one day she'll be part of the Tribulation Force," Judd said.

Chang's voice broke up and the phone finally went dead. Judd ran to the Hummer and plugged in the recharger, then found Mr. Stein and the others. The sun had gone down and Judd closed his eyes and listened to the noise of thousands of Israelis talking among themselves. Judd checked his watch. It was only an hour before the lifting of the plague.

Will God allow Carpathia to bomb these people? Judd thought.

Mr. Stein motioned to a robed figure at the other end of the fortress. The man's head was bowed in prayer. Mr. Stein joined hands with Judd and the others. "Righteous Father, those gathered here have not known you, but we ask that you will open ears and eyes tonight, and give your servant a strong voice and mind. We ask in the name of Jesus, amen."

As Mr. Stein finished, Dr. Rosenzweig stood on high ground and raised his arms. People around the fortress pointed, and Judd noticed that those outside became quiet.

"My friends," Micah said with power, "I cannot guarantee your safety here tonight. Your very presence makes you an enemy and a threat to the ruler of this world, and when the plague of sores upon his people is lifted at nine o'clock tonight, they may target you with a vengeance."

Judd watched the man's lips move. It looked like a foreign movie dubbed into English. Mr. Stein leaned over and whispered, "He is speaking in Hebrew, but we understand in English."

"I will keep my remarks brief," Dr. Rosenzweig said, "but I will be asking you to make a decision that will change your destiny. If you agree with me and make this commitment, cars, trucks, and helicopters will ferry you to a place of refuge. If you do not, you may return to your

homes and face the gruesome choice between the guillotine or the mark of loyalty to the man who sat in your
temple this very day and proclaimed himself god. He is
the man who defiled God's house with murder and with
the blood of swine, who installed his own throne and the
very image of himself in the Holy of Holies, who put an
end to all sacrifices to the true and living God, and who
withdrew his promise of peace for Israel."

Judd looked at the people around him. No one
strained or acted like they couldn't hear.

"I must tell you sadly that many of you will make that
choice. You will choose sin over God. You will choose pride
and selfishness and life over the threat of death. Some of
you have already rejected God's gift so many times that your
heart has been hardened. And though your risky sojourn to
this meeting may indicate a change of mind on your part, it
is too late for a change of heart. Only God knows.

"Because of who you are and where you come from,
and because of who I am and where I come from, we can
stipulate that we agree on many things. We believe there is
one God, creator of the universe and sustainer of life, that
all good and perfect things come from him alone. But I tell
you that the disappearances that ravaged our world three
and a half years ago were the work of his Son, the Messiah,
who was foretold in the Scriptures and whose prophecies
did Jesus of Nazareth, the Christ, fulfill."

Vicki was mobbed as she walked into Colin Dial's home.
Mark gave the full story of Manny's decision to stay with

the gang and the kids prayed for him, his sister, and that Hector would respond to the truth.

Darrion burst through the door, hugged Vicki, and urged the kids to follow her downstairs to hear the meeting at Masada.

"How are you getting it?" Mark said.

"Chang found a way to send it," Darrion said.

Mark guessed by the tinny sound that they were using a cell phone. However they were doing it, Dr. Rosenzweig's voice was clear.

The room was electrified as he spoke of Jesus as the Messiah the Jews had long awaited. He gave prophecy after prophecy from the Scriptures that Jesus had fulfilled. Vicki noticed Tom and Josey Fogarty furiously taking notes.

"He is the only One who could be the Messiah," Dr. Rosenzweig declared. "He also died unlike anyone else in history. He gave himself willingly as a sacrifice and then proved himself worthy when God raised him from the dead. Even skeptics and unbelievers have called Jesus the most influential person in history.

"Of the billions and billions of people who have ever lived, One stands head and shoulders above the rest in terms of influence. More schools, colleges, hospitals, and orphanages have been started because of him than because of anyone else. More art was created, more music written, and more humanitarian acts performed due to him and his influence than anyone else ever. Great international encyclopedias devote twenty thousand words to describing him and his influence on the world. Even our calendar is based on his birth. And all this he accomplished in a public ministry that lasted just three and a half years!

"Jesus of Nazareth, Son of God, Savior of the world, and Messiah, predicted that he would build his church and the gates of hell would not prevail against it. Centuries after his public, unmerciful mocking, his persecution and martyrdom, billions claimed membership in his church, making it by far the largest religion in the world. And when he returned, as he said he would, to take his faithful to heaven, the disappearance of so many had the most profound impact on this globe that man has ever seen.

"Messiah was to be born in Bethlehem to a virgin, to live a sinless life, to serve as God's spotless Lamb of sacrifice, to give himself willingly to die on a cross for the sins of the world, to rise again three days later, and to sit at the right hand of God the Father Almighty. Jesus fulfilled these and all the other 109 prophecies, proving he is the Son of God."

Vicki closed her eyes and tried to picture the gathering in Masada. She wondered if, at that same moment, Manny might be speaking to the gang, using different words, but giving the same message.

"Tonight, Messiah calls to you from down through the ages. He is the answer to your condition. He offers forgiveness for your sins. He paid the penalty for you. As the most prolific writer of Scripture, a Jew himself, wrote, 'If you confess with your mouth the Lord Jesus and believe in your heart that God has raised him from the dead, you will be saved. For with the heart one believes unto righteousness, and with the mouth confession is made unto salvation. For the Scripture says, 'Whoever believes on him will not be put to shame.' For there is no distinction between Jew and Greek, for the same Lord over all is rich to all who call upon him. For 'whoever calls on the name of the Lord shall be saved.'

"For years skeptics have made fun of the evangelist's plea, 'Do you want to be saved tonight?' and yet that is what I ask you right now. Do not expect God to be fooled. Be not deceived. God will not be mocked. Do not do this to avoid a confrontation with Antichrist. You need to be saved because you cannot save yourself.

"The cost is great but the reward greater. This may cost you your freedom, your family, your very head. You may not survive the journey to safety. But you will spend eternity with God, worshiping the Lord Christ, Messiah, Jesus."

The kids didn't make a sound. Vicki prayed silently for the people in Masada and that Judd and Lionel would soon return.

Judd stood, his mouth open, excited at what was happening around him. Seeing Chaim Rosenzweig speak with such authority to so many Israelis was worth any danger he would face. Judd knew the Bible predicted that Jewish people would one day recognize Jesus as Messiah. Could this be the day?

As Chaim listed more prophecies Jesus fulfilled, Judd noticed people standing, responding to the message.

People hung on every word. As Dr. Rosenzweig came to the end of his presentation, he invited people to pray with him. All around the fortress, inside and out, Israelis repeated the prayer. Judd looked over the crowd and saw many with the mark of God on their foreheads. Dr. Rosenzweig walked down the steps and thousands followed him.

Judd drew close as Mr. Stein talked with Rabbi Ben-Eliezar and his wife.

"Jesus is the fulfillment of all of those prophecies," Mr. Stein said.

The rabbi put a hand through his hair. "To say that Jesus is the Jewish Messiah is to go against everything I have been taught. I don't know . . ."

Mr. Stein lowered his voice. "Which is better? To continue believing a teaching that is in error or to believe the truth?"

Mr. Stein turned to Mrs. Ben-Eliezar. "You have heard the evidence. You know Nicolae Carpathia is anti-God. God has spared your lives for this time. But you must make your decision."

The woman huddled close to her husband. "I don't think we have a choice, Ethan. To put our trust in Jesus seems like spiritual suicide, but I feel in my heart that we may have been wrong all these years."

The rabbi gave Mr. Stein a terrified look. His eyes flashed as he turned to his wife. "How could I have been so blind? I have trampled the gift of God all of these years."

"Give your lives to the master now," Mr. Stein said. "Don't wait another minute."

"I can't remember the prayer," the rabbi said. "Will you help us?"

Mr. Stein nodded and the rabbi and his wife repeated his words. "Dear God, I know that I am separated from you because I am a sinner. I believe Jesus is the Messiah and that he died on the cross to pay the penalty for my sins. I believe he rose again the third day and that by receiving his gift of love I will have the power to become a son of God because I believe on his name. Thank you for hearing me and saving me, and I pledge the rest of my life to you."

Rabbi Ben-Eliezar and his wife looked up, and Judd saw the mark of the believer on their foreheads. Mr. Stein wept with them and Judd turned away. What he saw both thrilled and horrified him. Dr. Rosenzweig moved toward hundreds of vehicles and helicopters that waited in long lines. But thousands of others ran from Masada. They looked hopeless, like people with no direction, fear etched on their faces. They called out, looking for rides back to Jerusalem.

Judd shuddered when he thought of all those people turning their backs on God. Judd had done the same thing many times when he was younger.

Is this their last chance? he thought.

34

LIONEL and Sam helped Mac and the others tear down the medical tent and load it in a truck. People streamed out of Masada and into helicopters, cars, and trucks.

When the supplies were loaded, Mac yelled for new believers to get in the back of the truck. "Next stop, Petra!"

Israelis streamed toward them. One grabbed Sam by the arm. "When we pray to God now, should we pray to Jesus?" he said.

As Sam talked with him, Leah, a member of the Tribulation Force, turned to Lionel. "Are you coming with us?"

Lionel looked around for Judd. He didn't want to leave again without talking with his friend. Before Lionel could answer, Sam said, "I'll go."

"Then get in," Leah said. "And you?"

"I have to talk to my friend," Lionel said. "Go ahead."

Leah ran to the front and hopped in. Sam shook hands with Lionel and smiled. "Thanks for everything you've done. I hope to see you at Petra."

"If not," Lionel said, "call or write us. I want to hear about everything."

Sam jumped in the back of the truck. As they drove away, the Israelis peppered Sam with questions.

Judd and Mr. Stein joined Lionel at the loading area. Westin honked the Humvee's horn and waved.

"Somebody should go with these people back to Jerusalem," Lionel said. "Maybe they can be convinced of the truth."

Mr. Stein frowned. "I'm afraid they have hardened their hearts. If what they heard from Micah did not persuade them, I fear they are destined to choose Carpathia over God."

Judd studied the scores of choppers and vehicles recruited from around the world. The amount of work to get all these people together was staggering.

Lionel looked at Judd. "What do we do?"

Before Judd could answer, GC vehicles rumbled up with loudspeakers mounted on top. "The entire state of Israel has been declared a no-fly zone by the Global Community Security and Intelligence director. All civilian aircraft, take fair warning: Any non-GC craft determined to be over Israeli airspace runs the risk of destruction.

"The potentate himself has also decreed martial law and has instituted a curfew on civilian vehicular traffic in Israel. Violators are subject to arrest.

"Due to the severity of the affliction that has befallen GC personnel, these curfews are required. Only a skeleton crew of workers is available to maintain order.

"His Excellency reminds citizens that he has effected a relief from the plague as of 2100 hours, and the populace should plan to celebrate with him at daybreak."

Judd looked at his watch. It was a few minutes before nine. If these announcements were correct, new believers loading into the helicopters were flying to their deaths.

Mr. Stein started toward a quickly filling chopper. "Are you coming?"

Westin honked again. "I've got two more spots, guys, come on!"

Judd hesitated, knowing the decision he was about to make might change the course of their lives forever. In the dust and noise of motors and GC announcements, Judd grabbed Lionel by the shoulder and pulled him toward the Hummer.

Over the din of the helicopters, Judd heard Mr. Stein yell, "He is risen!"

"He is risen indeed!" Judd and Lionel yelled back.

While Mark got some needed sleep, Vicki pulled Shelly aside and told her about her conversation with Judd.

Shelly put a hand over her mouth. "How do you feel about it?" she said.

"Excited. A little scared. I've liked Judd as a friend for a long time. It feels like something's changed with him."

"Did he talk about the girl he was involved with?"

"Nada?" Vicki said. "No, he didn't mention her. But I'm sure he'll tell me all about it when he gets back."

Shelly ran her tongue over her lower lip and tilted her

head back. "Since we're being honest about guys, I have a confession."

Vicki grinned, anticipating what was coming.

"Conrad and I have become pretty good friends since our trip out west. We've been doing a Bible study together. And he writes me letters. Isn't it romantic?"

"If anything can be romantic these days, it's writing letters to somebody staying in the same house with you. Does anybody know?"

"We've kept it pretty quiet, but I think Charlie does."

Vicki smiled. "I have to remember that when Judd comes back."

Conrad knocked on the door and peeked in. Shelly winked at him. "I just told Vicki."

"I'm happy for you two," Vicki said.

Conrad nodded. "Vicki, there's something on the news I think you'll want to see."

Darrion turned the sound up as Vicki came into the main meeting room. ". . . found in an alley behind this building. Some experts believe there is a possible border war brewing among the gangs. But Global Community Peacekeepers don't think that's the case. They say the death of this man is payback for information he gave authorities after his arrest a few weeks ago."

Manny Aguilara's photo flashed on the screen. "Global Community Peacekeepers have revealed that this man escaped from a Global Community jail, aided by gang members. This happened after he gave information incriminating gang leader Hector Rodriguez. Aguilara's death—"

Vicki put a hand over her mouth, waved, and asked them to turn the TV off. When she could talk, she said, "Manny would be alive if he had come back with us."

Conrad put a hand on her shoulder. "He sent an e-mail for you. We just found it."

Vicki took the printed page, wiped her eyes, and read.

> *Vicki, Mark, and the rest of the Young Tribulation Force,*
>
> *I want to thank you for being so kind and helping me. You forgave me for not telling you the truth, but I believe it has turned out for the best.*
>
> *They've called a meeting and I'm to speak in front of a large group of gang members in a few minutes. I'm praying that God will open their eyes. I've been talking to my sister about God, and she listens but has not yet prayed. I wish one of you could be here or Zeke Sr. You would know exactly what to say.*
>
> *I will write and tell you what happened afterward. I hope you were able to find Claudia and get her to safety. Please remember to pray for me, as I will be praying for you.*
> *Sincerely,*
> *Manny*

Vicki stared at the letter and wondered what had happened in that meeting. Had the group planned to kill Manny all along? Had he even been able to tell them about God? Vicki closed her eyes and pictured Zeke welcoming Manny in heaven. She would see them again. The only question was, how soon?

Judd waited outside the Humvee as long as he could, admiring the line of helicopters and vehicles headed for Petra. Westin shouted for him to get in when everyone was ready, and Judd made sure he had a seat by the window. Several Israelis who had not prayed with Dr. Rosenzweig jammed into the vehicle, acting fidgety about the three believers on board.

"You don't have to worry about us," Westin said. "We'll get you back to Jerusalem in one piece. What you do from there is your business."

The sky filled with Operation Eagle choppers. Soon, what Judd assumed was a squadron of GC choppers approached. A few GC airplanes also flew cautiously above the line of Operation Eagle aircraft.

Lionel nudged Judd. "What are we going to do in Jerusalem?"

"See if we can get back home before another war breaks out," Judd said.

"Do you really think there will be war?" a young man beside Lionel said.

Westin looked in the rearview mirror. "Knowing how much Carpathia hates followers of Jesus *and* Jewish people, and seeing as how the Bible predicts another great war, I don't think there's any way to deny it."

Judd glanced at his watch. It was now well past the 9 P.M. deadline, and as Judd had feared, GC Peacekeepers and Morale Monitors seemed on a mission to head off the fleeing Israelis. Westin flipped on the video scanner, and Judd couldn't believe how many cars, buses, and trucks were on the road. GC squad cars passed them with lights flashing.

"Can you hear any GC transmissions?" Judd asked Westin.

Westin tuned in a GC frequency. Officers gave commands and coded communication Judd couldn't understand.

"I know what they're saying," an Israeli who had worked for the GC said. "They're telling them to block the traffic heading toward Petra first. The initial squad cars are supposed to stop them. The second wave, up ahead, is supposed to stop us and search our vehicles."

For ten minutes GC squad cars passed. There were so many that Judd lost count and wondered how many aircraft the GC had sent.

"I thought they were supposed to celebrate getting over their sores," Lionel said.

Westin leaned forward in his seat and peered out the windshield. "I think they *are* celebrating."

"But Micah was clear," Lionel said. "They're not supposed to hurt any of God's chosen people or there's going to be a worse plague."

"Does that mean us too?" one of the men in the back said.

"If you want God's protection," Westin said, "ask Jesus to forgive you—"

"Never!" the man shouted.

"Then I can't promise you won't suffer the same fate," Westin said.

The Israelis talked among themselves about the

locusts, the fiery hail, the water turned to blood, and other plagues they had experienced in the past few years. Judd wanted to shake them, repeat Chaim's message, anything.

A line of bright lights spread out on the road ahead of them and Westin slowed. "I don't like the looks of this." He rolled down his window and Judd heard loudspeakers.

"By order of Potentate Carpathia, each vehicle must stop immediately. You are violating a curfew established by the potentate himself."

A few vehicles in front slowed and came to a stop. Westin gunned the engine and pulled off the road, kicking up dust behind them.

Again the GC speakers came alive. "By authority of the Global Community and its risen potentate and lord, His Excellency Nicolae Carpathia, you are commanded to stop at once and surrender. Your passengers and cargo will be impounded by the Global Community. If you are in compliance with the loyalty mark, you will be free to go."

"Which means we're dead if we stop," Judd said.

"You got it," Westin said. "They take us in and they'll make us take Carpathia's mark or face the blade."

"I don't get what's so wrong with an identifying mark," an Israeli said.

"After what that monster did in the temple today?" another said. "I'll never comply."

"Anybody who wants to get out and follow the GC, do it right now," Westin said. He slammed on his brakes and slid into a huge culvert Judd assumed had been made during the wrath of the Lamb earthquake.

Westin unlocked the doors but no one moved. "All right then, fasten your seat belts. It might get a little bumpy."

Judd's mind raced, trying to remember all Tsion Ben-Judah had said. Judd believed Petra would have God's protection, but what about believers headed for Jerusalem with a vehicle filled with unbelievers? Judd closed his eyes and breathed a brief prayer as Westin put the Hummer into four-wheel drive and barreled out of the crater. The vehicle seemed to go straight up, then straight back down a rocky hillside.

Judd remembered going on a ride at a mall when he was younger. The video display and the motion of the car made it feel like he was actually hurtling through space. Now he was experiencing a thrill ride of another kind on the ground in Israel.

Judd leaned forward to watch the 3-D viewer in front. A line of choppers stretched miles behind them. He focused on one aircraft that seemed to hover above the others, and a smaller chopper pulled in beside it. The smaller helicopter appeared to be a Global Community craft and Judd wondered if it was armed.

Westin careened over curbs and torn-up streets. They passed the line of GC squad cars along with other vehicles following Westin's lead. Behind them, half the GC force was in hot pursuit.

Judd glanced at the grid again. Choppers remained in line except for the two choppers hovering above. The smaller one quickly moved back, like an angry bull ready to charge. The larger chopper held its position until something flashed onscreen. *Bullets!*

The smaller craft fired at close range. Judd closed his eyes and waited for the explosion.

JUDD looked again in horror as bursts of gunfire appeared on the screen in front of him. Judd had seen movies where these types of guns blew planes and helicopters out of the sky.

The bullets entered the rear of the bigger chopper, flashed inside the cabin, and exited the front, but there was no explosion, no ball of flame, no helicopter falling from the sky like Judd expected. Instead, the Operation Eagle bird hovered as if nothing had happened.

A Global Community chopper in front of the Operation Eagle bird veered crazily, its tail rotors struck by the bullets. It fell end over end and finally spun into the ground. A plume of smoke mushroomed from the wreckage.

"What was that?" Westin said.

Judd told him what he had seen and Lionel sat forward. "Maybe this is part of the protection God promised."

"Will we have that same protection?" an Israeli said.

"It's a trick," the man next to him said. "They're trying to scare us into believing."

"How could bullets go through metal and have no effect?" Westin said.

"The boy's making it up," another Israeli said. "I saw the screen and I don't think the bullets went through the first chopper. It was an accident."

Accident? Judd couldn't believe it. God had clearly done another miracle in front of their eyes and these people weren't seeing.

Westin continued around slower vehicles, avoiding traffic jams by jumping curbs, shooting around barricades, and spinning through loose rocks by the roadside. When they crested a hill, lights of vehicles headed toward Petra shone in the darkness. Judd wondered if they had made a mistake going back to Jerusalem. Could they remain safe that close to Carpathia?

Sam Goldberg held tight to a railing in the back of the vehicle driven by Mac McCullum. The truck bounced and weaved on and off the road as they tried to outrun GC vehicles. Sam answered questions from the new believers around him. Some seemed angry that they had not listened earlier, while others simply wanted to know more.

"When did you become a believer?" one asked.

"How long until Messiah comes back?" another said.

"Will Carpathia attack Petra?" a woman behind Sam said.

Sam answered the questions as best he could as they rumbled south. "How many of you have read Rabbi Tsion Ben-Judah's Web site?" A few raised hands. "When we get to our destination, we'll see that you have teaching that will answer all your questions."

Sam glanced out the window as Operation Eagle vehicles evaded more GC Peacekeepers and Morale Monitors. Sam didn't understand why they hadn't been fired upon. How was God protecting them?

Leah Rose climbed into the front seat to talk with Mac, while the other American, Hannah Palemoon, remained quiet. Sam turned and was blinded by flashing lights behind him. GC Peacekeepers called through their PA system to pull over, but Mac kept going.

The car sped forward and Sam looked at Mac. He was still talking, not paying attention to the GC vehicle. Sam glanced over and saw a guard pointing a submachine gun at Mac.

Sam ducked, waiting for the gun's bullets to rip through the vehicle. Mac had picked up a cell phone and was talking with someone, but Sam couldn't make out the conversation.

"Are we going to be killed?" an Israeli next to Sam said.

Sam clenched his teeth. "I don't know."

Mac stopped in the middle of the road and the GC squad car pulled in front of them. When a Peacekeeper got out, Mac quickly reversed and shot past them and the chase began again. When the squad car pulled alongside, Mac slammed on the brakes and Sam shot forward.

"Sorry, friends!" Mac yelled. "Shoulda told y'all to buckle up!"

Judd phoned Chang in New Babylon again and the boy seemed harried, audio blaring in the background. Judd learned of Tsion's broadcast and had Westin turn on his radio. Sure enough, GCNN radio was airing Tsion, though they were trying to talk over him.

"Are you putting Tsion on the air?" Judd asked Chang.

"Who else?" Chang said.

"Any idea how Carpathia is reacting?"

"He's not happy. He executed Walter Moon for not getting Tsion off the air."

"He killed the supreme commander? How do you know?"

"We have a bug on his airplane, remember? And he's ranting like mad, ordering troops in Israel to shoot to kill. He wants every civilian plane destroyed." Chang paused, turning up Tsion's audio. Carpathia's voice rose in the background. "Listen to him," Chang said.

". . . Run them down. Crash their vehicles. Blow their heads off. As for Petra, wait until we know for certain Micah is there, then level it. Do we have what we need to do that?"

"We do, sir," someone said.

"In the meantime, someone, anyone, get—Ben-Judah— off—the—air!"

"I will pray him off, Your Worship," Leon Fortunato said.

"I will kill you if you do not shut up," Carpathia said.

"Quieting now, Highness," Leon said. Then, a gasp.

"What!?" Carpathia said.

"The water!" Fortunato said. "The ice!"

"What's happening?" Judd said, but Chang had put down the phone. Judd heard a faucet running.

Chang returned, out of breath. "Judd, the water has turned to blood!"

Vicki sent a reply to Manny's e-mail, hoping somehow Manny's sister would see it. As she surfed for any new information about what was going on in Israel, she noticed someone familiar on the television monitor and called the others together.

"Is that Dr. Ben-Judah?" Shelly said.

"Turn it up!" Conrad said.

Tsion sat in front of a mostly empty wall. "Greetings. It is a privilege for me to address the world through the miracle of technology. But as I am an unwelcome guest here, forgive me for being brief, and please lend me your attention."

Conrad switched channels, but Tsion was on every one of them. "I don't know how the Trib Force did this, but I'll bet Carpathia will go nuts when he sees it."

"I want to give my encouragement to all believers in Messiah," Tsion continued. "What we have witnessed at the temple should leave no doubt as to the identity of the man who calls himself potentate. His actions prove what we have been saying all along is true. Jesus Christ is the Messiah the Jews have long awaited, and he is coming back in power and majesty to rule and reign. Nicolae Carpathia is the Antichrist.

"As new believers gather in a place of safety, I would remind you that time is running out. If you have not yet taken the mark of Nicolae Carpathia, avoid it at all cost. God has seen fit to warn us and get our attention by sending plagues among us. They are his divine way of getting our attention. More are coming as God judges the evil one and his followers."

Dr. Ben-Judah spoke of the events of the past few days and commented on Carpathia's unbridled evil. In the past, Tsion had spoken much longer, and Vicki was surprised when he wrapped up his broadcast after only a few minutes.

"I close with a word to those who are right now traveling to Petra. I wish you Godspeed in your journey, and I promise to travel to meet you there personally and address the one million brothers and sisters in the Messiah."

"I wonder if they'll show *that* on television," Shelly said.

Sam had never felt so energized and terrified at the same time. He was busy helping believers understand their newfound faith, while their vehicle was pursued by GC Peacekeepers.

A GC squad car flew past them again and stopped within inches of Mac's bumper. Two men bounded from the car, yelling and waving their weapons. Mac drove past them again, and Sam watched the two level their weapons, then jump back into their vehicle. As they accelerated, Mac swerved left and braked, the rear of their vehicle sliding on the sand. Before the Peacekeepers knew what was happening, Mac had pulled in behind them.

"All right, we're going to try and . . ." Mac's voice trailed off as the taillights ahead flashed bright red. He slammed on his brakes and the truck slid a few feet.

Sam peered through the dust, wondering when the shooting would begin, but the squad car was nowhere in sight. It had somehow disappeared.

Operation Eagle cars and trucks roared in the distance, and behind them another line of GC cars approached. Suddenly, one of the new believers screamed, "The earth has opened up!"

Sam gasped at the chasm that had formed behind them and to the right, and before the pursuing GC officers could stop, they plunged in. The screech of its siren grew faint as the car dropped out of sight.

Mac had jumped out and was now back in the vehicle, his voice quavery. "Our front tires are right on the edge. The thing must be hundreds of feet deep." Mac carefully backed up, using the four-wheel drive, and slowly tried to find a way around the opening.

"Here comes another one!" someone yelled behind Sam.

A GC car raced up to the edge and braked. Before the car slid into the crevasse, two Peacekeepers leaped out and rolled on the ground, their guns clattering. Everyone in the vehicle waited breathlessly as the two rose, found their rifles, and took aim at the truck.

"Duck!" Mac shouted.

Sam and the others dove for the floor of the truck, bumping heads and landing on one another. The guns cracked and Sam put his hands over his ears, not knowing what else to do. But the firing quickly stopped.

Sam peeked out the window as Mac opened his door. The Peacekeepers lay lifeless on the ground, their guns at their sides. Everyone got out and inspected the truck. Miraculously, there wasn't a scratch.

Mac's phone rang and Sam walked a few yards away to look into the chasm. He stood at the edge of what looked like the Grand Canyon.

"Better not get too close," Leah said. "Come on, let's get out of here."

Before they got back in the car, Mac told them he had just talked with the leader of Operation Eagle, Rayford Steele. "Dr. Ben-Judah is on the air right now, no doubt telling people the truth." He pointed into the air over Jerusalem. "And back there a war's going on."

Something in the distance burst into flames and fell to the earth in a fiery heap.

"War?" Sam said. "They're shooting down Operation Eagle helicopters?"

Mac smiled. "They're trying, but Rayford says they're only hitting each other."

Judd yelled as GC helicopters pursued a dozen Operation Eagle choppers above them. "They must not know they're protected! They're heading to Israel."

A GC chopper was hit and fell from the sky. Westin

swerved and nearly hit a boulder as the ball of fire crashed twenty yards away. Debris from the impact scattered over the area and bounced off the roof of the Hummer.

The sky lit up with gunfire from GC attack choppers. It was an all-out war, but God was protecting his people.

Judd was excited when the radio feed had switched to Chaim Rosenzweig's message recorded at the Temple Mount. He hoped some of the Israelis in the car would reconsider their position about Jesus, but all he heard from them were groans and complaints to turn the radio down. Westin, of course, left it blaring.

Judd didn't want to bother Chang again, but he was so curious about Carpathia and Operation Eagle that he dialed him.

"We've got a problem here," Chang said. "Someone told Carpathia that Dr. Ben-Judah is coming to Petra. They're going to destroy Petra when he arrives."

"But Petra is safe, right?"

"I hope. And the blood problem is international. Be listening for reports. It's affecting the seas this time." Chang grew quiet. "I need you to pray."

"What for?" Judd said.

"They know someone's been listening to them from inside the Global Community. They're going to give lie detector tests here. And they say they'll kill the person who's guilty."

36

JUDD wanted to talk with the Israelis in the Hummer one more time, but as Westin pulled into Jerusalem, the men jumped out and ran for their homes. They had listened to Dr. Rosenzweig's entire presentation and prayer over GCNN radio and still didn't respond.

Judd was terrified as hunks of molten steel, burning out of control, fell on roadways, buildings, and open fields. It looked like half the GC forces had been lost.

Chang called back and explained that he was safe from the GC for a while. "I hacked into the personnel files and created a record of my hospital stay for the last two days. They won't suspect a mole who's been recovering from boils."

"What about your computer?" Judd said. "If they search that—"

"It's fried. I saved everything, then crashed my hard drive. The laptop is stashed in my closet, so even if the

GC find it, they won't be able to trace the broadcast or any of my activity. I'll be at my desk in the morning, ready for work."

Vicki and the others watched the Israel coverage from the safety of Colin's home in Wisconsin. Live shots showed the falling GC aircraft. The GC was mistakenly killing its own by shooting at Operation Eagle.

GC forces on the ground fared no better, with reports that many vehicles had simply vanished. When it was learned that great holes had opened in the earth, rescue efforts were abandoned.

Vicki thought of Judd and hoped he would go with Lionel to Petra. From there, he might be able to find a flight home with a Tribulation Force volunteer.

Though the Global Community tried to downplay them, reports from around the world flooded in about the seas turning to blood. Beautiful vacation resorts became death sites as whales, fish, sharks, and every imaginable sea creature perished and rose to the surface. Ships radioed Mayday signals, saying they had run out of drinking water and were unable to get back to land.

Nicolae Carpathia spoke to the world from a secret studio in Israel, claiming that his Security and Intelligence personnel had identified Micah and his companion. As Carpathia spoke, Leon Fortunato stood in the background in his silly outfit, his lips moving in an unholy prayer.

"This Micah claimed to represent the rebels, but we

now know he is an impostor who has used his trickery to create the great seawater catastrophe," Carpathia said. "Do not be dismayed. The enemies of the Global Community will be brought to justice, and just as the difficulty we have faced with the sores has passed, so this problem with the earth's waters will be overcome."

Aerial shots of the plague were unbelievable. Thick, gooey blood washed up on shores around the world. Fishing vessels were stuck, as if they were trying to sail through red syrup.

Vicki went to the computer to search for any word about Claudia Zander. With the help of Jim Dekker, who knew some of the GC passwords, Vicki was able to find a personnel report saying Claudia had been reassigned to another Morale Monitor division outside the Midwest. No further information was available.

"With the way the GC operates, she's lucky to be alive," Dekker said.

An alarm sounded inside the hideout. Colin had installed a motion sensor with video capabilities around the perimeter of his property. It usually went off around dusk with the movement of deer and other animals searching for food. Colin pulled up a camera shot and hit the reset button. "It's nothing, I'm sure."

Sam was exhausted and running on adrenaline when Mac McCullum finally stopped their vehicle. Sam had talked with the new believers around him until his throat felt sore. The desert dust hadn't done much to help, but Sam thrilled at the taste of clean, clear water while the rest of the world was getting blood when they turned on a tap.

Sam had finally dozed after the GC chase ended and Mac had settled into the long drive through the desert. Mac relayed reports from Operation Eagle over his cell phone. Sam was excited to be part of the massive transport of a million Israelis to Petra, and he was eager to talk with Mr. Stein. The man had become like a father to him.

Hannah Palemoon had been quiet throughout the trip. She turned to Sam while most of the others were sleeping and asked if he was traveling alone.

Sam briefly told his story and how his father had been killed during the plague of horsemen. Hannah listened and wiped away a tear when Sam talked about his grief.

"Did you lose someone close to you?" Sam said.

Hannah nodded. "While I was in New Babylon, I met David Hassid, the one who organized this whole operation. He was killed by GC troops yesterday."

Sam put a hand on her shoulder. "Can I pray for you?"

Hannah nodded, too overcome to speak.

"Gracious Father, we thank you that we can come to you with our hurts. Thank you for the safety you provided tonight, and I pray for my new friend, that you would comfort her with your peace through this great sorrow over losing her good friend David. Encourage her in the days ahead, for we know it won't be long before Jesus returns in his majesty, and we will again see our friends who have died."

When Sam finished, Hannah wiped away tears and whispered, "Thank you."

Judd and Lionel waited in the lobby of a posh hotel while Westin parked the Humvee in an underground lot. Though it was late, people milled about watching video coverage from the Global Community News Network. Hotel workers scrambled to supply their guests with soft drinks and juice. All of their bottled water was bloodred.

Westin returned and grabbed a key from the front desk. The three took an elevator to the fifth floor and found an envelope taped to the door. Westin opened it as they walked inside, shook his head, and handed the note to Judd.

> *Wes,*
> *Call me as soon as you get in. We're performing for His Excellency at the celebration of the lifting of the sickness tomorrow morning. Have the plane ready in case we need it afterward.*
> *Z.*

"You going to call him?" Lionel said.

"I have a better idea," Westin said. "Let's get a few hours' sleep, and then we'll fly out of here before sunup and get you two back to the States."

"Are you serious?" Judd said.

Westin smiled. "I'll drop you guys, then bring the plane back here and clear things up. He promised to get you back home, and I'm going to see it happens."

Sam was overcome with emotion when he saw the growing multitudes at Petra. It looked like the Israelites fleeing
Egypt during the Exodus. Except this time they would not
need to part the Red Sea to get to safety—they would
enter through a narrow passage called a Siq.

Sam thanked Mac and the others for risking their
lives.

Mac smiled and patted Sam's shoulder. "You need a
ride anywhere, I'm there."

In the darkness came singing and rejoicing. Hundreds
of thousands of escapees praised God for their deliver-
ance and celebrated his goodness. Helicopters carried
older people and some who were disabled, but most
lined up for the walk that would lead them through the
narrow passage to safety.

Sam looked for Mr. Stein, but he knew it would be
too difficult to find one person in such a gathering. He
guessed that Dr. Rosenzweig was somewhere preparing
to speak to the throng. Sam could hardly contain his
excitement over the prospect of welcoming Dr. Tsion
Ben-Judah.

Nicolae Carpathia and his followers had tried to stop
this gathering from ever happening. The shouts and cries
of joy mocked the evil ruler and showed how impotent
the world system was against the plans of God.

As night fell in Wisconsin, Vicki watched her friends head
to their bunks or mattresses placed on the floor.

Colin had spoken briefly with Vicki about moving some of them to a church that had begun on the western side of the state. Vicki said she was open to it and that it was certainly needed, seeing how crowded the house had become. "But how do we choose who goes and who stays?"

"Let's talk about it in the morning," Colin said.

Shelly and Darrion stayed with Vicki until late, then went to their cots. Vicki watched the continuing coverage with a sense of awe and terror. The love and protection of God overwhelmed her, but she couldn't believe people still clung to the hope that Nicolae Carpathia was the answer to the world's problems.

In the midst of stories about the bloody seas and the GC's defeat in the air over Israel, Vicki saw an announcement for those who had not taken the mark of Carpathia. New application sites were opening, and Dr. Neal Damosa had scheduled a young people's rally at different sites around the world where kids could watch the next day's celebration *and* receive the mark.

Vicki shook her head. Only the Global Community could celebrate when there was so much death and destruction.

The motion alarm rang again and Vicki quickly flipped a switch, turning it off. She pulled up video of different sensors around Colin's property and noticed something moving in one of the frames. She enlarged the picture and saw an animal with a long tail crawling up a tree near the camera. She focused on the two eyes and long snout and recognized an opossum, with several little ones clinging to its back. The animal moved up and out of the frame and Vicki smiled. They were ugly creatures, but the babies were sort of cute.

The sensor beeped again so Vicki clicked back to the full list of camera shots. Some showed the dim glow of lights in houses several hundred yards away. The activated sensors were in the wooded area behind the house.

Vicki was about to turn everything off and go to bed when something caught her eye in a corner of the screen. A tree branch moved. Was it the wind? She enlarged the picture and moved closer. The image was grainy and slightly green.

A shadow moved in the moonlight. Was it another animal?

Vicki noticed something strange hanging behind one of the branches. At first it looked like Spanish moss, but the more she studied it, the more convinced she became that it was moving forward. The branch moved again— was that someone's arm?

A face!

It filled the screen, and long, black hair covered the camera. Vicki jumped back and knocked some books off the table behind her. When she turned, the screen was blank.

Judd awoke early to a flurry of activity in the hotel room. Though it was still dark, Westin had a bag packed and Lionel was eating a bagel and some fruit he had brought from downstairs.

"Get dressed," Westin said. "It's time to go."

Westin took them underground to the Humvee and they drove into the smoky streets. Debris from downed choppers littered the roadside. Rescue crews worked on several buildings damaged by falling aircraft.

"Did you talk with Z-Van?" Lionel said.

Westin shook his head. "I didn't want him to know I was in town. But I did see his buddy, Lars Rahlmost."

"The guy making that movie about Nicolae's resurrection?" Judd said.

"Yeah. And he says he got some great footage last night. He's supposed to be at the celebration this morning, but I have my doubts about them pulling it off, what with half the GC troops injured or unaccounted for."

Judd's heart raced as they neared the airport. When they were back with their friends, they wouldn't have to worry about Carpathia's attacks. Judd was sure there would be danger, but nothing like they had seen in Israel and New Babylon. He didn't know how Chang could stand working in the same building with the most evil man on earth.

Judd thought of Vicki. He hoped she hadn't changed her mind about him. She had seemed excited about the possibility of them working on their relationship, and he wanted one more chance to prove himself.

Westin pointed out more wreckage, and Judd feared there might be debris on the airport runway. He sighed when a plane rose into the air.

"Won't be long now," Westin said.

They returned the Humvee and took a shuttle to the

terminal. Westin showed his pass at the checkpoint and located the hangar where Z-Van's plane was stored. The three jogged toward it.

"I'm going to get in touch with Chang as soon as we're in the air," Judd said.

Westin stopped. "Oh no."

"What's wrong?" Judd said.

Westin gestured to the hangar. From the side it had looked okay, but now, as they neared the front, Judd saw a gaping hole in the roof and emergency crews at work.

The familiar insignia of The Four Horsemen lay on the ground, burning.

Z-Van's plane had been destroyed.

ABOUT THE AUTHORS

Jerry B. Jenkins (www.jerryjenkins.com) is the writer of the Left Behind series. He owns the Jerry B. Jenkins Christian Writers Guild, (www.ChristianWritersGuild.com), an organization dedicated to mentoring aspiring authors, as well as Jenkins Entertainment, a filmmaking company (www.Jenkins-Entertainment.com). Former vice president of publishing for the Moody Bible Institute of Chicago, he also served many years as editor of *Moody* magazine and is now Moody's writer-at-large.

His writing has appeared in publications as varied as *Time* magazine, *Reader's Digest, Parade, Guideposts*, in-flight magazines, and dozens of other periodicals. Jenkins's biographies include books with Billy Graham, Hank Aaron, Bill Gaither, Luis Palau, Walter Payton, Orel Hershiser, and Nolan Ryan, among many others. His books appear regularly on the *New York Times, USA Today, Wall Street Journal,* and *Publishers Weekly* best-seller lists.

He holds two honorary doctorates, one from Bethel College (Indiana) and one from Trinity International University. Jerry and his wife, Dianna, live in Colorado and have three grown sons and three grandchildren.

Dr. Tim LaHaye (www.timlahaye.com), who conceived the idea of fictionalizing an account of the Rapture and the Tribulation, is a noted author, minister, and nationally recognized speaker on Bible prophecy. He is the founder of both Tim LaHaye Ministries and The PreTrib Research Center.

He also recently cofounded the Tim LaHaye School

of Prophecy at Liberty University. Dr. LaHaye speaks at many of the major Bible prophecy conferences in the U.S. and Canada, where his prophecy books are very popular.

Dr. LaHaye earned a doctor of ministry degree from Western Theological Seminary and an honorary doctor of literature degree from Liberty University. For twenty-five years he pastored one of the nation's outstanding churches in San Diego, which grew to three locations. During that time he founded two accredited Christian high schools, a Christian school system of ten schools, and Christian Heritage College.

There are almost 13 million copies of Dr. LaHaye's fifty nonfiction books that have been published in over thirty-seven foreign languages. He has written books on a wide variety of subjects, such as family life, temperaments, and Bible prophecy. His current fiction works, the Left Behind series, written with Jerry B. Jenkins, continue to appear on the best-seller lists of the Christian Booksellers Association, *Publishers Weekly*, *Wall Street Journal*, *USA Today*, and the *New York Times*. LaHaye's second fiction series of prophetic novels consists of *Babylon Rising* and *The Secret on Ararat*, both of which hit the *New York Times* best-seller list and will soon be followed by *Europa Challenge*. This series of four action thrillers, unlike *Left Behind*, does not start with the Rapture but could take place today and goes up to the Rapture.

He is the father of four grown children and grandfather of nine. Snow skiing, waterskiing, motorcycling, golfing, vacationing with family, and jogging are among his leisure activities.

Coming Summer 2005

Look for the next two books
in the Young Trib Force Series!

areUthirsty.com

well . . . are you?